I0609533

Here *comes* Mercy

A Faith-Filled Redemption Story

Book 2 of the Second Chances Christian Romance Series

Cindy Luke

ISBN 13: 978-1-955485-04-3

This is a fictional piece of writing. Though some
of the characters and events have been inspired by
real people with their own stories to tell, all names
and situations have been changed to protect the
privacy of those parties. The resulting work you see
is a product of the writer's imagination.

Contact the author:
cindy@cindylukeauthor.com
On the web: cindylukeauthor.com

Dedication

To women:

mothers, sisters, daughters who have
believed the lie that God could never love
and rejoice over them because of the things
they have done or had done to them.

God sees you.

He cares so much

that He sent His only Son to make a way
for you

to be free.

*You can't go back and change
the beginning,*

*but you can start where you are
and change the ending.*[1]

One

The SUV moved smoothly in evening traffic as Carver drove home to his intercity apartment. A renovated hotel in downtown Oklahoma City, the Aberdeen was about 80 years old and boasted large flats with old antique details. Carver had first moved here when he was a medical student. It was ten minutes from the downtown teaching hospital system and at that time the rent for a one-bedroom had been doable. Last year, Carver had moved into one of the bigger end units. His apartment looked out over a major street, which meant he could hear ambulances with full lights and sirens transporting patients to the area hospitals, but those sounds were familiar and comforting to him. And he was on the top floor—no one making noise overhead. His current unit had two bedrooms, an acceptable galley kitchen, and a huge living area with windows on three sides. It was all he needed for now. Carver had thought about buying a home now that he was out of medical school and making money, but that had always been something he'd thought he would do with a wife. Not much luck in that department. Once again, the date had been a flop. They had nothing in common. He had not dated at all until finishing med school. Now he was playing catch-up, but there wasn't much of what he was looking for out there in dating land. So much so that he was still able to number his dates. Number One had been very... accommodating...*too accommodating*, he thought, remembering how she had plastered herself to his side from the moment he had picked her up until the final knoll as he dropped her off. He'd been more careful asking Number Two out, but she had ended up texting him the night before their date and explaining that she was going to refocus on her ex. Carver was happy for her, even though she had seemed to be someone he thought he could connect with. Date Number Three was nice, but she had a snorting laugh that was too distracting for him. Number Four never let him get a word in during the entire night. And tonight was just more of the same. Number Five was high maintenance if the incident at the restaurant was any indication. She had complained about the time to be seated—it was less than ten minutes, and once seated, she complained that the waitstaff had taken too long to arrive—it was moments. Number Five had complained through the whole meal, when really, they could have taken the time to get to know one another. She was nice to look at. But his dad's mantra was always playing like a record in the back of Carver's head.

"Boys, just remember, marriage is forever;

character is lasting; beauty? Not necessarily. Except, of course, in the case of your mother." Then a gentle smile would climb his dad's face until a look of utter contentment shone from his eyes and his dad would make his way to Carver's mom's side and pull her into a gentle embrace. "Except your mom, boys, find a woman like your momma, and you'll be set."

Carver sighed as he pulled his vehicle under the covered parking. *I feel old.* Despite what his best friend, Adam Noble, thought, Carver did want to find 'the right one' and get married. Adam had found 'the right one'—twice if they were counting. Adam and Grace had just celebrated one year of marriage with a backyard party. *How is that fair, God? Adam finds two wives with which he matched perfectly and I'm still waiting. Okay, so I am picky and a little gun shy.* Immediately he felt the burn of soured hopes in his gut as the memory of the last time he had trusted a woman flashed through his mind. He was in high school. He had always been quiet—serious, according to his classmates. They had given him the moniker "Doc Brown" during the middle school science fair, after the eccentric scientist from Back to the Future. He had always loved the science of things. But he had always been shy. His stuttering in grade school had taught him to keep his words to a minimum. Apparently, the Bible was right when it said you'd be considered wise if you kept your mouth shut. Everyone had decided he was smarter. The reality was that because he was shy, he spent more time reading and working on school things and thinking and dreaming. He hadn't wanted to be popular per se, but the idea of having a girlfriend had been welcome—as it would for most high school males. So, when Cassie Caruthers had

3

shown up in his junior year, fresh from another state thanks to the movements of her military family, Carver had been looking.

Cassie had been the new girl in town. All the guys had been hovering around her like a bunch of flies after a honey sandwich. She'd been cute. And most importantly, she had noticed him. *I don't know what she saw in me, but when she made her move, I just rolled over like a puppy wanting his belly scratched.* He had become her ride, her prom date, anything she wanted. Until the time he forgot his wallet and had headed back to his house after picking her up for Junior/Senior prom. He had intended to just run in the house and retrieve the wallet, but good training had him offering to have her meet his parents. His Dad was a family physician and later Carver realized that Cassie liked the idea of being connected to a doctor. Carver hadn't had the skill to understand that Cassie meant to date him because of his dad. That came out later, after Cassie had been introduced to Mom, Dad, and Georgie. Carver sighed. Meeting Georgie had been devastating. Cassie had been all graciousness and beauty queen until Georgie had come into the room. When Cassie laid eyes on Georgie, her whole demeanor changed. She hadn't said anything in front of his parents, but the first words out of her mouth when they had gotten back in the car for the trip back to the prom had been, "He's not normal."

The date had gone downhill from there. Other than those first words, Cassie had been silent all the way back to the high school gym. As soon as they had arrived, Cassie jumped out of the car before Carver could get around to open her car door like Mom had taught him. Carver wasn't surprised; he had been aware of an impending sense of doom.

4

Cassie had bolted out of her side of the car, meeting him at the hood of the car. "Look," she had said. "I can't date someone who has a brother like that."

Carver never could think on his feet. An early problem with stuttering in grade school had resulted in Carver spending years holding his words back so that he wouldn't embarrass himself. Before he could get his words together, Cassie had continued.

"It's not like we're getting married or anything, but *that's* in your genes. I don't want to even be dating anyone who has that in their family tree. So, thanks for picking me up and bringing me to prom, but no thanks for the rest of the party. I'll find my own ride home." And she had turned and practically sprinted to the party—without him.

Reflecting on that night, Carver was mostly ashamed that he'd not had the words to stand up for Georgie right there on the spot. He'd spent the next hour processing the events of the evening. The meanness of people. And then he had driven to an arcade near home and played games for the next two hours so he wouldn't show up at home too early and be subjected to awkward questions. There was no way he was going to tell his parents what happened. Georgie was his brother. He was special and important to their family. And Carver decided right there, he would always protect his brother from the 'Cassie Caruthers' of the world.

I just want to make sure I do this right. The Ellises have a history of long, happy marriages. I need to choose well. He mentally reviewed his list. *She needs to love God—not just call herself a Christian. She needs to be a good role model. She needs to be able to handle living with a doctor and the shift issues and days or nights on at a time. So...*

5

she can't be too needy. And she needs to be okay with Georgie. Scratch that, she needs to value Georgie. Anything less is a deal-breaker. I'd like her to care about the underserved and it would be nice if she was willing to be involved in some way in mission work. It would be nice if she had some fire, or, as Grandma Ruby would say, some gumption. Carver chuckled quietly thinking about his spitfire Grandma. She could probably set a bone in place with a look. *But the perfect woman can't be someone from work—if it doesn't work out and I have to work with a Cassie Caruthers...no, definitely no one from work.*

Two

Joelzi picked up her pace as she made her way to the employee entrance of Oklahoma Memorial Hospital's Emergency Room. *I wonder if Carver's on today.* Heaviness fell on her chest with the thought. *I thought we had something after working together to get Grace and Adam back on the right track. But he was very stand-offish at Grace and Adam's one year celebration on Saturday. Nothing but careful reservation.*

Last year, Joelzi's best friend, Grace James, had met and married Carver's best friend, Adam Noble. Joelzi and Carver had been instrumental in Grace and Adam's initial meeting, subsequent courtship, and eventual wedding. Joelzi would have been the last one to expect Grace to agree to a marriage of convenience. But Grace's tragic history had demolished well laid expectations. Safe, steady

Grace had launched into a relationship with Adam. And although there had been times Joelzi had worried about the outcome, Grace and Adam were trekking along happily in their new relationship. Joelzi bit her lip and blinked away her blurring vision. *Carver acts like we have no history outside of work, even after all the time we spent helping Grace and Adam.*

The only time I see him is at work and he seems so "professional" like he wants walls. I am so sick of caring what he thinks. It's just emotional angst. Why do guys get to do all the choosing? Why doesn't he see me? Am I really that unacceptable? Joelzi sighed. God, I want to trust You. You know I don't want to be single forever. I know, it's not forever... but it feels like it. Grace has been in love twice now. Two times you've brought wonderful men into her life. Okay, so the first one didn't turn out that well, but she's had two great loves—and I'm still waiting... Joelzi clocked in with her name badge and moved to her locker to store her purse. *I know I messed up with Myron. That fiasco took me down a road of regret... But the Bible says You've forgiven me for that. How long does a girl have to wait for You to bring her the real thing—a man who will love me for me? It's been seven years, God. I know I wasn't ready back then, but watching Grace fall in love... twice... Couldn't You just find me one Godly man?*

Joelzi shut and locked her locker door, then turned to check out the bulletin board. A small blue unassuming sign caught her eye and she moved closer to read it.

HOPE CLINIC
A medical clinic for the underserved needs
volunteers.
There is a place for everyone.
More information and application details can be
found at
www.hopeclinic.org

This is just what I need to keep me busy. I've always wanted to be involved in mission work and this is right here in my back yard. Quickly, she memorized the website. *I'll check it out today after work.*

"Hey Joelzi, strange seeing you here on the swing shift. Are you picking up?" asked Kelli-Lynn, one of the new externs.

Joelzi turned from her locker and set her thoughts aside. "Hi, Kelli-Lynn," Joelzi smiled her confident smile, "yes, I'm picking up. Are you ready for another shift?" Joelzi could see the admiration in Kelli-Lynn's face. *Kelli-Lynn thinks I've got it all together. That's the trouble with being the seasoned staff. Everyone thinks you've got it all together.* Six years in the ER did make Joelzi more comfortable. *But being comfortable with your job and being comfortable with your life—well, the two didn't compare. I'd like my personal life to be more comfortable, Lord. I've got plenty of people in my life—but I'd like more relationships. I'm tired of going home alone. Only Grace really knows me, and since marrying Adam, she's been very busy with family. Rightly so. I'm not jealous, but I'd like family. I'd like a full life. Is that too much to ask?*

Joelzi heard the volume increase as she walked out on the ER floor and headed to her assigned area

9

to get report. The next twelve hours would be filled with excitement and hard work. Time to set aside her feelings and take care of her patients.

Later that night after arriving home, Joelzi was too wired to go to sleep, so she grabbed her laptop and Googled the Hope Clinic website. The two founding doctors attended the Methodist church across the street. When their retirement began looming, they started looking for 'a project'. They didn't want to work full time, but neither did they want to go play golf every day. Being mission-minded, they went to their church board and convinced the church to purchase the building and do the basic renovation needed to turn the small storefront into a clinic. The two doctors agreed to run the clinic on a volunteer basis and to cull their peers for help. They called it Hope Clinic. A peace settled over Joelzi as she read the information. This would be a great place to give back. *I'm going to volunteer.* She quickly filled out the required forms and signed up to start this Thursday.

Three

Thursday, September 2nd
Hope Clinic
Joelzi

Joelzi pulled her car into the back parking lot and turned the car off. Vera Bledsoe, an administrator for Hope Clinic, had texted Joelzi this morning asking her to bring her credentials this evening when she showed up to volunteer, so they could have a copy in their records. She was excited about helping people who didn't have access to medical care. Of course, this would be nothing like the ER. This clinic would deal with non-emergency, daily-living kind of medical care. More mundane, but not less needed. She got out of her car and walked around to the front of the clinic. It looked small from the outside, but the building she had walked around to get to the front had been deep. She walked around the line of people waiting to get in and knocked on the front doors. A woman with silver threaded through her fading dark brown pixie cut unlocked the door and poked her head out. "Joelzi Parker?" she asked.

"That's me," said Joelzi.

"Come on in, Joelzi, and welcome to Hope Clinic," the woman said. "I'm Vera Bledsoe, call me Vera."

"Nice to meet you, Vera," said Joelzi.

"Let me show you around and introduce you to some of the volunteers," said Vera. She proceeded to show Joelzi around. The front area was a rectangular space with a small desk located at one side. "We use this area as the waiting/check-in area. A volunteer who doesn't need to have any medical background sits at that desk and checks people in. Most people have an appointment, because they are returning patients, but sometimes there are walk-ins. This hall leads to our three exam rooms and our pharmacy," Vera pointed to a Dutch door on the left. "When it's open, you will see that all of the walls are covered in shelves and filled with generic medicines that are most common to our clients' needs. Obviously, the volunteer Pharmacist and the Pharmacy tech dispense the medications. Each room has an exam table and supplies in cabinets. And we have two restrooms: one for the patients and one off the break room for volunteers." As they neared the back of the hall, Vera led the way into a kitchen. "And this is our break room. You can leave your purse in here in one of the lockers and use the refrigerator to store any food items you bring." Vera turned to the others who were already in the room. "Everyone, this is Joelzi Parker, our newest volunteer. She's a registered nurse who works in the emergency room." Everyone turned and introduced themselves. Some were older, some younger and from different specialties, but all were friendly and wore smiles. *This is going to be fun and rewarding,* thought Joelzi.

Four

Friday, September 3rd
Merci

Merci paused and wiped a long, stringy blue lock away from her cheek as she read the sign over the door across the street again. *I've gotta do something. This is not going away. And I don't know how I can take care of a baby.* HOPE CLINIC. The sign over the door was simple: red block letters with a cross between the two words. Merci took a deep breath and then checking traffic—not that there was any; this clinic was situated on a back street behind the old Methodist church in downtown Oklahoma City— made her way across the street. From the outside, it appeared more like an afterthought. But Merci had been here watching for the past two weeks, trying to gather her courage, trying to come up with another alternative.

She was a 'good girl'. She had been raised by a good momma. But Merci had wanted the popularity of the dangerous crowd. When she had been accepted into their group, they had whittled down her resolve until she had accepted the hits from their smokes and accepted the arms of the players. The first time it had happened Merci had tried to stop him. But she hadn't had the strength—her 5'2" to his 6'0" was not a winning combination. And he had just laughed and told her she didn't really mean it—she had been asking for it for weeks. He had been rough, and it had hurt even though the marijuana had dulled some of her senses. She cried later. But Merci craved the acceptance of the group and had told herself she had nothing to lose now. She kept those friends, *if you can call them friends*, until she missed her period. A Dollar Store pregnancy test had confirmed it. Merci had told Jose she was pregnant, and he had boasted that he was good at that—getting virgins pregnant. "You can get rid of it down at the abortion clinic on Brockett Road. I certainly don't want anything to do with your kid." *Talk about being swallowed up in numbness.* Merci didn't know what to do. Her mom was a single parent and had told Merci that being a single parent was the hardest thing she had ever done.

Merci had looked up an abortion clinic on her mom's computer when her mom was in the shower. She had even bummed a ride and stood across the street watching the abortion clinic door. But there had been people there holding signs about not killing your baby and that had given her pause. She had walked the four miles back to the apartment she shared with her mother in turmoil.

There was one other girl in the group that was pregnant. April was farther along and showing. Although she had been the 'one to be' when Merci joined the group, she was now a backseat

15

contender, pushed to the side by the girls in the group who still had their young, unpregnant bodies. *That's what will become of me. I'll be outer ranks, less than, all because I'm pregnant. They don't really care about me. I feel used.* Merci kicked the empty beer can on the sidewalk and wiped the tear leaking out of her right eye. *God, are you still there? I remember they talked about You in Catechism like You were real. Can You hear me? I need help. Oh, what am I doing? God isn't real and He certainly wouldn't help someone like me.*

A sign in the window of the clinic showed the clinic was only open on Thursdays from 5:30pm to 9:00pm. *Maybe I could come back on Thursday while Mami's at work.* She turned and continued her mindless shuffle down the street not wanting to get home too soon. *I'm going to have to tell Mami. I'm not looking forward to that.*

Five

Merci

Merci heard the key turning in the front door and felt her stomach clench into a knot. *Mami's home from work.* Merci could taste the bile rising in her throat. *I have to get this over with. Please let tonight be a good night.* Merci's mom worked at a local bar. It paid better than a regular chain restaurant. The tips alone were keeping them under a roof. At least that's what she told Merci. There wasn't a lot left over. It was just the two of them— Merci's dad had moved on shortly after Merci had been born. They had managed okay, until now. Merci had no idea how her mom would take the news. She had practiced the options in her head:

Hey, Mami, I'm pregnant. No, too blunt.

Remember how you told me not to get hooked up with the wrong crowd? Well, I guess I didn't do that so well...

Merci's mom dropped to the couch with a deep

sign, sliding her feet out of her crocs and propping them up on the coffee table beside her purse. "Oh, my feet are killing me, but I made the rest of this month's rent in tips tonight. Totally worth the sore feet." Her head leaned back against the couch and her eyes closed with exhaustion.

"Mami," Merci stood at the corner of the hall, her head down, examining the hole in the toe of her left tennis shoe determinedly.

"Si, mi hija?" Merci's mom murmured from the couch in her native language.

"I'm pregnant," Merci said softly in English.

"You are a prig nut?" her mother said, a frown of concentration flitting over her face, indicating her confusion. "Is that a part in the school play?"

"No, Mami, *pregnant*. Estoy embarazada," Merci added in frustration to cut through the English-Spanish translation.

The reaction was immediate. Liliana Lopez sat up on the couch and looked at Merci as though she were an alien. "You are pregnant?" It took several seconds and then she erupted in Spanish. "Embarazada? How could you? I told you not to hang around with those kids—but you did it anyway. How am I supposed to pay for a baby? I can barely keep us in this dump," she said, her arms out, eyes wide as she looked at the walls of the tiny living area. "It's a one-bedroom efficiency, for God's sake. Where would I put a baby—not to mention how will I feed one. And what about school—you're a sophomore in high school. Who's going to watch a baby while you go to school and I go to work?" Liliana stood up, her lips pressed together and her jaw set. "No. You know the rules. I told you what would happen if you got pregnant." She jabbed her finger in Merci's direction. "No, no, no. I am not doing this." She walked toward the front door and then spun back to Merci. "Who got you pregnant? He has to pay for the abortion. I cannot do this. I *will not* do this." She pointed her finger at Merci. "Having you ruined my life. I will not repeat this with you. You will get an abortion and that boy will pay for it or you will not live in this house. Do you understand me?" She was so close to Merci that her spit misted across Merci's face. "We are not having a pregnancy in this house. And that is final." She picked up her keys and purse and went back out the apartment door, slamming it behind her.

Merci heard the sounds of her mother's cursing as she slid down the wall to the floor and rolled into a ball right there in the hall. She was too tired to cry. *Having me ruined her life? What have I done? God, is there really a God? I need help.*

Six

"What ever happened between you and Carver?" asked Grace. "I thought there were sparks at our wedding." They were sitting around Grace's huge kitchen bar sharing a well-deserved morning coffee. Times like these had been harder to achieve since Grace and Adam had gotten married.

Joelzi rolled her eyes. "I don't know how you could pay attention to anyone but Adam at your wedding," replied Joelzi. "Despite it being 'a marriage of convenience'," Joelzi used her fingers to indicate quotes, "you two were googly-eyed for each other."

Grace laughed softly, her eyes clocking to her upper left as her memories seemed to take over her face and a shy smile rested there. "That was a lovely day," she breathed delicately.

Joelzi grinned and took another sip of her

coffee. "Reel it back in, Grace, you're off in another world. I'd have thought two kids and a workaholic husband would have rubbed some of the honeymoon bliss off." Adam and Grace had been married for eleven months now.

"Adam doesn't work the same kind of hours since we've been married. He likes coming home," Grace said, her eyes shining and a grin stretching her face. Leaving her memories and returning her gaze to her best friend, Grace said "I'm sorry, Joelzi, I'm being insensitive. We were talking about you and Carver," Grace prodded. "According to Adam, Carver's eyes 'bugged out' when he first saw you before the wedding." Grace giggled. "Adam was seriously impressed with Carver's undivided attention to you during the wedding."

"I'm sure it had something to do with that beautiful raspberry dress you picked out as my maid-of-honor outfit," Joelzi said. "And my irresistible persona," she added sarcastically.

"Stop it Joelzi, no self-deprecation among friends. You are beautiful, but more importantly you are caring, generous, and loyal." Grace paused to take a sip of her coffee. "Adam thought you might be the one to 'shake up Carver's safe and steady modus operandi.'" Grace raised her eyebrows suggestively and grinned at Joelzi.

"And then you two tag-teamed to help us when Adam and I had our blow-out." A frown flitted across Grace's face. Grace and Adam had hit a major roadblock in their marriage when Grace had been accused of dealing in drugs. Adam had walked out and Grace had called her best friend in tears. Joelzi and Carver had worked together to help their friends work through the situation and had spent the day at the zoo with Carver's brother, Georgie, and Adam's daughters, Zoe and Remi. It was a memory that Joelzi cherished. Not because of the painful situation for Grace and Adam, but because it had given her a chance to be with Carver. Even though she and Carver had not been dating or involved, she had felt like a couple. They had worked well together and she had secretly hoped something would come of it.

"Carver is not interested," Joelzi said flatly. "I have no love life. And there are no 'men after God's heart,'" she used air quotes again, "out there—well, none that I'm interested in," Joelzi said with a disgusted snort, her normally happy grin twisted into a smirk. "If a man is interested, he should pick up the phone and call, or at least take opportunities to chat at work," Joelzi said dully. "No. Dr. Ellis is not interested."

Grace frowned in thought. "I know Carver is reserved, but you two aren't exactly strangers. Have you offered any encouragement? You do come across as self-assured and not in the market sometimes."

"No, I don't," said Joelzi, crossing her arms over her chest.

Grace's eyebrows raised and her mouth popped open before she recovered and a smirk appeared on her face. "Oh, the arms crossed, that fake smile thing you do when someone you like—like Carver Ellis—is in the area—" Grace's hand raised and flipped toward her friend. "The, 'I'm not on the market' image?" she asked, crossing her arms in front of her and leaning back in her seat. "Yes, Joelzi," Grace continued with a sharp nod of her head. "You do that. It's like you've got a decorative brick wall built up high around you," Grace's arms raised as though stretching for the top of the wall.

"And you've thrown concertina wire on the top for good measure." Grace's arms dropped to the countertop. "Men can see in through the decorative brick, but they can't get in to the real you. The real you is so wonderful, Joelzi. I don't know what I would've done without your friendship," Grace finished her tirade with gentle pleading.

"If there's concertina wire on the top of my 'decorative brick wall,' there's a good reason for it," Joelzi said enigmatically, ignoring the compliment and leaning her arms on the countertop.

"See? Just like that." Grace nodded toward Joelzi's body language. Putting her coffee cup down in front of her, she leaned toward her friend. "Who hurt you, Joelzi? You are sabotaging your life for something that the people who love you can't see." Grace paused, searching Joelzi's face, her words hanging in the air between them. "I know you've been hurt, Joelzi." Grace stretched her hand out to touch Joelzi's arm. "And when you're ready to talk it out, I'm ready to listen."

Joelzi felt her eyes burn and her vision clouded with moisture. *Grace is the kindest person. She's been a real friend. You can trust Grace with your past. Maybe. Soon. Grace would definitely be the one to share the sordid details with. But not today. I'm not ready.*

"I'm sorry you've been hurt, Joelzi." Grace took a sip of her coffee and looked straight into Joelzi's eyes. "Truly… but one thing God has impressed on me after all my own chaos, is that I shouldn't be so disappointed with the last season of my life that I stall my forward momentum. Don't be afraid to move into the next season. Last season's trauma, however simple or complicated, can grow tenacity, character, and purpose for the next season. It

23

doesn't need to be wasted hurt—not if you let God into the mess. I should know. I'm not saying your past isn't painful, Joelzi. I don't know your past. But I am reminding you, as your friend, that God can take ashes and give you beauty. Jesus is still with you, Joelzi. He's got a great plan for your life. And whatever baggage you're carrying around—it doesn't have to derail your future."

Joelzi and Grace were quiet for a moment, sipping their coffee and mulling over their conversation, while Joelzi tried to get the pools in her eyes to reabsorb.

"What about online dating?" asked Grace. Joelzi laugh-snorted. *Leave it to Grace to shift the conversation so directly.*

"Excuse me. You wouldn't do online dating, but it's okay for me?" Joelzi asked.

"Point conceded," Grace said, lifting both hands in a show of surrender. "Let's talk about something else—since this is a sensitive subject," Grace said with a gentle grin. "Tell me about this new clinic you're volunteering at."

Relief poured over Joelzi at the chance to change the subject. "Oh Grace, I'm really enjoying it. It's a sliding scale clinic for people who can't afford health care. All the providers are volunteers and it's so rewarding. I feel like I'm a part of helping people who are desperate for care. It's small, but sufficient," Joelzi finished, taking a sip of her coffee.

"That sounds like something I would like to be involved in," said Grace.

"You should check it out, Grace, you might like it," said Joelzi.

"I think I would," agreed Grace, "and it would help me keep my credentials up, too. I'll have to mention it to Adam."

Seven

He heard Joelzi's voice before he saw her. Its upbeat lilt called out to him, energized him, even as he struggled to ignore the joy that surged in his chest. It felt like the deep breath you take at the end of a hard run. *Why am I so aware of her?* He asked himself as he sat down at the computer in the doctor's area and looked over the patients on the computer screen. Gallbladder waiting for surgery... Young pregnant female waiting for an ultrasound... He heard Joelzi's laugh over the din of the ER. *She is off limits.* He began ticking down the mental list he'd made in desperation to keep her off his radar. *Number one: she is a co-worker and you don't date co-workers. Number two: she is Grace's best friend and things could go all kinds of south and interfere with my friendship with Adam if I dated her and it didn't go well. Just pull yourself together, man. God,*

I could use some help here. Maybe bring along someone who fits the requirements. But Joelzi and Georgie are fast friends. His inner voice prompted. *Isn't that an absolute must-have? Argh. I've got to stop thinking about her and concentrate.* Thankfully, Dr Cohen, the doctor Carver was replacing appeared at his computer. "Hey Carver, are you ready to take over? I just got the ultrasound back on the pregnant female in Room Six, she's got an ectopic pregnancy..." The details of work pulled him in, and Carver focused on the job in front of him.

Eight

Tuesday, September 7th
Adam

"Hey man," Adam greeted Carver with a brotherly hug, "How have you been?" Adam and Carver were in their favorite booth at their favorite sports grill. Carver had gotten there a bit earlier so he had placed their regular order of hamburgers and fries. Their sodas were already waiting for them on the table when Adam arrived.

"Things are good," said Carver. "I'm checking out an opportunity to volunteer at a free clinic."

"A free clinic?" asked Adam.

"I saw the sign at work. They need all kinds of volunteers. Medical people obviously, but the site says they'll take anybody...I'm thinking about seeing if Georgie would like to volunteer with me."

"Georgie would be a great greeter," said Adam.

"You mean interrogator," said Carver with a grin, "Georgie can get all the details from people without even trying."

"It would be a great way for Georgie to be involved in an outreach," said Adam.

"Yes, I've always wanted to find a way to do something like this with him. I've always thought I would end up doing medical missions of some kind and that Georgie would have a part in that project," said Carver.

"When will you check it out?" asked Adam.

"They're only open on Thursday evenings, so either this Thursday or next. I need to run the idea past my parents and make sure they are on board before mentioning it to Georgie. I'm confident Georgie would be 'all in'."

"That sounds exciting, Carver, new adventures and all that..." Adam unwrapped his straw and stuck it in his drink. "How's the dating quest going?"

"My dating life is a flop," said Carver.

"You need to ask Joelzi out," said Adam, "You two got along exceptionally well during my debacle with Grace."

"No way. I work with Joelzi," said Carver, beginning to drum his fingers nervously on the table, "You know I don't date people I work with."

Adam took a long pull through his straw, letting the sharp taste of pure Pepsi Cola pepper his taste buds. Adam didn't get soda very often these days. Grace was determined that they eat healthily. Adam was a fan of eating healthily, since it meant Grace cooked. And Grace could cook. Still, it was nice to get away with his best friend and enjoy a soda and a burger every once in a while. Adam set the glass back down on the table, noting that Carver had not stopped hammering the table with his fingertips, and returned to the conversation at hand. The drumming fingers were a sign of stress for the quiet man sitting across from him. Carver had been his friend for a long time now, and Adam was privy to Carver's stress-relieving techniques. "So, the online dating is working?" Adam asked.

"Not exactly," Carver said. "Number Five was a disaster."

"Number Five...you're numbering them?" Adam asked, leaning forward in disbelief.

"I'm not exactly trying to remember their names—they were all flops," said Carver.

"It seems to me Joelzi's a prime candidate," Adam continued, leaning back in his seat. "Joelzi loves God. You, Grace, and I all know how loyal she is. She's been a real friend to Grace—for a very long time—and now me. You even attend the same church and singles group. Seems like an obvious choice."

"It's complicated, Adam," Carver said, a frown drawing his eyebrows together and the rhythm on the table becoming stronger.

Adam ducked his face until he could control the smile that wanted to escape. "Of course, it's complicated, Carver. You make everything complicated," Adam said pointedly.

"Just because I'm careful doesn't mean—"

"Carver, you're so careful you'd take God out of the equation if you could."

"That's not fair," Carver protested.

"Carver, we're friends—real friends. You've seen me at my absolute worst. You've supported me and told me the truth when I didn't want to hear it." Adam leaned forward. "So, I'm going to return the favor," Adam said *sotto voce*, "you're scared." The drumming stopped, but Adam continued in his regular voice. "You don't want to date the woman that's right in front of you because it doesn't fit your rules." Adam held his hands in front of him to stop

Carver from interrupting, "Rules that are logical—I'll give you that—but a woman on paper is not the same as a woman in person." Adam's chin and eyebrows lifted in unison as he continued, "You date all these other women. But only once, because they don't have the grit and integrity you're looking for in a woman. You've asked God for a wife. Seems to me He's put a spotlight on this one and you balk. What's that about?" Adam leaned back in the booth and spread his hands open before Carver. "Afraid you'll lose control? What would happen if you had feelings for Joelzi? What if she stirred up your heart? Got under your skin? Made you cry out to God?" Adam laughed softly, his eyes lifted to the ceiling, his memories flowing. "Marriage is a beautiful, terrifying journey... You don't realize how fiercely you can love another person and how deeply they can hurt or disappoint you—just because you care. It's exhilarating and it's humbling and it's worth the struggles when they come. I read somewhere that marriage isn't there to make you happy, but to make you holy. That may be true, but I'm mostly happy too, Carver. If God's put it on your heart to be married—then marriage is a good thing. Don't let your rules about working with someone from the same department at your hospital stop you from checking out the possibility that Joelzi is the one. There are plenty of hospitals in the Oklahoma City area, either of you can move to another one if your dating relationship gets untenable."

Carver leaned back and rested his head against the back of the booth cushion. "Okay."

"Okay?" Adam's head cocked to one side and both eyebrows rose in question.

"Okay. You convinced me. I'll think about asking her out," Carver said with a sigh.

"Don't look so down in the mouth about it, dude." Adam's eyebrows rose and he skewered Carver with a direct look. "Joelzi is a lovely person. More than good enough for the likes of you. Her fun-loving nature could take on your staid one and bring some life to your sorry existence. And lucky you, she's easy on the eyes, too."

Carver sat up and took a sip of his drink, the hint of a smile on his face. "Did you enjoy that takedown, brother? Cause it sure looked like you did."

Adam grinned at his friend. "Do you know how good it feels to be on this side of the table after all my troubles with Grace? I'm not complaining." They both laughed in relief as their burgers and fries were served.

Nine

Friday, September 10th
Joelzi

She was supposed to be having coffee with Grace. They were seated around Grace's big kitchen bar and Joelzi was sipping her coffee and carrying the conversation about last night's activity in the ER. "You'll never believe what happened last night." Joelzi paused for effect, but Grace only smiled in a distracted way. "A young pregnant woman came into the ER screaming. I thought she was in labor, but she wasn't holding her stomach and I couldn't see any amniotic fluid leaking on the floor. Besides, she was holding her head and screaming 'It's eating me, it's eating me.' You cannot make this stuff up." Joelzi paused to take a sip of coffee and noted that Grace had yet to taste her coffee. "You haven't even sipped your coffee," Joelzi said. "It's gonna get cold. You hate cold coffee," Joelzi said.

"Coffee doesn't sit on my stomach very well

right now," Grace said quietly, taking a long breath through her nose with eyes closed. "Go on," she said.

"Well, we got the girl in a room and got her calmed down enough to realize she had something in her ear. So, Carver came in and looked in her ear. You will never believe what he saw..."

Grace's smile is decidedly off, thought Joelzi. *I'll just cut to the chase.* "It was a cockroach!" Joelzi said lifting her hands in emphasis. "A cockroach in her ear. Have you ever heard of such a thing?" *Grace is definitely not looking well. In fact, she looks a tad green around the gills,* thought Joelzi. *Maybe she's lost her edge. I never thought it would happen to her. She was always so calm in the turmoil of the ER.* "Well, anyway, Carver drowned the cockroach with oil and then picked it out with alligator clamps."

Grace swallowed and nodded slowly; her eyes closed while she took another slow steady breath through her nose. She opened her eyes and looked at Joelzi intently, and then a panicked look came over her face and she ran to the kitchen sink and heaved over it.

"Grace, honey, are you sick? Why didn't you say something? We didn't have to have coffee today." Joelzi ran to the cabinet where she knew Grace kept the kitchen towels, grabbed a fresh towel, and ran cool water over it as Zoe entered the kitchen from the living room where she had been playing.

"Momma's sick 'cause she's having a baby," Zoe said matter-of-factly, making her way over to where Grace stood hanging over the sink. Zoe patted Grace on her hip, "I'm sorry you's feeling naus-ated, Momma. You need to lay down on the couch?"

The cool kitchen towel hung in Joelzi's hand and

33

a ball of nausea began roiling in her stomach as Zoe's words sank in. *Grace is pregnant.*

Ten

Joelzi paused just outside Grace's front door and took a deep breath. *I have to get this under control. I can't keep having panic attacks every time someone I know tells me they're pregnant or hands me a baby to hold.* Joelzi pressed her right hand over her heart and took another deep breath through her nose. *Better.* She stepped off the landing and headed to her car, wiping a hand across her face to clear her blurred vision. It came away damp. Joelzi swallowed hard and straightened her posture in determination as she made her way across the circular drive to her car. She buckled in and put her car in drive, pulling slowly out of the drive and onto the residential street, but her vision blurred so badly she had to pull over and park one block later. Joelzi laid her head down on the steering wheel and let the tears flow. *When am I ever going to get over this, God? I've been dragging this stuff around for years now. I thought it would go away, but every turn it's there. Haunting me. Reminding me of my failures.*

And what must Grace think? She tells me she's pregnant and I leave her house as quickly as I can get her settled on the couch. Grace doesn't even realize how easy she has it. Her life is so perfect. Grace would never do what I've done. "Argh!" Joelzi groaned out loud. *When am I ever going to get past this? It's been seven years and it still feels like yesterday...*

Eleven

Seven years earlier
Joelzi

"Oh, come on Joelzi, people do this every day. I've already paid the fee. The rest of it's up to you," Myron said in frustration, glancing at his wristwatch impatiently. They were sitting in the front seat of his car, pulled up to the clinic "I don't have all day, Joelzi. Your appointment was for 15 minutes ago. I've got football practice in an hour."

"I...I can't just walk in that place. I'm not that kind of girl...I..."

Myron turned in his seat behind the wheel, rolling his eyes at Joelzi, "Well, I guess you are that kind of girl, 'cause we're here..."

Joelzi shuddered at the harsh words. *I guess I am that kind of girl. I wasn't supposed to be. I was raised right.*

Mema Anna's frank voice wafted through Joelzi's mind with another rendition of The Talk. "Now you listen here, Joelzi, there's plenty of folk out there who'd trash you for the sheer pleasure of the trashin.' But you were intended for better, girl. Um hum. God's got a call on your life—since the beginning, Joelzi. Your momma sure had a hard time getting you. We prayed you in, Honey. Don't you ever forget that. You were a prayed-in child. Born to be a blessing. Born to bring honor to the Lord. Lots of people out there—they just want to see the Lord's children swimming in dirt. The deeper you fall, the more you hear their self-satisfied 'I knew you would fall—you're just like the rest of us.' No joy in seein' a body come through. In seein' righteousness. Um hum. So, you keep your eyes straight, girl. Don't be letting the things of this world tempt you to go soft with your calling. I've got eyes. I can see the Lord blessed you with beauty—but don't be letting that go to your head. We never had no fancy cheerleading when I was comin' up—no football team either. I guess it's fine to be cheering on your team. 'Specially since it gave you that scholarship to get your nursing degree. That's a fine thing. Education can help you go far. Might even get you a doctor for a husband," Mema Anna had cackled as though she had made a good joke, but then her face had turned fierce, "Just you watch yourself, girl. Nuthin' good comes of focusing too much on how we look or how much leg we can show. Oh, my mercy," Mema Anna had muttered to herself, raising her eyes to the ceiling as though she and God were having a face-to-face conversation, "the girl's too fine lookin' by far. Jesus, help us now." Joelzi remembered rolling her eyes at the ceiling every time she and Mema Anna had had some form of The Talk. But now...

"Oh, Jesus, help me now," Joelzi muttered to herself.

"What?" Myron asked, exasperation coloring his words.

"Nothing," Joelzi said, opening the car door and climbing out with resignation. *What would Momma say if she were here?* Joelzi's feet were like lead, but the hopeless chasm sucking her to the clinic door was unrelenting.

A woman greeted her at the front desk, smiling a reassuring smile at Joelzi, "Did you have an appointment?"

"Yes, I'm a little late..." Joelzi offered, hoping they might have to reschedule, although she didn't know why that was a reassurance. She was already twelve weeks along. If she waited much longer, she would start to show. She had missed three periods, her breasts were sore, and Joelzi had been nauseated and heaving over the sink every morning with disturbing regularity for weeks now.

"I'll just go check and make sure they're ready," said the woman, standing from her desk and walking through to the back area.

Joelzi's thoughts would not slow. At first, her sorority sisters had teased her about the constant hangovers, but now they just looked at Joelzi with a sad understanding. Joelzi had been proud—confident it would never happen to her. So, she hadn't been on the pill, or even had Myron use a condom—not that that had been an option, Joelzi recalled. *I asked him to stop. I begged him, and he just kept on. How could I have thought he cared about me? Even now, he's waiting for me to 'take care of this' so he can get back to football practice.* She and this pregnancy were an inconvenience to Myron. *But who can I turn to? This would have broken Momma's heart. Thank God, Mema Anna and Momma aren't around to witness my total failure. I can't go home. I would have to quit school when I lack one year. Everyone at home is expecting me to finish and get out of the house. They're counting on me to not be another mouth to feed—not bring another one home. I have to finish school. And I can't afford to take on a baby right now—it's the hardest part of the program. There's just no other way.*

"They're ready for you now," the receptionist came back through a door into the front area.

Joelzi firmed her jaw. It was time to get this over with. One thing was sure—Myron was no good for her. Joelzi would take responsibility for her part of the situation. But Myron was good for only one thing now, taking her home when this was done. Then she would   cut   all   ties.

Twelve

Thirty minutes later

Joelzi slid gingerly into the front seat of Myron's waiting vehicle.

"Finally," Myron said throwing the car into reverse before Joelzi had had time to fully buckle her seatbelt. "I barely have enough time to get you back to your sorority house before heading to football practice," Myron snarled in frustration, "We could have done this better if you'd just gone in when we first got here."

Joelzi buckled into her seat and stared straight ahead saying nothing.

"So, it went okay? You took care of it?" Myron asked as he backed out of the clinic parking spot and made the turn towards the campus.

Twin tears made their way slowly down Joelzi's cheeks, but she said nothing. *I feel violated. Again.* The nurse's condescending words had assured her. "You'll be fine in a few days—good as new. We'll want to get you on birth control, so this doesn't happen again. And we'll give you a doctor's note so you can take it easy for the next couple of days, but you'll be surprised at how quickly you'll get back to your regular routine." But Joelzi ached deep inside. It had hurt. And now she was cramping and aching, but that was nothing compared to the ache in her heart. She was so disappointed in herself. Clutching her hands over her stomach, she began slowly rocking back and forth. *How could I have killed my baby? I'm no better than a murderer. This can never happen again.*

The deep shame of that day washed over Joelzi again like a familiar tsunami. Without realizing it, she wrapped her arms around her stomach and began the slow rocking that had comforted her for the past seven years. *I deserved what I got.* She pulled the feelings over her and wrapped them tightly around her heart like a bandage that should have soothed it. *I'm used goods. No good man will ever want me if they know what I have done. Worthless. Broken. Stupid.* The voice's familiar monologue began its rant. Joelzi sat in her car seven years later and sank into the memories of that day and all the days since.

Thirteen

Sunday, September 12th
Joelzi

She couldn't help herself. Joelzi glanced to her left and let her gaze track over the middle section of the church auditorium as she looked for a place to sit. That's where he usually sat when he attended. Her attention became more concentrated when she didn't see him. *Maybe he had to work today*. She had given up on seeing him today when her eye caught the shiny pate and closely trimmed full beard of the tall, sinewy, brown-skinned man she worked with; her heart skipped a beat. *Carver Ellis is in the house*. Joelzi looked away quickly in case he had seen her...but how could that be, he would have to turn around in his seat to see her checking him out. She felt the tug of her emotions, wishing Carver would notice her and simultaneously struggling to keep her mind on the whole reason she was in church. *I'm so double-minded. I'm anxious to find him every*

Sunday I'm here, but then frustrated with myself for getting distracted. She found a seat in the right center section of the auditorium and moved to the middle, relieved when a heavy-set couple moved into the row after her, blocking her view of Carver Ellis. *Time to get your mind on worship, where it belongs.*

Fourteen

Carver pulled his SUV into the parking lot and turned off the ignition.

"Is that it?" asked Georgie, peering around Carver and the steering wheel at the unassuming wood-clad storefront building. "It says Hope Clinic. This is where we're going to volunteer?"

"Looks like it." Carver nodded his head. Already a queue of people lined the sidewalk. It looked like there was truly a need. After seeing the sign at work, he had gone on the website. They were looking for all kinds of volunteers. They needed doctors, nurses, admin people, pharmacists, translators, cleaners. 'There is a place for everyone,' the site had said. Carver had checked with his mom and dad that it would be okay for Georgie to volunteer with him and they had agreed; it would be good for Georgie to be involved. If Carver ever ran a clinic like this, he would want the 'Georgies' of the world to be involved. And volunteering in this clinic would be a small way for Carver to give back and get his feet wet in medical missions. Carver and Georgie got out of the car and Carver grabbed his medical bag from the back seat before locking the doors.

"We're gonna help people, right, Carver?" Georgie asked, bouncing on the balls of his feet with excitement as they walked toward the entrance.

"Absolutely." Carver looked down affectionately at his younger brother and put a hand on his shoulder. *What would I do without him, God? He's made such an impact on my life. He's so honest and caring. When I forget, he reminds me how good You are.*

Fifteen

Carver

To say he had been surprised to see her there was an understatement. More telling was the jolt of pleasure that coursed through him at the moment she turned in the hallway and made eye contact with him. *Joelzi is here?*

"Hi, Georgie. Hi, Dr. Ellis. Are you here to help?" Joelzi had asked. Carver had taken a moment to catch himself, afraid he might stutter if he rushed his words. *Afraid I might stutter.* Yes, stuttering had been an issue in the past, but he had learned to slow himself down and modulate his breathing. It was rarely a problem these days. But still, when caught off guard his tongue could get the better of him and he hated feeling inept. By the time he was prepared to speak, Georgie had answered. Georgie may have Down's Syndrome, but he was not shy, reticent, or concerned about feelings of ineptness. And Georgie had never had a problem with stuttering. Carver sighed. He usually worried about women his age disregarding or dismissing Georgie. But not Joelzi. Joelzi and Georgie had always had a connection—from their very first meeting during the Adam and Grace disaster.

"Hi, Joelzi. Carver and me are volunteering. It's our first time," Georgie said, standing his full five-foot height, a grin stretching across his face and his hands on his hips.

"Well, you'll be wanting to talk to Dr. Lang. He's one of the clinic founders," Joelzi said, her beautiful smile exposing straight white teeth, made more appealing with her red lipstick. *Stunning.* "Come on back this way, Dr. Lang's in the break room. We usually open doors for the patients fifteen minutes before we start and then have a simple corporate prayer with everyone—patients and volunteers—before starting the schedule." Joelzi walked them back to the kitchen area, pointing out the exam rooms and the pharmacy on their way. Joelzi left them with Dr. Lang and went back out to finish something she had been working on. Carver and Dr. Lang had quickly exchanged background details before Carver introduced Georgie to Dr. Lang.

"Well, Georgie, we're pleased to have you on our team," said Dr. Lang.

"I'm happy to be here, sir," said Georgie, "I like helping people." Georgie crossed his arms in his normal stance, feet wide, and added, "I like people."

"Well, you're going to like it here, then. We've got lots of people, and they all need help," said Dr. Lang. "Carver, why don't you two follow me? Let's get Georgie situated at the front to help greet people, and then I'll run through our standard procedure with you to get you comfortable."

Sixteen

Later that evening outside Hope Clinic
Carver

Carver's mind was running rampant with ideas on how to improve the clinic flow and patient care as he and Georgie walked Joelzi out to the parking lot where their cars were parked. Three physicians had seen a total of forty patients in the past three and a half hours. The nurses had improved those numbers by taking detailed histories and getting simple lab results where it was possible. It had been satisfying work, Carver reflected as they paused in the spot between his and Joelzi's cars. Carver zoned back into the conversation in time to hear Georgie extend the invitation.

"You should come to Ellis Saturday Supper with us, Joelzi. It's not this Saturday, we had it last Saturday, but it's on Saturday at my house," Georgie said. "Tell Joelzi when the next Saturday Supper is, Carver," insisted Georgie.

*He is a thorn in my side*r. "Georgie, you can't just invite people over for family dinners."

"She needs to be there," Georgie insisted, looking up at Carver as though Carver had no common sense.

"But you haven't asked Mom," Carver tried to stall the conversation. "Remember she told you the last time you did this that you had to ask first."

"Joelzi is supposed to be there." Georgie crossed his arms over his chest and gave his best Superman focused stare, his bottom lip slightly protruding.

"I'm not the bad guy, Georgie, you can stop the laser focus thing," Carver said.

"Mom and Dad need to meet her," Georgie said, repositioning his crossed arms. "She's the one."

Carver felt his heart leap in his chest as a wave of heat began rushing over his face. *Did she hear Georgie's last statement?*

"Hey, guys," Joelzi said at the same time Georgie made his declaration. She was waving a hand between them. "I'm right here."

"So you are," Carver said under his breath, closing his eyes in an attempt to maintain his calm. *It's dark and she can't see my face.*

"What's that supposed to mean?" Joelzi asked, crossing her arms over her chest, her voice raising a notch as her eyebrows rose and moved together.

"Don't you like Joelzi?" Georgie prompted Carver a little too loudly, stepping a bit closer to Joelzi's side, but maintaining the protective arms-crossed stance.

"Yeah, Carver, what's the matter with me?" Joelzi lifted her crossed arms and repositioned them across her chest, and her left eyebrow angled up in an appealing way as she tilted her head in question.

Carver didn't miss the way she stepped over to match Georgie's stance or the smile she tried to control before she grinned down at Georgie.

Carver was momentarily distracted by the eyebrow thing. Two other women in his life had that ability. *It's like walking through a mine field.* And now she and Georgie were like a team. Together. Against him. "Of course I like Joelzi," Carver chose to address Georgie. "She's a nice girl...l...l...lady...she's nice, okay?" Carver refused to make eye contact with Joelzi.

"Do you 'want-to-hold-her-hand' like her?" Georgie persisted, his eyebrows meeting in the middle and his mouth a straight line.

Carver felt heat slide up his chest and flush his face again. *I haven't blushed since high school, but tonight I'm on a roll. Not sure Georgie will live long enough for me to have the brother-to-brother straight talk that's definitely happening when this is over.*

"Or is she just like the other girl-ladies at church that laugh funny and talk to you all the time?" Georgie continued; a frown of concentration perched on his face.

Joelzi's laughter floated across the parking lot, and Carver glanced her way. She grinned impishly at Carver before turning to hug Georgie. "I'd be pleased to attend an Ellis Saturday Supper with you, Georgie. Just clear it with your mom and call me— your brother has my number." She turned to Carver with that eyebrow lifted his direction, "Unless you've deleted me since the Grace and Adam issue?"

"I didn't delete you," Carver said in frustration, blowing out a noisy breath.

"Okay then, boys, I think I'll remove myself from

this testosterone-ladened environment and go home. Later." Joelzi rippled the fingers of her right hand in good-bye as she unlocked her car and climbed in.

Carver and Georgie stood together watching her drive away. *She is mesmerizing,* Carver thought before he could wrestle the idea to the ground. *Too bad she works in the same ER.* His rationale slid into place with the ease of constant use.

"Carver?" Georgie said, reminding Carver they were still standing there watching the taillights of Joelzi's car fade into the night.

"Hmm?" said Carver. *It's not a bad idea having her over for an Ellis Saturday Supper. And I did tell Adam I'd consider asking her out...*

"What's a testosterone ladder environment?"

Carver focused on Georgie, wrapping him in a side hug and patting his cheek a little rougher than necessary. "Let's get you home, buddy."

"But Carver..."

"Home, buddy. Now. You can ask Mom and Dad about that later."

Seventeen

"So..." Sharon Ellis paused and looked at Carver after passing him a fresh glass of her homemade iced tea across the counter, "you're bringing a young lady to our next Saturday Supper?"

Carver had just taken the first swallow of his favorite drink—sunbaked tea, not too sweet, with a hint of lemon and basil—when his mother posed her question. His throat spasmed and he coughed, spewing some of the drink across the counter. *That Georgie. I'm going to clobber him the next time I see him.* Carver took the napkin his mom passed him and wiped his mouth and then patted the front of his clean polo shirt. *Well, it had been clean.* There was silence in the kitchen as he busied himself cleaning the countertop. But the silence remained even as he made his way to the trashcan to throw the used napkin away. Carver chanced a glance at his mother. Sharon Ellis stood calmly. Her left eyebrow lifted in question when he looked her way. She had always done that—just lifted that eyebrow and waited patiently for her questions to be answered. She had picked it up from Grandma Ruby, perfected it on her elementary school students, and later used it on her own children. It didn't matter that he was a grown man. It still worked. Carver went back to his seat and took a slow steady drink of tea, before meeting his mother's eyes.

"Georgie invited her," Carver said.

"Yes, Georgie mentioned that. He said something about how she needed to be here and that you liked her..."

"She's one of the nurses I work with."

"I believe Georgie said it was the 'handholding kind of like,'" Sharon Ellis said firmly. "He might have even said 'she's the one.'" His mom's left eyebrow remained poised.

No more easy wins for Georgie during our wrestling matches; I'm going to pin him immediately—and not let him up till he cries 'calf rope'. Carver waited, letting his eyes trace the pattern of the granite veins on the counter before lifting his gaze and meeting his mother's eyes. "I do like her. I just..." The silence hung in the air as Sharon Ellis took a sip of her iced tea and waited.

Carver sighed in resignation. *Might as well get this over with.* "Joelzi Parker is larger than life, Mom. She's got the whole ER wrapped around her little finger. People love her—and for good reason— Joelzi brings life and laughter wherever she is. But if I date Joelzi and it doesn't work out—for whatever reason—I'm the one who's gonna be the outcast. Working in the ER will be next to impossible if it doesn't work out." Carver watched his mother take another slow sip of her tea, before setting her glass back down. She ran her finger up the glass, catching the condensation as she examined the glass carefully. Carver knew she was gathering her words. After a moment, she lifted her gaze, a thoughtful expression on her face.

"Carver, honey, you've always been so careful. And your dad and I are glad that you take things slow and steady. You've been a model son. You work hard at everything you do, and you don't treat others' emotions lightly. Those are all commendable characteristics." She paused.

"But...? I hear a 'but' in your voice," Carver said.

Sharon Ellis sighed and placed both hands around her glass of tea. Looking up, she continued, "But I would also say you haven't put yourself out there. You haven't risked anything—not your work environment, not your heart. Do you want to find someone and settle down and get married?"

"Of course I do. But I've been busy with school and then getting settled in my job and..."

"And now you have time to find 'the one'," Sharon Ellis said softly.

"I date," Carver said, noting his voice had risen and working to speak calmly.

"I wonder...when was the last time you went on a second date?" his mother pondered.

"There's been no one I've wanted to take out a second time. They all seem so superficial. It's like they have no depth—no life goals beyond finding someone who can buy an expensive house and give them two kids, one dog, and a lifetime membership to the country club," Carver defended himself.

"Well, that *is* off-putting. But there is someone out there for you. Sometimes you have to step out in faith and let God do the rest. Sometimes you have to get in over your chest in order to let God move,"

Sharon offered quietly.

"What does that mean?" asked Carver.

"It means you have to risk sharing your heart—your dreams. Carver, you're looking for a woman of character. Have you ever shared with any of your dates your dream of running a medical mission? Sharing a detail like that could quickly cull the women waiting in the wings. Why don't you just let it be known you're not looking for a trophy wife? Or better yet, pay attention to young ladies involved in that mission work you started volunteering at and see who shows up there."

Carver took a slow sip of his tea. He had done that. Joelzi had been volunteering at the Hope Clinic before he had had the time to get involved. But Joelzi didn't know it had been a dream of his. And his mother didn't know that Joelzi had been at the clinic before he had. That was telling. He loved these talks with his mom. She was a woman of grace and wisdom. She was a model of the kind of character he was looking for in a wife. She had a point. He wasn't going to find the kind of woman he was looking for in the regular places.

"That being said," his mother continued, "your dad and I are looking forward to meeting your friend at the next Saturday Supper. I believe you have three weeks to firm up the invitation and get used to the idea of bringing a woman to your parents' home to meet your family." Sharon grinned. "I recommend you prepare for your brothers' reactions. Just know that your father and I have your back," she added with a wink.

Okay, maybe she's a little too gleeful sometimes. Carver took a sip of his tea so he wouldn't blurt out anything that might be telling. If he were keeping score, the scoreboard would read: Georgie two:

Carver zero. *But there's still time to decide,* Carver assured himself. *I'm not going to be pushed into ruining a good work relationship to keep my family happy.*

Eighteen

She was working one of the trauma rooms when the call came in from 911. It was non-emergent in the sense that it wasn't heart- or trauma-related, but the smell that permeated the entire ER as the paramedics brought in the older man was eye-watering and causing general heaving in the main area. *Well, that's what most of the others said.* Joelzi wasn't really known for her keen sense of smell. It had always been that way for her. And at times like these, when all of her teammates were gagging and running to put a wintergreen-covered gauze pad inside the masks they had chosen to wear for themselves, Joelzi was reminded of the plus side to having poor olfactory glands. The smell was bad, even she could tell. She slid a mask on and took the time to add her own wintergreen-covered gauze to the inside—she wasn't oblivious to the odor—and stepped into the room for report. Apparently, the patient had stopped taking care of his diabetes. And when his feet started oozing, his wife had gotten tired of the mess and started covering them with plastic grocery bags. The charge nurse, Tom, had braved the triage process with her and they were gingerly removing all the plastic grocery bags to better assess the legs when Dr Ellis opened the door.

The look on his face was priceless; his eyes widened and then began tearing up. Joelzi saw him swallow hard. Then he quickly pivoted and left the room. Joelzi smirked behind her mask and went back to work.

They finished vital signs and Joelzi had her patient comfortable when she exited the room. Carver Ellis stood at her nursing station, masked like all the other staff, apparently waiting for her assessment.

"How do you do that?" Carver asked quietly.

"What, exactly are you asking about?" asked Joelzi.

"How can you handle the smell?"

Joelzi grinned up at him, her cheeks pumping up the sides of her mask. "Unlike most of the world, I have a poor sense of smell."

"Apparently," Carver said dryly.

"I did take the time to put some of the wintergreen oil on a piece of gauze and stick it in my mask so I'm not above using every trick in the trade, but with my bad sense of smell and my mask, I'm doing pretty well."

"That's nice," said Carver. "Do you have any suggestions for someone who has an excellent sense of smell?"

"Sometimes excellence is overrated," said Joelzi

with a laugh as she finished inputting vital signs in the electronic medical record. "Let me get you a piece of gauze with some wintergreen oil on it and then you're just going to have to man up and doctor your way through your exam," she said with a grin.

"You're all charm and caring," Carver said, his eyes crinkling at the edges in humor. "But I will take you up on your offer. I'm going to need all the help I can get."

"Follow me and I'll get you all set up," said Joelzi.

"Right beside you," Carver replied, matching his step with hers as they headed to the medication dispensing section in the middle of the ER.

Wouldn't that be lovely to have Carver right beside me? Joelzi thought.

Later that night, Joelzi triaged a young man in his thirties who had been working in his garage and had somehow impaled an Allen wrench through his hand.

"Wow. That's impressive," said Joelzi when the patient calmly entered her triage room and held up his hand. The short end of the Allen wrench was wrapped around the outside of the boney part of the palm, but inside the skin, so that the short end poked up, holding the skin of the hand up in a tent-like fashion.

"I know, right?" agreed the patient.

"Does it hurt?" Joelzi asked as she checked his pulses and recorded his vital signs.

"It's definitely uncomfortable—it feels weird, but not really painful," the patient said.

"Tell me what happened," Joelzi said, working to get the details for the triage note and keep the patient engaged.

"I was working on a project and tried to use the

Allen wrench in my drill. I don't really know how it happened. Just that I dropped the drill and saw this," he said.

"Well, we've got you covered. Let's get you to a room—are you able to walk or are you feeling lightheaded?"

"I can walk. I drove myself here," he said.

"I'm ordering an x-ray and the doctor will be in to see you shortly. We'll see how this plays out, but if we give you anything for a procedure, you're going to need a ride home. Is there anyone who can do that? You might want to give them a heads up," Joelzi said.

That had been an interesting case. Carver had worked with the young man to try to remove the Allen wrench. Surprisingly, none of the hand bones had broken when the injury had occurred. It was testament to Carver's skill, that he had managed to remove the Allen wrench without further injury. *I love watching him get creative with the unique situations that come through the ER doors. There's no question; Carver Ellis is a brilliant physician.*

Nineteen

Joelzi breezed into Hope Clinic, looking around the crowded front waiting area with a smile. She had been volunteering now for the past four weeks and was beginning to recognize 'the regulars.' "Hi Mr. Williams," Joelzi nodded at the thin older man waiting for his appointment, his walker positioned carefully in front of him. Mr. Williams' face brightened at her greeting, and he smiled a shy smile, minus several key teeth. He was a dear. His wife Addie had died last year and without her subsidies, his income had dropped in half. He'd had to move out of the small home they had rented and was now trying to make ends meet while living in government housing. He had hit the 'donut hole' with his medicines, and he had resorted to coming to the clinic where he could get the medicines free—

not the name brand ones—but effective ones all the same.

Joelzi turned to her right and saw a young teen with light brown-colored skin and serious ebony eyes. *She is new.* The girl looked away when Joelzi's gaze lingered, her fingers moving to the strand of faded blue hair that stood out against her natural dark brown hair color, as she began twisting that one section repeatedly.

Hmm, she looks like she lost her best friend, thought Joelzi. *Well, I'll find out soon enough, I'd better get checked in and find out who I'm working with   tonight.*

Twenty

Thursday evening, Hope Clinic
Carver

I wonder if she'll be here tonight. The thought wafted through Carver's consciousness as he pulled his SUV into the Hope Clinic parking lot.

"Joelzi's here," said Georgie.

"How do you know?" asked Carver, looking around for the woman who was never far from his thoughts these days.

"That's her car," said Georgie, pointing to the blue CRV parked under the parking lot light.

His heart lifted and he grinned over at Georgie. "I think you're right. Good eye, bro," and he offered his hand for a high five.

"You like her," said Georgie.

Carver felt his breath catch. "Of course I like her, Georgie. She's a great nurse."

"You get a funny kind of smile on your face when you talk about her," said Georgie. "It's okay, Carver," Georgie patted Carver's leg. "Joelzi's a really nice girl. I like her too. But she doesn't make me smile funny like you." Georgie opened his door and climbed out, slamming it behind him as he made his way to Carver. "I won't tell Winston or Luther-Martin," he said seriously.

Carver felt his chest release with the words. His older brothers would rib him mercilessly if they thought Carver was interested in any woman. He had been the younger brother when they had been dating their respective wives and Carver had pulled innumerable stunts on them when they brought their then girlfriends home. But Georgie said he wouldn't tell. *It's going to be a good night volunteering beside Joelzi.*

"But I might tell Momma!" said Georgie with a loud squeal, before turning to hurry across the parking lot toward the clinic.

"Georgie!" Carver called, picking up his pace in hopes of catching his brother who was quickly making his way to the clinic front door. "Georgie!" But Georgie had disappeared into the clinic. Carver felt the slight tightening of his chest muscles as he walked through the front door. Georgie's mouth could blow secret things out of hiding. Carver's simple statement would be misconstrued by Georgie's missing filter. *Georgie just says what he thinks. I'd better catch him before he sees Joelzi.*

Twenty-One

Hope Clinic
Joelzi

Joelzi was in the break room talking to Dr. Lang when Georgie appeared in the doorway. Immediately, she felt as if the sun was shining. *If Georgie is here, Carver is not far behind.*

"Georgie, it's good to see you," said Joelzi. Like a choreographed natural event, Georgie and Joelzi made their way towards each other and hugged.

"Hi, Joelzi," said Georgie, resting his head on Joelzi's chest. "Would you like to be my sister?"

"That's a lovely thought," said Joelzi, looking up to see Carver, breathless and watching his brother with a grimace on his face. She tilted her head in question at Carver. "What does that look mean?" she asked.

Carver's eyes met hers and he shook his head slightly.

"He's afraid I'll tell," said Georgie.

"Afraid you'll tell?" asked Joelzi, her eyebrows

lifting in question.

"I promised not to tell Winston or Luther-Martin. But I didn't promise not to tell Momma." Georgie paused. "And I didn't promise not to tell you..." Georgie peeked back at his brother from the safety of Joelzi's hug.

"Georgie," Carver almost growled. And Joelzi laughed. It was the most natural she had ever seen Carver act.

"Carver said he likes you," said Georgie with a grin.

"Oh, that is interesting," said Joelzi, raising her eyebrows at Carver.

"No I didn't," said Carver forcefully, his hands going to his hips as he frowned at Georgie.

"Yes, you did," crowed Georgie, with a loud laugh.

"What I actually said," said Carver looking at Joelzi, "was that you were an excellent nurse. Georgie just over-interpreted my words."

Joelzi untangled herself from Georgie's hug and struggled to appear serious as she looked between the brothers. "Work starts in five minutes," she said, leaving the break room to go prep her rooms. *Those two are something else,* she thought with a smile. *I'm so glad they're volunteering here too.*

Twenty-Two

Hope Clinic
Merci

She waited, her right leg in a constant bounce. *Will they see me? What will this cost? I'm being stupid. What can they tell me that I don't already know? Mami's right. I should just go back to the abortion place. But I don't want to walk in with those people outside holding signs saying I'm killing my baby. What am I going to do?* Merci stood and looked around the clinic. *I should just go. I just need to get over myself and go take care of this. These people all look like they need a lot more help than I do.*

"Mercedes Lopez?" The pretty, dark-skinned lady Merci had noticed when she first entered the clinic stood just outside the hallway that led to the back of the clinic. She held a clipboard in hand and looked straight at her. "Are you Mercedes?" she asked with an encouraging smile. Her eyes crinkled at the sides and she looked...kind.

Merci felt a surge of hope. *I might as well see*

what she says. Merci nodded her head two times, rapidly to indicate her "yes" and made her way through the feet and walkers crowding the narrow waiting area, her head down in concentration and shame. When she arrived at the spot where the lady was waiting, she chanced a look up. "It's me. I'm Mercedes Lopez, but everyone calls me Merci." Merci expected a terse, "well, come on then." But the lady looked straight into Merci's eyes, "Hi Merci, my name is Joelzi. I'm one of the nurses here. Let me show you to a room."

Twenty-Three

Joelzi

Her heart squeezed as the young Hispanic girl stood up and carefully made her way to where Joelzi stood. Questions raced through Joelzi's mind. The information sheet Merci had filled out on signing into the clinic indicated that it was her first visit to the clinic and the information she wanted to be seen for was "private." Instantly, Joelzi was transported back to her trip to the abortion clinic. She too had gone by herself on that first visit. This girl looked too much like Joelzi had felt on that horrible first visit. Joelzi hadn't done anything but talk to the people at the clinic that day. But the dread in the pit of her stomach could be drummed up with just the memory. *Oh, I don't even know why she's here and I'm projecting all over the place,* Joelzi chastised herself.

"Let's put you here in Room Two." Joelzi let Merci go in before her and shut the door behind them, indicating with her hand that Merci should take one of the two chairs. The exam table stood like a behemoth in the small room, but Joelzi just scooted her chair closer to Merci's and set the clipboard on her lap. "It says here," Joelzi indicated the clipboard, "you're sixteen and you're not on any medications, and you're not allergic to anything. How can we help you today?" Joelzi glanced at the girl's hands, twisting expressively in her lap, before settling her gaze on Merci's beautiful dark eyes.

"I missed my period," Merci said bluntly, a quiver in her voice.

"Okay," said Joelzi. "When was your last period?"

"About three months ago," Merci said.

"Is there any chance you're pregnant?" Joelzi asked.

Merci nodded, her eyes on the floor. "Okay," said Joelzi. Her mind was racing. *It's like déjà vu. I was older, a senior in college, but the fear—not knowing what to do, who to tell. I remember that.* "Have you told your parents?"

"I told my mom," Merci said softly. "Mami says I have to get an abortion or I can't stay with her in the apartment. I went to an abortion clinic...but I'm not sure. I saw your clinic sign from the street." Merci indicated the general direction of outside with her hand. "I was walking home from school and...it said 'Hope Clinic'...I guess...I wanted to check with someone else. My mom says my boyfriend—well, Jose's not my boyfriend anymore—Mami says he has to pay to get rid of the baby. But he says it's not his problem and that I can't prove he's the one. But he is the one. He's the only one I ever did it with." Tears pooled in Merci's eyes as her voice trailed off.

Sorrow, dread, and anger swept over Joelzi.

"Oh, Merci. I'm so sorry." Joelzi's eyes filled with tears. "I'm so sorry you are going through this. How can I help you? What do you need me to do?"

"Tell me what to do?"

Joelzi paused. It would be so easy to step in and organize all the things that she had needed as a pregnant senior in college. Merci was just sixteen years old. No one would fault Joelzi for moving beyond guidance to insisting that she not get an abortion. *But there is a better way,* Joelzi thought. *Do I dare care enough to get involved?* Joelzi swallowed hard and took a deep breath. *Yes, I dare.* "Merci, I'm not going to tell you what to do...but I will tell you my story and maybe it will help you decide your next step."

"Okay," Merci said softly.

Joelzi paused. She had never shared this with anyone, not even Grace. But it was time to move out of the dark and into the light. If her dark places could shed light for others, she was willing. "I didn't sleep around. But I had a boyfriend. We had dated since high school. My parents didn't like him. They said he was overconfident. He was on the football team and he got a scholarship to University of Oklahoma. I was on the cheerleading squad in high school and it helped me get a scholarship to nursing school at University of Oklahoma. My scholarship wasn't as good as his, but it was enough to get me through college if I paid attention and did my work. My parents both worked, and I had a younger sister and brother, so money was tight. I needed that scholarship. Anyway," Joelzi refocused on the point of her story, "I was doing well. I was at the start of my senior year of nursing school. It was a difficult program—I was focused and doing my work when two things happened. First, my grandma died. Mema

Anna was the one I always went to when I needed to talk out my feelings. She was the best listener—never made me feel stupid or cheap. And she would give her advice without holding back and then chuckle and remind me I was made in the image of God. 'Go make Him proud, girl,' she would always say to me." Joelzi paused, remembering. Seeing Merci lean in with interest, Joelzi continued. "I did okay that first week that Mema Anna passed, but the week after Mema Anna died, my mom had a freak car accident. She died instantly. I was devastated. I went looking for comfort in the wrong place—straight into the arms of my boyfriend who was determined to fit in with the football team. I'm not going to pretend I was innocent. I wasn't. I showed up in his dorm room late at night. He had been drinking and one thing led to another...later when my period was late my worst fears were realized. I was pregnant." Joelzi sighed and sat back in her chair, "I'll just get to the point. I was right where you are..." At that moment, the door swung open, and Dr. Carver Ellis stood in the doorway. His eyebrows were raised in question as his glance switched between Joelzi and Merci.

"Uh...am I too soon?" Carver seemed to gather himself. "The chart wasn't on the door and I thought we might tag-team the history and..."

"Not this time," Joelzi said bluntly, "I'll come get you when we're ready."

"Okay," Carver said, his eyes tracking between the two females, before he quietly let himself out of the room.

Joelzi waited a moment to give Carver time to move on down the hall. *He cannot hear this*. In a quieter voice, she continued. "Merci, I understand where you're coming from. I've been there. I ended

up getting pregnant and deciding to abort my baby."
Joelzi shuddered remembering. "And I have lived to
regret it ever since. I know you're in a bad spot, but I
want you to think through the things that nobody
ever talked to me about. I never gave anyone a
chance to talk to me about my options. I think about
that baby every day. I just want better for you. And
as a woman who has gone through an abortion, I
want to protect you from the feelings and the
emotions that I have of never giving my baby a
chance to live. I won't force you to do anything you
don't want to do. But I want you to have the
information you need to make a decision you can
live with." Joelzi patted the shoulder closest to her,
"So I'm here for you."

"But I don't know what to do," Merci's face
twisted in anguish as she pleaded with Joelzi, "I
don't know where to go." Merci covered her face
with her hands and bowed her frame over her legs
as she spoke through her hands. "Mami says she's
gonna kick me out if I don't get an abortion. I
don't...I don't have anywhere to go." Merci's thin
shoulders shook. "I don't know what to do. What am
I going to do?"

Joelzi reached over and put her hand on Merci's
shoulder. "It's gonna be okay, Merci. I don't know
how it's gonna work out, but I promise you, I'm
gonna walk it out with you. We'll figure out what
that looks like together. If you'll give me a chance—"
Joelzi lifted her head to the unseen Son, shining
down on her heart and swallowed the lump in her
throat. She had a chance to make a difference. It
wouldn't change her past, but it might change the
future. "If you'll give me a chance to help, Merci, I'll
try to make a difference."

Merci

She didn't tell me what to do, but she's nice and she seems to want to help me, thought Merci. *At least she knows what I'm going through. But that doctor walking in seemed to upset her. I hope it doesn't stop her from helping me.*

Twenty-Four

Joelzi

"She thinks she's pregnant," said Joelzi.

Joelzi and Carver were in an empty room where they could talk privately, and Joelzi was bringing Carver up to speed on Merci's history.

"Did you get a urine pregnancy?"

"She's getting me a sample now. Carver, how do we help her? What are the resources available?

"Well, first of all, she's a minor and we're not going to do more than we can legally."

"You're just going to throw her out the door?" Joelzi whisper shouted.

"No. I'm not unfeeling, Joelzi, but we need facts and we need to think about the legal repercussions before proceeding. We don't even know if she's pregnant."

"Merci says she's had three positive pregnancy tests," said Joelzi. "Her mother insists Merci get an abortion or she's going to kick her out."

"Joelzi, people say things they don't mean in a

moment of anger or stress. You don't really know that her mom will kick her out."

Joelzi felt a surge of deep anger. Without warning, her finger came out of nowhere and poked Carver in the center of his chest. "And *you* don't know that she won't."

Carver grabbed her hand gently, holding it against his chest. His head slanted to the side and a caring smile curved his lips, showing his beautiful white teeth. Joelzi felt his calmness blanket her has she was pulled into Carver's personal space. She momentarily lost her train of thought. Her breath seemed too shallow as she became aware of his body heat and the movement of his chest as he spoke quietly.

"I think I woke a sleeping giant," Carver said with a chuckle. "I love that about you, Joelzi. You are such an advocate for your patients." He seemed to notice his grip on her hand and the closeness of their bodies before letting go of her hand. It dropped to her side with a disappointing loss of contact. "However, we have no facts. There's no need to get overly excited. Let's start with the facts and move forward from there."

I'm not sure if I've been complimented or set down, thought Joelzi as she watched Carver leave the room.

Later that night

"Joelzi, is that girl Merci going to be alright?" asked Georgie.

"I think so, Georgie," Joelzi replied. "She's sad right now, but I think we can help her."

"I heard the other nurse say she was pregnant, and she might not have a place to live," said Georgie.

"Yes, that's true, Georgie."

"Why can't she live with her parents?" Georgie asked.

"It's complicated, Georgie. I don't always understand why people do the things they do or say the things they say. I know people are broken and a lot of times we do things out of our brokenness and our actions are hurtful to other people."

"Her mom has broken bones?" asked Georgie.

"No, Georgie, her mom probably has a broken heart. A lot of us have a broken heart and that can make us do things that aren't nice. I don't think Merci's mother is happy that Merci has a baby growing inside her," said Joelzi.

"But babies are special. I'm glad you talked to Merci about how special babies are," Georgie said, crossing his arms over his chest and emphasizing his comment with a firm nod of his head.

"Yes, they are," said Joelzi softly, reaching out to rest her hand on Georgie's shoulder.

"Momma and Daddy were happy to have me, even though I'm different than Winston, and Luther-Martin, and Carver. 'Specially Carver—he's the smart one. He's a doctor like Daddy."

"So, he is," Joelzi agreed.

"We don't think it's right to hurt your baby," Georgie continued.

"No, you're right, we shouldn't hurt babies," Joelzi said, a deep burning dread rising in the pit of her stomach. Would Georgie forgive her if he knew what she had done? Would his brother?

Twenty-Five

Friday, September 24th
Carver

"Carver, how've you been?" Adam's bass rumbled over the phone.

"Adam. All's well on my side. Are we still up for golf tomorrow?"

"Well..." Adam paused, "actually, golf and dinner at the grill are going to be on hold for the foreseeable future...that's kind of why I'm calling. Grace has been under the weather and—"

"Grace is sick?" Dread slithered up Carver's spine and settled in his stomach. Adam's first wife, Sara, had died of pancreatic cancer. Surely God wouldn't put Adam through this again? "Have you taken her to the doctor?" Carver had his doctor cap on now.

"Well, she thought she had the flu. A lot of nausea and vomiting, you know—" Adam offered.

"But it's not flu season..." Carver interrupted.

"And that's why you're the doctor and I'm not,"

Adam said.

"So, did they figure out what it is? Is she going to be okay?"

"Yeah," Adam said solemnly, "if everything progresses normally, the nausea and vomiting should go away in another 6-8 weeks..."

"Six to eight weeks? Wait...is Grace pregnant?" Carver asked.

"You got it in one!" said Adam with a laugh. "We're expecting a new Noble in another seven months, give or take. We're not zeroed in on the exact date yet."

"You had me going there for a moment, Adam," said Carver with a bark of relief.

"I couldn't resist, Carver. We are over the top excited and..." Adam's voice became choked up. "I knew you would understand...and be happy for us," he finished softly.

Carver felt a frog in his throat and struggled to speak around it. His friend was alive again. Life was happening. "I'm thrilled for you, man. Congratulations to both you and Grace." As he hung up the phone, Carver was aware of a bittersweet joy. *God, I'm thrilled for my friend, but I want a family too.* He looked at the phone in his hand. Did he dare? He scrolled through his contacts and found the one he was looking for and then, taking a deep breath, he placed the call.

Twenty-Six

The same night
Joelzi

Joelzi stood in her kitchen looking at her cell phone in shock. *He called me. He actually initiated a phone call to me and asked to take me to church. It's not the official invite to the Ellis Family Saturday Supper, but I'll take what I can get.* A grin split her cheeks and she felt silly for grinning so big with no one around. But she couldn't stop it. "He asked me out!" She squealed out loud and then popped her hand over her mouth at the noise. *I should call Grace. No, Grace will tell Adam and it might get back to Carver. Oh, but I've got to tell someone. Pride be smashed, I'm calling.* And she speed-dialed Grace.

"Hi, Joelzi, how are you doing?" asked Grace in a decidedly upbeat voice.

"Oh Grace, I just had to share. He called me and asked me out."

"He did? Who did? Do I know him?" Grace asked.

"Carver. Carver Ellis called and asked me out. Can you believe it?

"Carver called you and asked you out? Our Carver? Mr. Slow-moving, Deep Water called you and asked you out? Finally!" said Grace.

"Oh, Grace, 'slow-moving, deep water'? He's not that bad," said Joelzi.

"Yes. He is. And you know it. You should stop looking at Carver Ellis through rose-colored glasses. That man could make a woman perspire just waiting for him to make a move." Grace laughed. Joelzi heard Grace's muffled voice talking to someone as though she had covered the phone with her hand. "Sorry about that, Adam was telling me something. So, did he say where he was taking you?"

"He asked to take me to church," said Joelzi, not sure if that was a good indication of actually wanting to date her now that she said it out loud.

"That's not a bad start," said Grace. "Adam met me at church to begin with."

"I hope it's a good thing. We both attend New Life Community, but we've made a point of not flashing our work connections. Well...I would be open to connecting, but Carver's always been sort of standoffish with me at church and the singles meetings. Mind you, he isn't too standoffish with other females that don't share a workplace. He's just so careful with me. I wonder what made him finally decide to ask me to church."

"I bet I know," said Grace.

"What?" asked Joelzi.

"Adam just mentioned that he called Carver tonight and told him we were expecting. I bet Carver is seeing the years flash before him," said Grace.

"Oh, I know how that feels," said Joelzi.

"Well, that's just an opinion," said Grace. "And it's sad because I want both you and Carver to find someone to love. I think Carver is ready to find his one and I think he struggles with wanting to control the way it plays out. But, as I can personally attest, life is messy, and there really is no way to know everything God has planned."

They talked for a few more minutes before Joelzi said, "It's late; you probably want to spend time with Adam and I need to go finish my laundry. I just wanted to share my news with my bestie."

"I'm glad you called, Joelzi. I'll be praying. I'm praying for God's best for both you and for Carver— whatever that looks like. Keep me posted."

"You know I will."

Twenty-Seven

Sunday, September 26th
Joelzi

This was another first. Although they both attended the same church and the same Pairs 'N' Spares group, Carver and Joelzi had never gone to church together. When he had called last night asking if he could pick her up for church today, Joelzi had said an immediate 'yes'. Now she was having second thoughts. "God, I can't be distracted from You. I really like Carver. But I don't want him to get between us," Joelzi whispered out loud, her breath fogging her apartment window where she stood watching for Carver's SUV.

Her phone pinged and she glanced down to read the text.

Pulling up now. Stay put. Coming to get you, Carver texted.

Well, that is gentlemanly, Joelzi reflected. *Daddy used to do that for Momma.* She moved over to the mirror to check her hair and lipstick. It wouldn't do for him to see her standing there watching for him if he was coming up anyway. Five minutes later, a firm knock sounded on her apartment door and Joelzi grabbed her purse and her Bible and moved to open it. Carver stood there in dark washed jeans and a crisp blue untucked long-sleeve shirt. Joelzi's heart sighed in appreciation. *Be still, my beating heart.* She smiled cheerfully his direction. "Good morning, Dr. Ellis!"

Twenty-Eight

Carver

He was nervous and excited at the same time. It's not like he didn't know Joelzi Parker; he worked with her in the ER. And he had mostly avoided any significant interactions with her. 'No work relationships' was his mantra and he had mostly stuck to it—until last night. After Adam had told Carver his news, Carver's disappointment with the status of his own love life had flared and he had called Joelzi, asking if she would go to church with him today. It's not like they didn't see each other at singles group, or in service. It was his little secret that he made a point to always look for her at church. He knew which service she attended. It was hard to miss her beauty. She had shoulder length dark curly hair, vibrant brown eyes, and a smile that was mischievous and kind at the same time. Straight white teeth graced her full lips, and she always wore a nice red or pink lipstick that just screamed 'happy.' His glance took in Joelzi's hot pink floral dress that defined her perfect curves and accentuated her glowing dark brown skin. *Wow*, he thought. *What was she saying? Oh, the doctor thing...*

Carver rolled his eyes, before returning her gaze, "Please. It's Carver. Unless we're at work," he added at the last moment.

Joelzi grinned. "All propriety will be upheld at work." She held two fingers up in the Brownie promise. "I will not be sharing our church adventure with the work force. I have my reputation to uphold," she added coyly as she locked her door. "I'm ready."

Carver offered his arm as they approached the stairs going down to the parking lot. "Those stilettos might need the stability of a strong arm," he said, eyeing her shoes seriously.

Twenty-Nine

Joelzi

Carver wasn't wrong. It took strong ankles to manage these shoes, but Joelzi hadn't been able to resist them. They were so pretty. And knowing she would be with Carver had pushed her over the edge. He was tall and sinewy and she knew she wouldn't be too tall. Like a true gentleman, Carver slowed his descent and was careful to help her maneuver the stairs. It was a simple thing really, but it made Joelzi feel cared for. They walked to his SUV and he opened her door and waited for her to get settled in the passenger seat before closing her in and walking around to the driver's side. It wasn't the first time she had been in his car. But this was the first time they were doing the actual date thing. The first time was when they took Georgie, Zoe, and Remi to the zoo so Grace and Adam could have time to work through their differences. Joelzi had been the one to instigate the outing then. But last night's call and today's church going were all the result of Carver choosing to ask her. And today had nothing to do with an intervention. Joelzi swallowed hard and took a deep breath through her nose before he opened his side and climbed into the driver's seat. Seatbelts were buckled, the car was in reverse with his foot still on the brake as Carver turned to her, a calm raising of his eyebrows. "Ready?"

As I'll ever be, Joelzi thought as she nodded her 'yes.'

Thirty

New Life Community Church
Joelzi

It feels awkward in an intimate kind of way to stand this close to Carver, Joelzi thought. They had moved to the middle section of the seats knowing that it would be easier for latecomers not to have to climb over them. Joelzi had thought there was plenty of room for others and had placed her Bible on the seat between her and Carver. But by the time the worship service was finished, the latecomers had filled the seats on either side of her and Carver, so Joelzi had to move her Bible to the floor beside her purse and scoot over. Now they sat side by side. Carver's body heat wrapped her in a warm hug and the smell of his cologne gently wafted her way, soothing her with comfort and presence. They sat so close that his arm brushed hers with every breath he took, the movement of his shirt sleeve against her arm was magnetic, pulling her ever closer to him.

How am I going to concentrate? Joelzi forcibly turned her focus to the front, where Pastor Tommy Jacobs was speaking.

"So today we're in Judges 6:11-14. You know, all these stories in the Bible are God's attempt to relate to us. I hear people say 'that's too long ago—I don't relate to that'—but I believe we can glean something from every story in the Bible. So today we're talking about Gideon. Gideon has an inferiority complex. He doesn't know who he really is." Pastor Tommy paused. "A lot of us don't know who we are. And Gideon's afraid of failure. A lot of us are afraid of failure. At this point in history, Israel has been ravaged by the surrounding countries for the past seven years. They plant stuff, these other countries come and ravage the crops, the livestock. They steal all their potential—all their harvest. Any of you feel like your potential is stolen from you?" He paused again for emphasis, then pulled out his readers, but held them out toward the congregation in emphasis. "These invaders impoverish the Israelites. It's so bad that the Israelites make shelters for themselves in mountain clefts, caves, places in the rocks so that they can 'disappear' from the enemy. Have you ever wanted to disappear from the enemy of your soul? Ever felt like you just can't get ahead? Your past just keeps raising its ugly head?" Pastor Tommy's readers were set down on the podium and his hand rubbed his lower jaw in thought. "All of this happened because the Israelites did evil in the eyes of the Lord, so—let's be honest—they weren't living their best life. But it gets so bad that the Israelites cry out to God for help." He looked over the congregation and picked up his readers. "It's not in my notes, but it's worth mentioning. God hears the cries of His people. He is always listening. It is His nature to care about us. He's listening to you today—right there where you sit listening to my voice. God hears the things you are concerned about and talking to him about." Pastor Tommy put his readers back on and checked his notes. "So, the Israelites cry out to God and He sends a prophet to remind them whose they are. That's my first point. Do you remember Whose you are? Do you know Who brought you out of slavery? Do you remember Who snatched you from the power of your oppressors?" The events from seven years ago flashed through Joelzi's mind in slow motion as Pastor Tommy's words penetrated her heart.

Pastor Tommy continued as though he was countering every negative memory, "We belong to God. He paid for us on Calvary. If you haven't made that decision yet, we'll discuss that before we leave here today. Because knowing Whose we are makes all the difference in how we approach life's battles. So back to Gideon. The oppression—the danger—is so bad that Gideon is threshing wheat in a winepress to keep it from the Midianites." The readers came off again. "Normally, wheat is threshed out in the open on a large flat area. Sometimes they would use the hooves of animals to separate the seed head from the straw by having the cattle walk over the wheat. If it was a smaller quantity, they could do this by hand. Some reports say it could take an hour to thresh a bushel of wheat by hand. So, threshing by hand is less than ideal. What we know is that Gideon was down in a winepress where no one could see him, threshing wheat so his family could have something to eat. It is safe to say that Gideon was desperate. Many would say he was a coward. But it is clear that his family needed food. And Gideon is doing what he can to get flour so they can make bread.

"Desperation is the beginning. In this story, the Israelites are desperate for God because of bad times. But why should we wait for bad times to be desperate? Why can't we promote a heart of desperation for God in the good times? But I digress." The readers went back on. "The angel of the Lord appears to Gideon and says, 'The Lord is with you, mighty warrior.'[2]

"Point number two: God calls out greatness in our lives. He created our DNA and He knows what He will do through us if we yield to Him. Search the scripture. What does God say about you?" Pastor Jacobs paused and smiled out to the crowd. "That's your homework. I could spoon-feed you, but you'll get more out of it if you read the Bible for yourselves." He grinned at his congregation; his readers perched on the end of his nose. "Let's see, where was I... here we go... God tells Gideon to 'go in the strength you have and save Israel out of Midian's hand. Am I not sending you?'"[3] Pastor Tommy looked out over the congregation. "In the Disney version, Gideon would put on his thinking cap and outwit the Midianites and come out the hero. But the Bible is not a Disney cartoon. It's real people with real insecurities. Of course, Gideon had second thoughts. My clan is the weakest. And of my weakest clan status—I'm the least of the whole family."

Joelzi lost awareness of Carver beside her, and Pastor Tommy's voice droned on in the background of her thoughts. *I feel like the most damaged one of my family. I'm weak. I didn't live out what was*

---

[2] NIV, Judges 6:12
[3] NIV, Judges 6:14

93

expected of me. I feel like I've been hiding in that winepress trying to stay under the radar. I'm tired of the secrets. Tired of hiding from my past. What is it You really want from me, God? I guess I need to rediscover what You say about me, God...

Thirty-One

Ludivine Restaurant downtown Oklahoma City
Joelzi

They left church and Carver drove them to Ludivine.

Wow. Just Wow, thought Joelzi. *Carver brought me to Ludivine for lunch?* Ludivine was located in the Midtown District and was known for serving some of the finest farm-to-table meals based on seasonal availability. It was an intimate but relaxed atmosphere. *I'm on a real date with Carver Ellis—not a family dinner, not church, but a real date.* He must have made a reservation, because the wait was short, and there was a long line when they arrived. They were seated across from each other in a cozy booth, given two waters and a complimentary charcuterie sample, and left to peruse their menus.

"So..." Carver's fingers beat out an unknown rhythm on the table in front of them, "...have you always lived in Oklahoma?"

"Yes," Joelzi said, looking over the charcuterie

sample. It looked good. She picked up the fancy skewer, eyeing the cheese cubes and the olives. Both looked appetizing. She stabbed a cheese cube.

"Where are you from?" Carver asked, taking a drink of his water.

Joelzi's hand stopped midway to her mouth with the cheese cube she had just stabbed with her toothpick. She thought about the little town she was from, how everyone knew everyone. It was very rural. Would he judge her for where she grew up? Joelzi had been hungry...until Carver asked about her hometown. She set the skewered cheese cube on her plate and clasped her hands under the table where he couldn't see her fingers tremble.

"I grew up in Meeker," Joelzi said. "Are you familiar with Meeker?" Joelzi asked.

"Not at all," said Carver, "tell me about growing up there." Carver's other hand picked up a complementary rhythm and Joelzi was momentarily mesmerized by his strong hands and long fingers.

"Did you play football?" she asked.

"What?" Carver stopped drumming his fingers and looked at Joelzi intently. "No. I spent all my time studying. Why do you ask?"

"Your hands," Joelzi said. "They look like hands that could catch a football."

There was a lull in the conversation, then Carver said, "Did you not want to talk about Meeker? I just wanted to hear about your growing-up years."

I guess he's right, I should tell him about myself. "Well, yes, I grew up in Meeker. It's a really small town east of Oklahoma City."

"You mentioned that," Carver said with a smile. "Were you born there?"

"No, I was born at the hospital in Shawnee, but

my parents lived in Meeker. My dad still lives there. My mom passed about seven years ago."

"I'm sorry. That had to have been hard," said Carver.

"It was. I didn't handle it well. But I needed to be strong for my dad, and Mary Margaret, and Sammy Jr. So, I basically pulled myself together and finished nursing school. That's where Grace and I met."

"I remember Adam saying something about that. Adam and I have been tight since college," Carver said.

"So, you were there when his first wife died?" Joelzi asked quietly, picking up her cheese cube and popping it in her mouth.

"Yeah. That was a bad season... but he got through it and he and Grace are doing well."

"You can never really tell what the end of terrible events will be when you're in the middle of the tragedy," Joelzi said. "My dad remarried pretty quickly after my mom died. It was shocking to me, but having watched Grace and Adam's story, I understand it better now than I did at the time. Mary Margaret was eleven and Sammy was even younger. They needed a mother figure. And Daddy was lonely and overwhelmed." There was a pause and then Joelzi continued, "I think it's a double-edged sword."

"How so?" Carver asked.

"If you had a good marriage, you wonder if anyone could live up to the last spouse's goodness and might hesitate to try marriage again. But if you had a good marriage, you want the chance to have another good marriage," Joelzi said.

"Wow, this is pretty deep...we could always talk about growing up in Meeker," Carver said with a smile.

"Let's see if I can satisfy your Meeker curiosity so we can move on...Meeker is tiny. If I were to go home today and simply stop to buy something at the grocery store, word would quickly get around that I was home. Everyone knows everyone. That's both a blessing and a curse." Joelzi tilted her head in thought. "I was a cheerleader and valedictorian of my class. I earned a scholarship to University of Oklahoma in Norman to continue as a cheerleader for the football team. I did that until my senior year when I moved to the Oklahoma City campus to finish nursing school." Joelzi skewered an olive and pointed it at Carver. "Your turn," she said and popped the olive in her mouth. *Let him do some of the talking.*

And Carver rose to the challenge.

"As you already know, I'm the third of four sons. My dad's in Family Practice, my mom is a retired Elementary school teacher—she quit when Georgie was born, for obvious reasons. And she's the reason Georgie is so well mannered and integrated into life. She never let us treat him like he couldn't. I mean, there are things he doesn't do well, but she always told him he could. My mom and dad have never let any of us boys play the victim. All of us know how to cook and do laundry and we've all been encouraged to 'find our softer side.'

"You know I want to hear more about that," said Joelzi raising her eyebrows and grinning at him. "The softer side."

"It's different for all of us," Carver said. "Winston loves photography, Luther-Martin enjoys landscaping—planning and planting, Georgie's into ceramics, and I like painting."

"Painting?" Joelzi asked.

98

"Acrylics mostly. I paint flowers," Carver said softly.

"You are a very deep well, Carver Ellis," said Joelzi thoughtfully. "Do you have any photos of said paintings?" she asked.

"No. But there are several in my apartment," he said. "And there's one hanging on the living room wall in my parents' house," he added.

"You never cease to amaze, Carver," said Joelzi.

"Tell me about being a cheerleader. Was it hard?" Carver asked.

The conversation flowed seamlessly through lunch. Carver told her about meeting Adam on the flag football field during college and discovering they both had difficult majors and would be spending most of their time in the library studying. They had become study buddies.

When Carver dropped Joelzi off at her apartment later that afternoon, he walked her to her door and waited for her to unlock the door. Joelzi turned around to thank him for a wonderful afternoon. She had no expectation of a kiss. Neither of them was free with affection like that on a first date. He smiled at her, took her hand and brought it to his lips, placing a simple kiss on her hand. "Thank you for a day that was truly fun, engaging, and worth repeating. Good afternoon, Joelzi." Then Carver turned and made his way down the stairs, whistling a tune that was familiar to her. Joelzi closed and locked her door, leaning against it as she tried to identify the lyrics of the tune Carver was whistling as he descended the stairs.

"At last, my love has come along, my lonely days are over..."[4]

---

[4] At Last · Etta James At Last! ℗ A Geffen Records

She couldn't stop the grin that spread across her face as she recognized the lyrics to 'At Last' by Harry Warren and Mack Gordan. It took very little imagination to hear Etta James belting out the song. She was tempted to put that in her phone as Carver's ring tone, but she would wait. *I wouldn't want to be presumptuous.*

Thirty-Two

Monday morning, September 27th
Carver

Carver checked his phone for the umpteenth time and growled in frustration as he realized what he was doing. *Why am I expecting Joelzi to text me? I haven't texted her. I'm a grown man and I'm distracted by the possibility she might contact me. I am so mixed-up, God. I want to be steadfast and focused on my job. You called me to this. I didn't spend all these years studying and losing sleep, just to throw it all away on an emotion. I really want to do this right. I don't want to get side-tracked by my emotions. But she is exactly what I've always thought my wife would be like...Joelzi is my polar opposite. She's outgoing, cheerful, encouraging. When she walks into a room—God, I'm mesmerized in a way that is both exhilarating and frightening. How can I let someone who so moves me interfere with my focus? Make me lose control?*

I might see her tonight at work. How to handle that? He could simply go on like he hadn't just had the most fantastic date of his life. He thought back over their time together. Joelzi Parker was easy on the eyes, easy to be with, kind to others, intelligent, and funny. *It's a wonder she's not already taken.* Fear raised its ugly head. *However, Joelzi is a huge distraction. Better get that under control before it gets out of hand...*

Thirty-Three

Monday, September 27
ER, evening
Joelzi

Joelzi walked into the emergency department break room with a spring in her step. Yesterday had been amazing. First, church together and then lunch at Ludivine's had been so fun and a real confidence booster. *I really like him.* She smiled, remembering sitting across the table from him. Carver was handsome of course, but handsome fades without character and kindness. And Carver Ellis had those in spades. *I hope he's working tonight. It will be good to show him I can be professional at work, so he doesn't need to worry about my changing the work rules.*

She clocked in and made her way to Team Two rooms for report. She had just finished getting bedside report on her last patient and was coming out of that room when she saw him in the hallway. Joelzi checked to make sure there was no one else around before smiling at Carver. "Hi," Joelzi said, feeling her cheeks grow warm. She was suddenly unable to come up with anything more interesting to say.

Carver looked at her without smiling, a pained look flitting across his face before he acknowledged her with an upward movement with his chin. Then he turned on his heel and walked into the physicians' desk area.

What? Embarrassment washed over Joelzi. Quickly, she made her way back to her desk area in shock. *Did I do something wrong? I only said "Hi." I would do that to any human being.*

Joelzi dropped her purse by her door after letting herself in her apartment and locking the door. She made her way to the couch and plopped down, toeing her tennis shoes off and putting her feet up on the leather coffee table. *I'm so tired. My feet are killing me.* She let her head drop to the back of the couch and felt a wave of sadness flow over her. She closed her eyes, replaying tonight's debacle. What happened? Where was the Carver of yesterday? The shift had not improved with time. Carver had been cold. Not mean, but rigidly professional. He had not joked, laughed, or been friendly. At first, Joelzi had tried to figure out what she had done wrong. "Dr. Ellis, your favorite frequent flyer is here to see you," Joelzi had said with a grin, looking up from her monitor where she was finishing up her note on said patient. She pretended not to have noticed the way he had ignored her earlier.

"Room ten? I've got it," Carver had replied without looking up from his list. It had been that way all shift long. No eye contact. Brief responses and no verbal orders—she'd had to check her computer for any inputs by him. It wasn't like Carver. Normally all the providers would give verbal orders as they passed by the desk to load them on the computer system. But not Carver Ellis. He had been like a recluse, determined to have minimal interaction—with her. Not so the other *nurses*. She had overheard him making small talk with another of the nurses. *So it's only me he's avoiding.* Her stomach sank and her cheeks warmed every time she thought about it. They had gone to church together, sat beside each other, done something so familiar like sing worship songs and listen to a sermon, and pray together and he had taken her out to Ludivine's. *What happened between yesterday and today?* When the other nurses commented on the change in Carver's behavior, Joelzi's confusion turned to anger. *Is this what it's like to be in Carver Ellis's life? He's like a chameleon. He runs hot and then cold. He's a friend and then a stranger. He's double-minded. The Bible has nothing good to say about that*, she thought petulantly. She had avoided him for the rest of the shift. But now she was home, and the feelings could not be held at bay any longer. A tear slipped down her cheek ignoring her best efforts to remain unaffected. Between the tiredness of a hard shift and the frustration of not understanding Carver's actions, she settled into having a good cry.

105

Thirty-Four

Carver

He let himself into his apartment and plopped down on the couch, the memories of tonight's shift running through his brain like a video. He had purposefully ostracized Joelzi. *I'm a jerk.* Joelzi's face came to mind, and he remembered her shock when he treated her like a stranger. Like they hadn't gone to church together and then lunched at Ludivine's afterward, where their conversation had flowed and he had talked ad nauseam. He was embarrassed by how much he had divulged to her. He'd never prattled on like that with anyone—not even his family. Joelzi had been so easy to talk to...but no one could accuse him of not being in control tonight. He was controlled to the point of rudeness. His mom would be sad, Georgie would be mad, and Carver would deserve their censure. But he was frustrated with himself. *I'm my own worst enemy, shooting myself in the foot. Joelzi Parker is beautiful, intelligent, kind and full of life—everything I want in a woman.* He liked her. A lot. Too much. He groaned and dropped his head into his hands. Hopefully, he could turn this self-censorship off long enough to get some sleep.

Thirty-Five

Thursday, September 30th
Hope Clinic
Joelzi

She had contemplated not going to the clinic tonight, but she had already signed up. *Besides,* Joelzi thought, *I'm not going to let Carver Ellis impact my schedule like that.* So, here she was, doing her best to take care of the patients and avoid unnecessary interaction with Carver. There were two providers and two nurses working tonight, so Joelzi had arrived early to make sure she was assigned to work with the nurse practitioner. Georgie and Carver arrived fifteen minutes before the clinic opened and Georgie immediately found Joelzi and gave her a big hug.

"Hi, Georgie," said Joelzi, rocking back and forth for a minute in Georgie's signature hug.

"Carver's grumpy," said Georgie.

Joelzi felt her insides relax. *Not that I want*

Carver to be grumpy, she thought, *but I like that he's having some reaction. Is it too much to hope it's because of his yo-yo emotions?* She grinned before catching Carver swing around the corner, his eyes clocking over the picture of her and Georgie hugging. He admonished Georgie as he turned away, "Time to get to your post, Georgie, we're here to work."

Georgie released Joelzi from their hug. "I just had to get a hug from Joelzi. I'm going."

Joelzi was determined not to speak to Carver unless he spoke to her directly. And she had managed to avoid him until the last patient had gone and they were leaving the clinic. Joelzi started around the building to the parking lot when Georgie ran to catch up with her.

"Carver told me to catch up with you so you don't have to walk to your car by yourself," said Georgie, grabbing Joelzi's hand and swinging it big between them.

"He did, did he?" Joelzi took a quick look back over her shoulder where Carver followed them about ten feet back. It was dark outside and difficult to catch Carver's expression, but he was not trying to catch up with them. The three of them walked quickly across the gravel parking lot, the crunch of their shoes echoing in the dark. Georgie stopped at her car door, waiting for her to unlock it and climb in.

"Good night, Joelzi," Georgie said with a wave.

"Good night Georgie," Joelzi answered before closing her car door and starting her car. *Good night Carver Ellis,* she thought as she pulled out of the parking lot. *I'm not sure a relationship with you is worth all this angst to get through your barriers. I wish I were willing to just walk away. But I just seem to keep hoping*

Thirty-Six

Friday, October 1st
The parking lot of Merci's high school
Joelzi

Joelzi parked her car outside the high school, rolled her window down, and sat back to wait for Merci. They were going to the Pregnancy Resource Center today. It was an area clinic that scheduled pregnant women for free ultrasounds and offered counseling and resources to promote life. Joelzi didn't know much about it, but Merci had done her homework and found the place online. She had shown Joelzi and Joelzi had to admit, it was worth a try. Merci was underage and her mother was not receptive to abortion alternatives. It looked like Merci was going to have to move out if she decided to keep the baby. *The statistics are horrible for girls who drop out of school to have a baby. Merci needs to stay in school.* Joelzi teethed her bottom lip as she tried to think of alternatives. She turned as the passenger door opened and Merci slid into the seat, a careful smile on her face.

"Merci, there you are. I was miles away in my head," Joelzi said, smiling at Merci. "Are you doing okay?"

"Yes, ma'am," Merci nodded.

"Are you still up for checking out the Pregnancy Resource Center?" Joelzi asked.

"Yes ma'am. I called and made an appointment," said Merci.

"You did?" Joelzi asked, her eyebrows rising in surprise as she turned to the young woman beside her. *She is one determined young lady.* "Well, let's get going, we don't want to be late."

Thirty-Seven

The Pregnancy Resource Center
Joelzi

The Pregnancy Resource Center or PRC as they called themselves, was not far from the high school. A woman with graying brunette hair met them at the front waiting area and after introducing herself as Gina, proceeded to show them around the facility, explaining what services were available for prospective parents. Because Merci had called ahead and made an appointment, they were given the full tour and then taken to a private area for deeper discussion.

"Do you have any questions for me?" asked Gina.

Joelzi looked over at Merci with a head tilt, her eyebrows raising in a 'here's your chance to figure this out' look.

Merci sent Joelzi a quick nod of her head. Then taking a deep breath, she turned to Gina. "I'm pregnant and my mom doesn't want me to keep the baby," said Merci, "but I don't want to have an abortion. Can you help me?"

"Yes, Merci," said Gina leaning forward, "we can help you. Occasionally, we even have housing on a case-by-case basis." Gina paused. "Do you know how far along you are?"

"Well, I know when I got pregnant. I think I'm a little over three months along," Merci said, looking over at Joelzi for validation." Joelzi nodded her head in agreement.

"Have you seen a doctor?" asked Gina.

"Yes," said Merci, "at the Hope Clinic. They figured it out on a paper wheel thing. But they don't have ultrasounds. I was hoping I could get an ultrasound of my baby."

"We can do that," said Gina. "Our ultrasound technician comes in on Mondays, Thursdays, and Fridays. Are one of those days good for you?" Gina asked.

"I have half days at school on Fridays," said Merci. "I could come on a Friday."

"Would two Fridays from now work for you?" asked Gina looking through a large calendar on the table. There's an opening that day at 2 o'clock."

Merci leaned toward Joelzi, her eyes sparkling. "Could you...would you be able to come with me on that Friday at 2?" she asked Joelzi.

Joelzi pulled out her phone and checked her schedule. "Yes, Merci," she said, a grin plastered across her face. "I'm free. Would you like me to pick you up?

Merci nodded her head rapidly up and down, a big smile shaping her lips. "Yes, please."

"Now Merci, do you have prenatal vitamins?" Asked Gina.

"Yes ma'am," said Merci "They gave me some at the Hope Clinic."

"OK then," said Gina, "we look forward to seeing both of you on Friday the 15th at 2 o'clock. Wear comfortable clothes, Merci, that will allow the technician to get to your abdomen and drink lots of water to make sure your bladder is full—it will help the ultrasound technician see things more clearly."

"Yes ma'am," said Merci.

Later, the two women left the Pregnancy Resource Center with two very different perspectives. The younger was hopeful that somehow there was a way through this dilemma.

The older had mixed feelings. How would her life have been if she had had access to a facility like this? What would her choices have been if someone had walked through her unplanned pregnancy with her? And now that she was on this side of things, how could she best support Merci through this journey? Could she make a difference? Joelzi was determined to try.

Thirty-Eight

Wednesday, October 6th
In the physician's lounge
Carver

Carver checked again to make there were no other providers in hearing distance as he tried the call again. He had moved Joelzi's number to speed dial on his phone, although it wasn't doing him much good; she wasn't answering. *I deserve that*, he thought. *Should I leave a message? I need to talk to her—to try to explain.* Carver waited for two more rings and just as he thought it would go to voicemail, Joelzi answered.

"Hey," Joelzi said, and the sun began shining. Planets aligned and rightness soothed his soul. If he hadn't recognized it before, he did now. She called to his inner person. Joelzi was like the joy to his sorrow, the genuine to his pretense.

"Hey," Carver said, knowing it was so much less than what he wanted to say. He should be saying more with that first offering, but that was all he could get out.

He could hear her smile through the phone, "Did you just call to 'Hey' me?" Joelzi asked.

He laughed softly. "No. For starters, I've called to beg forgiveness." There was silence on the other end of the line. "My behavior at work the other night was unacceptable." The silence was deafening. "Are you there?" Carver asked quietly, switching his phone to speaker so he could sink his face in his hands.

"I'm here," Joelzi said.

"So, I acted the fool," Carver continued his apology.

"Um Hmm," came across the phone.

Carver grinned at her minimalist response. Joelzi Parker was not a pushover. He was totally in the doghouse. *I'm glad she can't see me.* Then he remembered how he had acted, and his grin slid off his face. "So, I behaved badly—I...you..."

"What did I do that made you treat me that way?" Joelzi asked bluntly.

Now there was silence on *his* end as Carver thought through how he should respond. It didn't take much thought to decide the truth was the best path. "I am so uncomfortable with how to act at work with someone I really like," he started.

"*That's* the way you treat someone you really like?" asked Joelzi.

Carver rubbed his hands over his face. *How do I make her see?* "Joelzi, this is not about you. I mean, it *is* about you, but it's all on me. I'm just conflicted. I don't want to lose my focus. I've worked so hard to be where I'm at that it's difficult to be okay with just wallowing in this emotion called love and losing every iota of control that I've worked so hard to maintain."

"Wallowing in this emotion called love?" Joelzi repeated his words. "That sounds horrible."

"It's not horrible, Joelzi," Carver refuted instinctively as his hands began beating out a rhythm on the small island bar. *It wasn't. Actually it was a powerful feeling of belonging that he didn't want to let his guard down over. What would happen if it all just went away? It would be crushing.* "It's just...unfamiliar. I..." *Maybe I need to just put it all out there. Take a chance. Mom says I don't go in over my chest.* Carver took a deep breath, "look, Joelzi, I've only felt this way about one girl, and she was way back in my high school years..."

"Oh?" Joelzi asked.

"Look, she's history. She crashed and burned when she didn't appreciate Georgie, but..."

"What?" Joelzi asked, her voice rising in disbelief.

"It's a long story, Joelzi. I didn't think it affected me, but apparently it had some lasting repercussions. She basically told me she wasn't interested in me because of Georgie, and I've had trouble trusting girls—women—ever since. That, and my family and even Adam, insist that I like to make sure everything is controlled. Well, it makes me picky about dating."

"I'm sorry she hurt you like that, Carver. High school kids can be brutal sometimes, although I would never have said that. I think Georgie is wonderful."

"I know you do. He thinks the same of you. And...I do too. In fact," he rushed the words, "I've been thinking about Saturday Supper. It's this Saturday. I haven't really followed up with you—"

"No, you haven't," agreed Joelzi. "I guess I was

expecting a call from Georgie."

"Georgie will not be calling you about Saturday Supper; he's been very clear it's my part."

"Oh, I'm sorry if you feel put upon," said Joelzi.

"No, I don't feel put upon," said Carver feeling irritated that he had to explain himself. "I just need to follow through."

"It's okay," offered Joelzi, "I didn't expect it to be a thing, Carver. Thanks for calling to tell me not to save the date."

"I'm not calling you to cancel," Carver said with a huff of disbelief, aware that his voice was rising. *What is the matter with me? I'm never this touchy.* Carver worked to get his voice to sound calm, "I'm calling to ask if you're still available. We would love to have you come to Saturday Supper."

"We would?" There was a pause and emphasis on the 'we.'

He could hear the dryness in her tone and had to admit to a bit of pleasure over her lack of aggrandizement of his person. Joelzi saw him as a human being. A real person. She didn't put him on a pedestal, and that was refreshing. He was going to have to stop holding back and start communicating his willingness—no, maybe his enthusiasm—over asking her to this Saturday's supper with his family.

He cleared his throat. "I, Carver Ellis, would like to take you to my family's Saturday Supper," he said sincerely.

"Oh." She seemed surprised, taken aback by his directness. "Well, in that case, I, Joelzi Parker, would be pleased to accept your invitation to the Ellis Family Saturday Supper."

"You would?" he asked, almost in surprise.

"Was your invitation genuine?" Joelzi countered.

119

"It was," Carver said.

"Then I accept," Joelzi assured him.

"It's in three days," Carver added.

"I'm aware" Joelzi said.

"Then...okay," said Carver. "I'm on the floor in five minutes, so I can't talk long, but I wanted to make the invitation official—shall I pick you up at 5:30?"

"That would be wonderful," Joelzi replied.

Thirty-Nine

Telephone call to Grace
Joelzi

"I can't figure him out, Grace," said Joelzi.

"What do you mean?" Grace asked.

"After our date, Carver never once mentioned our going to church together or the wonderful time we had at Ludivine's. In fact, it felt like he was avoiding me at work. He was himself with all the other nurses, but curt and mostly non-verbal with me. Then the next thing I know, he's calling to 'officially' ask me to EFSS. I'm confused," said Joelzi.

"Trust me, Joelzi, so is Carver," Grace laughed. "What is EFSS?"

"Oh, that's the abbreviation I've given to the Ellis Family Saturday Supper—it's a mouthful, so I just shortened it," said Joelzi.

"And when is the EFSS?" Grace asked.

"It's this Saturday."

"In three days? Carver didn't give you much notice, did he?" Grace said.

"Well, Carver didn't actually ask me out the first time," said Joelzi.

"He didn't?" asked Grace. "Wait, I'm confused."

"Georgie actually asked me out the first time," said Joelzi.

"Oh...my goodness, that Georgie is unpredictable. What did Carver do?" Grace asked.

"Well, Georgie asked me to EFSS about three weeks ago. Carver was speechless to begin with and then started backpedaling as hard and fast as he could. Carver told Georgie that he had to ask their mom. And that was the end of it. I heard nothing until today when Carver called before work and made it official. I could hear all the ER noise in the background. And he basically told me he had to be on the floor in five minutes but wanted to make the invitation official—if I'd like to go, he and his family would love to have me. Almost like he's not sure he wants full responsibility for asking me."

"Saturday Supper with the Ellis family? Oh, to be a fly on the wall before you show up and after you leave." Grace giggled. "For a second date? Are you up for that? Did you say yes?" Grace asked.

"Yes, ma'am, I did," said Joelzi. "He may have been forced into it by proper etiquette. But I'm tired of waiting for Carver to act like I expect him to act. I'm gonna go meet his family and figure out if there's anything there that I'm willing to wait for."

"That a girl, Joelzi," said Grace.

"I'm not going to lie, Grace, this is scary for me," said Joelzi. "I feel terrified about meeting his parents. You know they have to be wonderful people to have sons like Carver and Georgie. What will they think of me?"

"They *are* wonderful people, Joelzi," said Grace. "And they will love you and probably see how great you would be for Carver. He needs some interaction with people who are independent and unconstrained."

"Oh, Grace, unconstrained doesn't sound very attractive..." said Joelzi.

"Then how about 'free'? Everyone who knows and loves Carver is aware of his preference for total calm and control. It's not that you're out of control, per se," said Grace, "but you don't limit yourself from having a good laugh or a good time."

"I think that's a compliment," said Joelzi with a chuckle. "I notice you sound a little bit chipper, are you feeling better?" asked Joelzi.

"Oh Joelzi, I have turned a corner. This nausea is only first thing in the morning when I brush my teeth, and when I get hungry and haven't eaten. For the most part I'm feeling great. "In fact, I'm ready to resume our coffee dates. Although I won't be drinking coffee. It's ginger tea for me right now. When's your next free morning?"

They settled on the next day and hung up.

Forty

It has been almost four weeks, thought Joelzi as she settled into the bar area in Grace's kitchen. She watched Grace fill water bottles for Zoe and Remi with the ease of a loving parent. The girls bickered over who had the right water bottle, before Grace calmly settled the argument and both girls went to the living room to watch a kids show.

"You handle them well," said Joelzi with a smile, watching the girls make their way to the living area.

"It's a funny thing. I never used to think much about adoption. But when I married Adam, I did so to protect Zoe and Remi. It was a surreal kind of willingness to give up everything for their wellbeing. I know God gave me a love for them that is like the love of a biological parent. It really brought home to me the love of the Father for his kids. I'm not Jewish. I'm adopted into God's family because Jesus made a way for me. God adopts us, and that's a beautiful thing."

"And that is not the end of the story," said Joelzi with a pointed look at Grace's still flat abdomen.

Grace laughed and her hand moved to her abdomen, "You're right, Joelzi, love bloomed between Adam and me, and...well..."

"Yes," laughed Joelzi, "well..."

"The love of the Father changes everything," said Grace.

"I want to believe that" said Joelzi, "but I am very below the mark." *If you only knew my past.*

"Joelzi, it's time to accept God's love and forgiveness for whatever it is that you believe He can't handle. It's time to forgive yourself. It's time to stop believing the condemning voices in your head that say you're not good enough—none of us is. The voices that tell you you're not redeemable—we all are. The voice that says God could never love you after whatever it is you have done; you fill in your worst in the blank. It's a lie. God loves the 'whole' you, Joelzi, not just the 'pretty' you. No one is perfect but Jesus. Not Carver Ellis, not Carver Ellis's family, not me or Adam—not you." Grace paused her mini sermon and looked at Joelzi, her head cocked to the side as she studied her friend.

Joelzi waited. *If you want to get some pieces of wisdom, sometimes you have to let Grace think it through.*

Grace nodded her head as though coming to a decision, setting her cup down on the counter in front of her. "Try to chill on the pressure, Joelzi. You're simply going to dinner. Go, meet Carver's family, and enjoy yourself. Have a good dinner with good people and stay out of your head. Carver hasn't asked you to marry him." Grace had smirked, picking up her ginger tea, "Technically, Carver didn't even ask you to dinner at his family's place until twenty-four hours ago." Grace giggled. "That Georgie is a wanna-be matchmaker."

Forty-One

Panicked excitement raced through her core as Joelzi took a calming breath and checked her image in the bathroom mirror. *They don't know.* She paused. *No one there knows,* Joelzi repeated to herself. She took another deep breath, watching her reflection in the mirror. *Remember who you are in Christ. You were an expensive purchase. He died for you so you could have life. Your history is just that— history.* She had worked all day long on those truths. *Maybe a little more lipstick.* Her hands trembled as she touched up the burgundy red that lightly covered her lips. She practiced a smile in the mirror but noticed it didn't reach her eyes. *Fake, fake, fake. How am I going to meet Carver's family—they'll see right through me.*

She remembered Grace's comment.

'Technically, Georgie asked you to dinner.' The craziness of the whole 'accidentally-on-purpose dinner invitation' replayed in Joelzi's mind and she grinned to herself, remembering Georgie's determination to have her at the EFSS. A knock at her apartment door alerted her that Carver was here to pick her up. Joelzi had offered to drive herself, but Carver had insisted on picking her up. Joelzi grabbed her purse and a light jacket and opened her door. Georgie stood in the doorway, a huge grin on his face. *Speaking of my real date*, Joelzi grinned at Georgie. Behind him and to the side, stood Carver, watching them with a soft smile on his face.

"Hi, Joelzi! Are you ready?" said Georgie.

"Hi, Georgie," Joelzi said as Georgie stepped into her space and captured her with her arms still at her side, hugging her fiercely. "Opft." The air escaped her lungs as Joelzi paused in surprise. She managed to pull one arm out of Georgie's grasp and hugged Georgie back.

"Umm. Thank you for the hug, Georgie. You make me feel like family."

"Do you have a family, Joelzi?" Georgie asked.

"I do," Joelzi answered. "I have a younger sister, Mary Margaret, a younger brother, Sammy Jr., and a baby brother Handsome." Joelzi turned to Carver, "Hi," she said softly, "thanks for coming to get me."

"No problem," Carver smiled. "Georgie insisted."

"On your picking me up or coming with you?" Joelzi asked.

"Both. He was determined," Carver said.

"Well, then," Joelzi turned to Georgie, "thanks for making sure your big brother got the job done."

"How old are they?" Georgie asked.

"Hmm?" Joelzi asked.

"Your sister and brothers—how old are they?" Georgie asked.

"Mary Margaret is eighteen going on thirty, Sammy is fifteen, and Handsome is two."

"You have a brother named 'Handsome'?" Georgie scrunched his nose up.

"Well, that's what we call him," Joelzi said locking her door and pocketing the keys. "John is my half-brother actually and he's been a pacifier for our family."

"He's still using a pacifier?" Georgie asked.

"Georgie..." Carver slid an apologetic glance Joelzi's way.

"It's fine, Carver," Joelzi said. "My family is what you might call blended—although technically that isn't right either." Joelzi took a deep breath, turning to Georgie. "My mom died when I was at the start of my senior year of college. It was a car accident—"

Georgie grabbed Joelzi's hand as they started down the stairs. "I'm sorry, Joelzi, what did you do?"

"I was very sad. So sad I made some bad choices. But I finished school and graduated and passed my boards and went to work in the emergency room where your brother works."

"I'm glad you work with Carver. Carver's a good doctor—like my dad. Carver's smart too."

Joelzi grinned over her shoulder at Carver, "Yes, he's a good doctor and yes, he's smart." *When he's not trying to decide whether to play hot or cold,* Joelzi thought.

"You can sit in the front seat with Carver," Georgie offered as they approached Carver's SUV. "I'll sit in the back seat 'cause you're a girl. 'Ellis boys treat girls special.' That's what Momma says," Georgie said. "You're gonna open her door for her, right, Carver?"

Forty-Two

Carver

"It's like having Mr. Manners direct the show when you're around, Georgie," Carver rolled his eyes as he followed Joelzi around to the front passenger side and opened her door, watching her slide gracefully into her seat before closing her door firmly and walking around to the other side of the car where Georgie stood watching, a gleeful look on his face. "Do you need me to get your door too, Georgie?" Carver asked pointedly.

"Nope. I was just making sure you did it right. Gotta tell Momma," Georgie said, climbing into the backseat and buckling up.

It's going to be a long trip to the house, Carver thought.

But it wasn't. The conversation flowed and Joelzi and Georgie were cutting up the whole way. It was refreshing how comfortable Joelzi was around Georgie. Usually Carver was on edge, watching to make sure Georgie was treated respectfully. But Georgie and Joelzi had had a special connection from that first meeting when they took Georgie and Adam's girls to the zoo. Carver relaxed back in his seat, hands firmly on the steering wheel, and let the conversation flow around him. *Leave it to Georgie to get the details.* All he had to do was drive and listen.

"So, Mary Margaret is thirty?" Georgie was a master interrogator.

"What? No," said Joelzi, "Mary Margaret is eighteen. She just acts like she's thirty."

"I'm twenty-five," said Georgie. "I'm older than she is. Is she pretty like you? Where does she live?"

Carver noted a wry smile splashing across Joelzi's face as he checked for oncoming traffic out Joelzi's window and quickly averted his eyes so he didn't make eye contact. He was curious about the details of her family and confident in Georgie's ability to extract those details without undue stress on his or Joelzi's part.

"My family lives in a small town to the east of Oklahoma City called Meeker. And, yes, Mary Margaret is beautiful. She's headed to OU when she graduates."

"Is she going to be a nurse like you?" asked Georgie.

"No, Mary Margaret's current ambition is to be an event planner," said Joelzi.

"What's an event planner?" asked Georgie.

"It's someone who plans and organizes big parties," said Joelzi.

"Oh," said Georgie. It didn't appear to impress him that Joelzi's sister wanted to go into the hospitality field. Carver felt the corners of his mouth rise and he worked to keep them steady. "What about Sammy?" Georgie changed the subject.

"Sammy is fifteen and plans to make it as a basketball player."

"Is he good at basketball?" Georgie continued in a serious tone.

The interrogation continued as they drove to his parents' home, and Joelzi handled the full court press like she was made for it.

She sure is good with Georgie. In fact, I'm not sure I have any friends that are as easy with him. Joelzi seems to genuinely like Georgie. Why was I so reluctant to get to know her? Carver felt a soothing peace cover him and he settled back in his seat, hands resting lightly on the steering wheel, prepared to soak in every word.

Forty-Three

As he pulled the car into the circular drive of his childhood home, Carver felt his neck and shoulder muscles tighten up again. They were all here. Waiting. Carver had never brought a female to the Ellis Saturday Suppers. There was an unspoken understanding that you didn't just bring a casual date to Saturday Suppers. And yet here he was— bringing someone he had only dated once. Well, they had been to the zoo that one time. But he didn't count that as a date. Although that had been a good day...exceptional, come to think of it...Joelzi had handled Georgie, Zoe, and Remi like a capable and caring mother would. He had done his best to help, pushed the stroller, paid for all the snacks and food, and helped answer the dozens of questions Georgie and Zoe had asked. He and Joelzi had worked together like a well-trained team. They *had* gone to church together and lunched at Ludivine's afterwards, but that was just lunch after church, wasn't it? He would do that for any person he took to church, wouldn't he? Maybe. Possibly. No, probably not. He had taken Joelzi to Ludivine's because he wanted to...and he had enjoyed every minute of it, but one dinner did not constitute 'dating.' It was just an 'after church lunch.' He wasn't counting that as an official date. *It was...well, it wasn't official*, he told himself.

"Look, Joelzi..." Georgie pointed out the front windshield. "Winston's here—that's his blue van. He's married to Annie. So that means Winnie and Angie are here. And that's Luther-Martin's silver truck. He's married to Catherine. That means Jr. and Marti are here too." Georgie hurried out of the car and headed to the front door. "Hurry up Carver, what are you waiting for? Get her out of the car," Georgie called from the front stoop. He disappeared for a moment and then reappeared at the landing. "I rang the bell," Georgie announced. "Momma told me to ring the bell when we got here so she would have time to take her apron off before meeting Joelzi." Georgie promptly turned and disappeared inside the house.

Carver took a deep breath and made his way to Joelzi's door. "Sorry about that..." he started. "Georgie's pretty excited about you being here for Saturday Supper." Carver held out his hand to help Joelzi out of the car when he noticed she was trembling. "Heeey," Carver said, drawing the word out. "You okay?" he asked softly, appreciating the soft, yet firm texture of her hand in his.

Joelzi stood and nodded firmly, just once. "Terrified."

Carver felt a protective tenderness breach his control and rise to the surface. "Oh, they're not that bad," he chuckled. "You'll do fine. I'm the one who needs to be on my best behavior," he said.

"Why is that?" Joelzi said, smoothing her hands down her dark wash jeans.

"I've never brought a girl to my parents' house.

My brothers are both going to grill me."

"But this doesn't count—Georgie invited me," Joelzi said.

"Not according to my family," Carver answered softly.

Forty-Four

Joelzi

Carver followed Joelzi to the large double door entry where a middle-aged couple waited.

"Mom, Dad, this is Joelzi Parker. Joelzi, these are my parents, Sharon and Lincoln Ellis."

"Dr. and Mrs. Ellis, Georgie has told me a lot about both of you! Thank you for having me over for your Saturday Supper," said Joelzi.

"Of course Georgie has told you all about us," laughed Sharon Ellis, "Georgie has no secrets. He's told us a lot about you as well. You have made a friend for life in Georgie. It's nice to finally meet you, Joelzi," said Sharon Ellis reaching out two hands and holding Joelzi's hand with one hand while patting her with the other. "Call me Sharon."

"And call me Lincoln," said Dr. Ellis with a friendly smile. "Welcome to our home, Joelzi, we're glad to share our Saturday Supper with a friend of Carver's..." he cleared his throat, "and Georgie's," he added almost as an afterthought.

Sharon led the way into the living room where

two additional couples lounged on the oversized couch in front of a television with a children's movie playing. The two men rose as they entered the room. Sharon held out a hand in the direction of the closest tall, brown-skinned man. He had more hair on his head than Carver and darker eyes that flitted carefully between Joelzi and Carver, a serious look on his face. "This is my oldest son, Winston, and his lovely wife, Annette," said Sharon indicating the woman still seated on the couch. Annette was a light-skinned, blue-eyed woman with fiery red hair that curled riotously on her head. She remained seated with her large belly obviously preventing easy movement off the couch. Annette smiled and wiggled her fingers in Joelzi's direction. "Please forgive my beached whale modus. Getting off the couch in this condition is a bit delicate. And call me Annie—everybody does."

Joelzi fought the familiar stomach twist as she took in Annette's pregnant belly. *She reminds me of Grace. So real*, thought Joelzi. "Oh, please, don't get up on my behalf. It's nice to meet you." *I wonder when she's due. I can't seem to get away from pregnant women.*

"Next month," Annie volunteered cheerfully as she followed Joelzi's quick glance at her abdomen. "This mound represents eight months down and one to go." Annie patted her belly, "It's number three for us. Our other two are over there with their eyes glued to the TV. Winnette—we call her Winnie or sometimes Pooh Bear—is the one in the pink jumper, and Angel—we call her Angie—is in the blue with the purple tutu. She wears that tutu with everything, so you won't have trouble remembering who she is..."

Joelzi grinned, relaxing a bit. "I like her dress

code."

"Trust me, Angie would wear that tutu to bed if we let her," laughed Annie. "It's nice to meet you, Joelzi, and about time Carver brought someone to Saturday Suppers."

Winston smiled at Joelzi. "Annie's right, it's nice to meet you, Joelzi. Welcome to your first Ellis Saturday Supper." Then he turned to Carver, and Joelzi noticed a silent look pass between them as Winston lifted his eyebrows in a meaningful gesture.

Joelzi turned her attention back to Sharon Ellis where she was indicating the other couple. The tall, brown-skinned man who looked a lot like an older version of Carver stood by a tall, slender, brown-skinned beauty with shoulder-length kinky black hair and large dark brown eyes. This woman was also sporting a small but significant belly bump. *Lots of pregnant women in this household*, thought Joelzi. "And this is Luther-Martin and his wonderful wife, Catherine."

"A pleasure to finally meet you, Joelzi," said Luther-Martin. "Georgie's regaled us with stories ever since the zoo outing—we weren't sure we were ever going to meet you. After all, Carver isn't known for speed in the dating arena..." Luther-Martin let his words hang in the air as he looked past Joelzi's shoulder and lobbed a smirk in Carver's direction. The family chuckled and Joelzi felt Carver squirm beside her. She kept her gaze on Luther-Martin and his wife.

"Oh, stop, Luther-Martin! Joelzi doesn't need to be in the middle of your brotherly ribbing," the woman at Luther-Martin's side interrupted with a smile. "Hi, Joelzi, I'm Catherine. And as a woman married to one of these brothers, let me just say, it's good to have another woman in the mix. Those two over there are ours. The boy is Luther, Jr., we call him Junior and the littlest girl in the yellow is Martina, but we call her Marti."

"It's nice to meet you," said Joelzi.

"And, of course," Sharon took over the introductions again, "you already know Georgie." Sharon smiled in Georgie's direction.

"She already knows me, Momma," Georgie said, crossing his arms over his chest and leaning back, his legs wide for balance. He looked over at Joelzi and sent her a perfunctory nod.

"Yes, Georgie and I are fast friends," Joelzi said to the group. *Oh, they're nice.*

"Have a seat, Joelzi. Would you like a glass of my Basil Lemon iced tea?" Sharon asked as she headed toward the open kitchen area.

"Yes, please," Joelzi said sitting down in the chair Sharon had indicated.

There was a small pause in conversation, before Catherine said, "Joelzi is such an unusual name. I don't think I've ever known anyone by that name. Is there a story there?"

"Yes. My mom's name was Joelene. Her mother's name was Anna. When I was born—I was the oldest—they combined their names and called me Joelzianna," said Joelzi. "But I've always felt it was too big and fancy. Over time it got shortened. Now, everyone calls me Joelzi. The Joel part is after the book of Joel in the Bible where it talks about "in the last days I'll pour out my Spirit upon all flesh... (Joel 2:28)," Joelzi looked around the room wondering if they knew what she was talking about.

"We know it," said Lincoln. "It's a good promise."

"Oh, that's lovely!" said Sharon coming back

into the room with Joelzi's iced tea. Handing the tea to Joelzi, Sharon sat down next to her. "So, I take it your people know the Lord?" she added.

"Yes, ma'am," Joelzi replied. "Mema Anna and my mom were both strong believers. My dad too. And I was raised in church."

"Well, that's always a good start," said Sharon. She paused. "You said 'were.'" Sharon tilted her head in thought. "Have your grandmother and mother both passed?" Sharon asked gently.

"Yes, ma'am. Mema Anna died a couple of weeks into my senior year of nursing school. My mom died in a car accident a week later." There were audible gasps and moans across the room at this.

"Oh Joelzi, I'm so sorry!" Sharon patted Joelzi on the knee closest to her. "That had to have been hard."

"Thank you, ma'am." Joelzi swallowed down the knot in her throat that appeared at the genuine concern from all the adults in the room. It had been harder than anyone knew. And Joelzi was still reeling in the aftermath of her choices following those sad days. She searched for a way to change the subject. "So, what's the story of Luther-Martin's name?"

"The Ellises like to name their children after well-known people from history. Lincoln's parents named him after Abraham Lincoln; they named his oldest sister Jemimah after one of Job's daughters. So, when we started having children, we continued the tradition," said Sharon. "We named Winston after Winston Churchill. Carver is named after the scientist and inventor George Washington Carver. We broke the rules a bit with Georgie," Sharon turned to look at her youngest son. "We named him

141

after George Foreman, the two-time world heavyweight champion and Olympic gold medalist, who is still very much alive and making his mark." A thoughtful look covered Sharon's face, "Georgie is our heavyweight champion."

"Yeah," said Georgie, arms up in a winner's stance, "I'm a champion. Who wants to take me on?" he crowed to his brothers.

There was general laughter as the older brothers agreed to some wrestling after dinner, before Sharon continued. "We named Luther-Martin after Martin Luther, but I still wanted him to have a unique name, so we switched it up. It was just a God thing that Luther-Martin ended up married to Catherine. Are you familiar with the story of Martin Luther and Catherine?" Sharon asked.

"Wasn't he the father of the Protestant revolution?" Joelzi asked.

"You know your history," said Sharon Ellis, a delighted smile on her face. Her three oldest sons groaned in unison but she continued. "Yes, Martin Luther ended up marrying a nun named Catherine." There was a pause before she continued. "They had six children," said Sharon, the hint of a smile appearing on her face.

"Okay, Mom, don't start with the number of children again," Luther-Martin interjected. "Three is a respectable number. We're not keeping up with Martin Luther," Luther-Martin said, eyeing Catherine's pregnant belly carefully. "There's only one in there, right?"

Catherine grinned up at her husband, "Babe, the ultrasound says one," she said. Catherine turned to Joelzi. "I'm a twin. With every pregnancy, Luther-Martin worries about the possibility of having twins. I don't know what he's worried about. He's crazy about every one of our kids. He's a great dad." She smiled at him before looking around the room. "All of the men in this family are great fathers. And there's no reason to believe Carver won't be a phenomenal father someday too." Initially, Catherine seemed oblivious to how her comments could be taken, meeting Joelzi's eyes with a guileless expression, before smirking in Carver's direction and winking at him.

Carver closed his eyes and groaned out loud as his two older brothers cackled in the background.

"Would you like a refill on your tea, Joelzi? I feel the need to step out of the room," Carver said.

Joelzi laughed along with everyone else. "That would be nice, Carver, but I haven't had a chance to finish it," she said, holding her tea glass to show him it was still full.

"It was worth a try," said Carver softly, slumping back down in the chair beside hers.

Joelzi smiled at Carver in understanding. Families were wonderful when they weren't terrifying. *They're a nice family.*

For supper, they sat around the large kitchen table and ate barbeque that Dr. Ellis had been cooking on the grill with Georgie's help for the better part of the afternoon. They dug into the meat and the sides that Annette and Catherine had brought, plus the coleslaw Mrs. Ellis had made. It was a relaxed meal with full of stories and laughter and a tour of the Ellis' backyard where a profusion of hydrangeas were coming into bloom.

As Joelzi and Carver prepared to leave, Sharon led them back though the family room toward the front door.

"Did you see my newest art piece, Joelzi?"

Sharon asked, pointing out a beautiful, three-foot square painting of hydrangeas.

Joelzi paused and took in the art piece. It was beautiful, with creamy whites, greens, and pinks. "It's amazing," Joelzi said quietly, her eyes studying the painting. *I need to invest in some art for my apartment. It just elevates the décor,* she thought.

"Carver painted this," said Sharon. "He fashioned it after the hydrangeas growing in the backyard. Those hydrangeas have been gifted to me over the years by Lincoln. This was Carver's Christmas present to me last year."

Joelzi turned to a sheepish Carver. "You painted this?" she asked.

"I told you I painted," he said.

"You made it sound like it was a hobby...not that you're a professional," Joelzi said.

"I'm not a professional..."

"Do you ever NOT do anything well, Carver?" asked Joelzi.

Carver paused, and his mother chuckled. "Carver works hard to be...*proficient*...at everything he tries," said Sharon.

"Carver works hard to be *perfect*," said Winston from the couch.

"He's been a thorn in our side from the day he was born," added Luther-Martin with a laugh, "he's hard to keep up with."

"I just want to do my best," said Carver, frowning in the direction of his brothers.

"And you *always* do your best," Winston and Luther-Martin said in unison.

"Well, I think the painting is amazing, Carver," Joelzi said touching Carver's arm lightly. "It could hang in a museum," said Joelzi turning back to give the painting a last look before offering Sharon a final

144

thanks for having her for dinner. The evening had been so much fun. It had been a long time since she had spent time with a family. *I miss my family. I should try to go home sometime soon.*

Forty-Five

Sunday, October 10th
New Life Community Church
Joelzi

It felt strange to be sitting alone again in the service. *We only came together one time. How is it so strange to be sitting here without Carver?* Joelzi asked herself. She didn't know. It just was. Worship time was finished and the worship leader was giving the announcements as Joelzi's thoughts drifted. *Maybe he had to work a day shift today. He hadn't said last night on the trip home from his parents' house. That had been so much fun.* A grin stretched her cheeks as the visual of their playing games flashed through her mind. The brothers were seemingly quiet and easy-going on first meeting them. But after dinner, when the games had been brought out, their competitiveness erupted. They became loud, table slapping, teasing men— comfortable in their parents' home with the people they loved, laughing and relaxed. It was a side of Carver she would not forget. *That was the real Carver—not the staid, serious-minded, super focused man she worked with in the ER. He had to be those things when he was working. But last night felt like the deeper, genuine side of Carver.* And he had taken her breath away and stolen her heart. Made her hope in possibilities again. *What would it be like to be loved by a man like that?*

"Good morning, everyone!" The announcements were over and Pastor Tommy had stepped behind the podium.

Joelzi pulled her Bible into her lap and focused on her pastor's words. *I'm here for you, God. Speak to me.*

"I had another sermon planned," said Pastor Tommy, "But the Lord woke me up last night with this one. God doesn't often do that..." he paused and looked out at his congregation over the readers perched on his nose, "but when He does, I've learned to listen and obey...that's a whole sermon of its own...listen and obey. Maybe I'll teach on that next." He found the bookmark he was looking for and opened his Bible there. We're in the book of John, the nineteenth chapter. Jesus is on the cross, dying for our sins." Pastor Tommy looked out over the people and lifted his hand up like a child in school trying to get the teacher's attention. "How many have sins that Jesus died for?" Joelzi's eyes watered and her chest tightened at the question. *Me.* She glanced out to all the people in front of her and saw a sea of hands lifted in recognition. She raised her hand with the rest. Truth be told, she wanted to raise both hands in acknowledgement. But she stayed seated and felt a tear roll down her right cheek.

Pastor Tommy lowered his hand. "'All we like sheep have gone astray; we have turned—everyone—to his own way; and the Lord has laid on him the iniquity of us all.' That's Isaiah 53:6[5]. It was a prophecy given during the time of Isaiah, telling us what would happen to Jesus the Christ. We did our own thing. We turned away from the way we were told to do things. And Jesus paid the price for our choices." Pastor Tommy paused, looking around. "We are guilty. Why would a perfect God let his son pay for people who ignored or defied his standards? Standards that would keep us healthy, safe, and most importantly, connected to him? Because the Bible says he is love. The Bible says he has always intended to have a relationship with us. The Bible says he didn't want any to perish.

"So, God came up with a plan. God's creative that way. The God who spoke and caused sun and moon, and stars and planets and galaxies, and amoebas and great whales—I could get sidetracked on the wonders of God--suffice it to say, this incredible, mind-blowing, creative God has always had a way to restore our lost relationship with him. So, whatever you've done that you think is unfixable, God has already done all that needed to be done for you to be restored to him.

"Let's get back to John, Chapter 19. Jesus is hanging on the cross. He's been tried unjustly and found guilty. He's been mocked, ridiculed, whipped, made to carry a heavy cross a long way. He has been fastened to said cross by nails in his arms and legs and is taking his last breaths. Let's start with verse twenty-nine.

'A jar full of sour wine stood there, so they put a

---

[5] ESV

sponge full of the sour wine on a hyssop branch and held it to his mouth. When Jesus had received the sour wine, he said, "It is finished," and he bowed his head and gave up his spirit.'[6]

"I don't know how he did it...but I'm so grateful he did," Pastor Tommy said, coming out from behind the pulpit and taking his glasses off. He reached into his pants pocket for a cleaning cloth and began cleaning his readers as he continued, "Notice that Jesus said, 'it is finished.' Those three English words don't do justice to the Greek. In Greek that phrase is 'tetelestai,' or 'it is finished." The tense in tetelestai is called the Parakeimenos tense. The closest thing we have to this in English is the Present Perfect. The perfect tense references an action or process that has been completed—in this case it's Jesus death that fulfilled the requirement of the law that condemned us to death. And it also references that the results of His fulfillment of the law are still in effect.

Pastor Tommy stopped his polishing and shook his head side to side. He took a deep breath and blew it out as he struggled to maintain his demeanor. "When Jesus said 'tetelestai,' He was essentially saying 'my death is payment for all the past...and it continues to be effective. It has been paid. Stop. Think about that. Everything that you have done that you're not proud of, all those things that haunt your heart and condemn you—things that come to mind making you think you aren't lovable or good enough or—you fill in the blank." Pastor Tommy's hand flung out toward the congregation. "It's all been paid. The only thing you and I have to do is take it to Jesus. It's a good practice to name it.

---

[6] ESV, John 19:29-30

149

Get it out of the closet where you hide all your ugly stuff. Pull out the stuff you've locked in that secret closet and give it to Jesus. I promise, you will never be the same. Today is a new beginning. It's time to let it all go.

"You can stay right there in your seat, or you can come to the front if you like, but whatever you choose. Take it to Jesus. 'Tetelestai.' It is finished."

Joelzi was weeping quietly as she made her way to the front. No one had ever explained it like that. She hadn't understood before. But she did now. And she was getting all her stuff out of that closet. No more secrets. No more shame. *Tetelestai.* It is finished.

Forty-Six

Merci was lying on the exam table, her belly exposed, and the ultrasound technician stood on Merci's right side with her arm stretched over Merci's belly. "Hopefully this is not too cold," she said squirting gel over Merci's belly. "We now have gel warmers to make it more comfortable."

Joelzi stood on Merci's left and held Merci's hand while they waited for the technician to get the ultrasound transducer in a position to give them a glimpse of the baby growing in Merci's body.

The technician ran the ultrasound transducer over Merci's lubricated belly a couple of times and then, as clear as day, the profile of a sweet baby appeared. Merci and Joelzi let out quiet 'Ohs' and 'Ahs' as the sonographer pointed out the nose, mouth, and ear. And then right there on the screen, they watched the baby pull its hand up to its mouth.

Joelzi felt her eyes burn as tears blurred her vision and dripped down her cheek. *It's a real baby. It's a real baby. And I killed mine,* Joelzi thought sadly. *Would I have made a different decision if I had seen mine?* She wondered. The sweet sound of a little heartbeat came through the audio and Joelzi felt deep wonder blanket her heart.

"Can you tell what it is?" asked Merci. "Is it a boy or a girl?"

The technician moved the ultrasound transducer in several swipes as she prefaced, "It's not 100% accurate this early in your pregnancy—we figured you're about fifteen weeks—but let's see if I can tell—oh, the baby is cooperating..."

"What do you mean?" asked Merci.

"Well, sometimes babies move around too much, or have their legs positioned so we can't see their privates," said the technician, continuing to run the ultrasound transducer over Merci's belly. "Here we go...it's a girl." The technician pushed a button to take a picture of the screen.

"A girl," said Merci. "A little girl...I want to keep her. She's mine. I'm gonna keep her," Merci said, her eyes never leaving the monitor screen.

Joelzi's heart couldn't decide whether to soar with joy or plummet with despair. *I'm glad Merci already loves her baby and wants her, but how can a sixteen-year-old raise a newborn on her own? She's still a child herself.* Joelzi firmed her lips. *One day at a time. God, I'm going to need help.*

"I'm going to keep her," Merci repeated.

"Okay, Merci. We can talk this out," said Joelzi, her eyes on the screen, watching the baby move around as the technician tried to keep up.

"You're not going to talk me out of it," Merci said

quietly. "You and Mami think I can't do it. I can. She's mine. I'm going to call her Esperanza."

"Esperanza?" asked Joelzi, trying to avoid the difficult discussion they would need to have at some point.

"It means hope. I'm going to call her Hope," said Merci.

Joelzi's heart sank. Merci was quickly bonding to her baby. *What if Merci couldn't keep the baby? What if Merci did keep the baby?* Both were challenging options. *What a difficult decision for a sixteen-year-old to face.* Joelzi nodded her head and looked into Merci's young eyes, "That's a beautiful name, Merci. Let's just walk this out one day at a time. Today, we're here seeing your beautiful baby. Let's enjoy it." *I'm not leaving you to do this alone. You're not alone, Merci—not as long as I have breath.* Joelzi muttered the last part under her breath and turned her attention back to the ultrasound screen.

Later, as they made their way out of the Pregnancy Resource Center, they saw Gina coming down the hall.

"Merci, Joelzi! It's so good to see you," Gina said cheerfully. "Did you get to see everything you wanted to see?" she asked Merci.

"Yes, Ma'am," said Merci. "I'm keeping my baby."

"Oh, well, that's wonderful news, Merci," said Gina. "Has everything worked out for you to stay with your mom, then?"

"No, Ma'am. Mami's still mad. She told me I have one week to decide before I have to move out." Joelzi and Gina looked at each other in concern. "You said you might be able to find me a place to stay," Merci said to Gina.

"I did tell you that, Merci. But the couple that I was planning on asking has just had an emergency family situation and they are going away for an extended period." Gina looked at Joelzi, "A family member was just diagnosed with late-stage cancer and they are going to help."

Merci's face crumbled. She turned to Joelzi. "You have to help me," she said bluntly through tears pooling in her eyes. "You promised."

"Let's go to the car and discuss this, Merci," Joelzi said. Joelzi watched Merci head outside, wiping her eyes on her t-shirt and sniffing as she went, before turning to Gina. "Thank you for all that you did today. That ultrasound was a breath of hope." Joelzi's eyes filled with tears. "It made me wish I had made a different decision," she added before clearing her throat when her voice cracked.

"Are you saying what I think you're saying, Joelzi?" Gina's gaze was warm and caring, but direct.

Joelzi felt her throat burn with sadness making it difficult to talk. "Yes," she whispered, "I had an abortion in college."

Gina's eyes narrowed. "Joelzi, you know we don't just give young pregnant women alternative resources? We also counsel women, who, for whatever reason, have had an abortion. We also counsel men who have gone through loss, by choice or without their agreement."

Joelzi caught her breath, her eyes wide, "Oh, but I..."

"Abortion either breaks a woman's heart, or it hardens it," said Gina. "I know. I'm one of those statistics."

"But you..." Joelzi looked around the clinic.

"I'm here because of what I went through. I was

a good Christian girl and I made some wrong choices and found myself pregnant. As a pastor's daughter, I thought I would ruin my father's career if I showed up pregnant. I didn't make wise choices when all I could think of were the repercussions of an unwanted pregnancy. What I didn't appreciate were all the consequences I would face because I made that choice. I don't want others to suffer the way I did. It wasn't until I understood God's forgiveness and got counseling that my outlook improved. I'm not trying to pressure you, Joelzi, just think about it. There's a group for women that meets here every Tuesday night at 6:00pm. There's a new class starting this week. The focus is healing—not shaming. The classes do a good job of helping you grieve and move forward. And, just in case you're interested, it's a required class should you ever decide to volunteer here."

"Could you tell I had an abortion?" Joelzi asked. "Before I told you?"

"I wasn't sure. Abortion is a trauma a lot of us hide well. But you remind me of my younger self, trying to make a difference but being torn up inside at the same time," said Gina.

Forty-Seven

In the parking lot
Joelzi

"You really have no place to stay?" asked Joelzi.

She and Merci sat in the front seats of her sedan with the windows rolled down. They were parked under the shade of a huge oak tree in the parking lot of the Pregnancy Resource Center.

"No," said Merci, staring at her hands. "Mami told me that 'I decided to leave the house when I decided to be sexually active'. But I didn't think that I would get pregnant. I was just trying to be part of the group. I messed up."

"Do you think your mom would reconsider?" asked Joelzi.

"I begged her. Two nights ago." Merci looked over at Joelzi, "She said, 'When you decided not to get rid of it, you decided to move out.' Mami got pregnant with me when she was sixteen. My dad gave her money to get rid of me, but she is a good

Catholic and that's wrong for Catholics."

"It's wrong for all of us, Merci. It hurts us all in the long run," said Joelzi.

"Mami decided to keep me. She says she can never get ahead. She works hard jobs and we live paycheck to paycheck. She doesn't want that for me. She doesn't want that for her either. She says she can't afford it. But I can't get rid of Hope, Joelzi. I just can't." Merci rubbed her still inconspicuous baby bump protectively.

"When do you have to be out?" Joelzi asked. *I can't believe I'm even asking this. What am I thinking? I'm just a single woman with no expertise in helping a young single pregnant girl manage the road before her. I'm so imperfect...so unqualified for the job.*

"Next Saturday," said Merci glumly. "I don't know what to do. I was hoping that family that Gina had mentioned would be willing to let me move in with them. But it doesn't look like that's going to work." There was a pause in the conversation as each one thought about the weekend. "Do you think God really sees me?" Merci asked out loud. "I mean, do you think He's really real and cares about someone like me?"

Joelzi thought about her next words. "God really does see us, Merci. But He's not a God that is manipulated. Even when we mess up, He has a plan. It usually involves coming back to Him and listening to Him. And most of the time, it doesn't involve an easy out for our mistakes. We still have to ask Him to forgive us. And we still have consequences for our choices. But God loves us better than anyone else can, and He's not a fickle friend. He's with us for the long haul—all the way to death."

"Why can't I hear Him? Why doesn't He answer me when I ask Him for help?"

"Good questions, Merci." Joelzi paused. "I think God uses ordinary people—people like me—to step in and help. But ordinary people like me are worried about how much things cost and how much time things take and we are really aware of how badly things could go."

"And I messed up," said Merci. "Mami said I asked to be kicked out when I decided to hang with that crowd...but my baby doesn't deserve all of this. Hope is innocent, Joelzi."

"Yes," said Joelzi reaching out to grab Merci's hand, "baby Hope is innocent. Do you think your mom would be okay if you moved in with me until we figure out how to best take care of you and your baby?" Joelzi asked.

Merci turned in her seat, her hand over her heart, "You would let me move in with you?"

"Just until we find a better way," said Joelzi. She looked at Merci, "And there will be rules," Joelzi added. "I still need to work and you still need to keep your grades up in school. You have to be willing to pull your weight."

"I think Mami would be okay with that," said Merci, "and I'll do whatever you ask me to do, Joelzi."

"Okay, you ask your mom and I'm going to run this idea by some friends to make sure I won't get in trouble for letting you stay with me. Deal?" Joelzi asked.

"Deal," said Merci with a sharp nod of her head.

Forty-Eight

The weekend had been full of mental lists and game plans. She had gone back to her one-bedroom apartment on Friday and reassessed the alcove that had been the game changer when she had rented. The alcove was a unique bump out, only found in apartments on the top floor of the building. It was big enough for a twin bed along the outside wall, that also boasted a large picture window. Joelzi pulled out her tape measure and quickly wrote down the dimensions. She didn't enjoy getting her hands in the dirt like Grace, but she loved interior decorating. The challenge of making the small space work as a bedroom thrilled her. The small table that held her laptop and office supplies would have to move to her bedroom. She found her furniture moving sliders and began moving the desk to make a space for Merci. Joelzi was in her element. She felt energized by the puzzle of reworking this area. A trip to a big box store had scored a blackout shade to fit the window, curtains, and a curtain rod, and she had even found a small area rug that would make the small alcove feel homey and inviting. *Now I need a twin bed*, she thought as she made her way into work.

The break room was full when Joelzi walked in. *Perfect*. She waited for a break in the conversation. "Hey, everybody, I'm looking for the loan of a twin bed. I'll need it at least six weeks, maybe longer."

"Sorry, I'm not your solution," said Kelli-Lynn, "what are you doing? Are you setting up for your sister or brother to visit?"

"No, I probably should have done that a long time ago, but...I have a young pregnant girl moving in with me while we figure out what to do. Her mom is kicking her out because she won't get rid of her baby. She's in her second trimester."

"Wow. How did you meet her?" The questions continued as Joelzi explained Merci's situation.

"And does anyone know how to handle a situation like this? I don't want to get in any legal trouble," said Joelzi.

"My brother's a lawyer," said Annabelle, one of her coworkers, "I'll text him and see what he knows."

"Oh, could you?" asked Joelzi, "I want to do the right thing, but I don't want to cause trouble."

"I have a twin bed up in my attic," said Simone, "all my kids used it until they 'grew up'." Everyone in the break room grinned. Simone was six foot tall. Her husband was six' foot four. All three of her boys were in high school and all were over six foot.

Simone could often be heard lamenting that her paycheck was simply keeping her boys in clothes and shoes. "I'm not going to be needing it anytime soon. You're welcome to use it as long as you need it. But you'll need new sheets and comforter and stuff. All my stuff was threadbare by the time the last boy moved into a queen-size bed. Besides, the stuff was all boy colors. That would never do for someone like you who loves the whole decorating thing." Everyone knew that Joelzi loved color and had a gift for decorating. "When do you need it? I can get my husband and the boys to drop it off for you."

"Are you sure, Simone?" asked Joelzi. "That would be such a blessing, but I don't want to put you and your family out."

"It's no problem," said Simone, "but we've got ball games tomorrow, so the earliest we can bring it over is Wednesday."

"Wednesday is perfect for me too," said Joelzi, "I have a meeting tomorrow night, so Wednesday is my first available." They finished all the specifics before making their way out on the floor. Joelzi felt the lightness in her step and a weight off her shoulders. Details were coming together.

Forty-Nine

Tuesday morning, October 19th
Joelzi

Joelzi pulled her body out of bed when the alarm went off at 9:00am. *Lots to do today.* She grabbed her laptop and made her way to the kitchen where she filled the coffee pot with water and ground coffee and got comfortable on the couch while the coffee perked. 'Twin bedding', she typed into the search engine. *What color would Merci like? If it's multi-colored, we could pull any number of colors out.* She added "multi-colored" to the description and began perusing the options. *Floral or geometric? Reversible?* The coffee pot beeped, indicating her coffee was ready. She poured the hot brew into her favorite coffee mug, a black and white-textured outside with a bold red on the inside and stirred in a splash of peppermint mocha. The smell alone was tantalizing, but the heated goodness sliding over her tongue made a sigh of pure pleasure escape her lips. *I wonder how Carver takes his coffee.* The thought leaped into her consciousness and she let it linger there for just a moment before rolling her eyes. *You've got too many things to get done today to be mooning about a guy and his coffee preferences,* she thought as she headed back to the couch and her laptop. *Time for some decorating therapy.* She had just ordered new bed linens that would arrive tomorrow when her cell phone rang and she looked at her screen. Grace.

"Hi, Grace," said Joelzi.

"Hi, Joelzi, is today a day off? I'm just calling to check on my bestie. I'm having a sans nausea moment."

"So the nausea is gone?" asked Joelzi.

"I don't know if I'd say it's gone, it's more like there are certain times that the nausea is not rearing its ugly head," said Grace.

"I'm sorry, Grace," said Joelzi, "I'm off work, but trying to get ready for Merci moving in."

"So you're going ahead with the move-in?" asked Grace.

"Yes," said Joelzi, "I mentioned what was going on at work on Monday and stuff just started coming together. Simone had a twin bed in her attic that she's letting me use—I just ordered new bed linens. And do you remember Annabelle?" asked Joelzi.

"Of course," said Grace.

"Annabelle's brother, Wes, is a lawyer. Annabelle asked him about the legalities of having a minor move in with me. Because Merci is pregnant, she is basically an emancipated minor. But Wes still recommended that we ask Lilianna, that's Merci's mom, to sign a letter giving Merci permission to live with me while Merci is pregnant or until other living arrangements are made. Wes even had a sample form typed up and sent to me. I printed it at work, and I'll swing by the high school today and drop it off with Merci. Assuming her mom signs it, Merci will be moving in on Saturday since I work Friday."

"So what's left to get ready for the move?" asked Grace.

"I've got a curtain rod and shade that needs to be mounted on the wall. I don't have a ladder to do that...or a drill...does Adam have any of those items that I could borrow?" Joelzi asked.

"I've got a better idea, Joelzi," said Grace, "I'll text Adam and see if he can bring the drill and ladder with him and install the curtain rod and shade for you."

"That would be lovely, Grace, but I don't want to inconvenience Adam," said Joelzi.

"Joelzi, did you or Carver feel inconvenienced when you helped Adam and me last year? I woke you up at dark-thirty in the morning after you had had a hard shift the night before, sobbing hysterically on the phone about how Adam had walked out. And you just got out of bed, called Carver to go find Adam, and came over to be with me. You and Carver ended up taking the kids for the day." There was silence as both women remembered the events of that day. "You don't inconvenience me, Joelzi. And I guarantee you, Adam feels the same way."

"Okay," said Joelzi, "if you're sure." Joelzi heard the familiar sound of someone typing on their cell. "Okay, I texted Adam," Grace said eventually. "If he's not in a meeting, we should know something soon," said Grace. "So what are you thinking about colors?" Joelzi began sharing her recent purchases and current ideas as Grace's cell chimed.

"Adam just texted me back. He says, 'he's on

it'," said Grace. "What time shall I tell him?"

"Simone's family is delivering the bed around 7:00pm. The bed only fits in front of the window where the shade and curtain are going, so maybe 6:00pm? That way he's finished before they bring the bed?" asked Joelzi.

"That sounds like a plan. I'll come with the girls if I can, but don't hold your breath, Joelzi, it may be more than my pregnancy stomach can handle—and I won't know till we're closer to the time to leave," said Grace.

"Don't worry about it, Grace," said Joelzi, "I'm just really grateful for the help."

They spoke a few more minutes and then hung up.

Fifty

Later that evening
Pregnancy Resource Center Hope and Healing Group
Joelzi

Joelzi sat in her car. It was 5:45pm. Hope and Healing, the post-abortion counseling group, was starting in fifteen minutes. *I feel strange sitting here thinking about attending a group like this all these years later. But I do think I need to give this a chance. Maybe all this jumbled mess of emotions is fixable. I owe it to myself to try this.* Joelzi's thoughts went back to the evening she had driven Grace to her first Grief workshop. Grace had been a mess. And it had only taken one group meeting for Grace's perspective to change. Grace's return to the 'land of the living' had been a process, but that first meeting had been pivotal. *Hopefully, that's what tonight will be for me,* thought Joelzi, *a new beginning.* She locked her car door and headed into the building.

The meeting was in a larger room in the back of the building with comfortable chairs placed in a circle. There were ten women in the group and if appearances were any indication, they were from all walks of life: young, middle-aged, some in jeans, one in a bohemian dress with lots of bracelets and earrings—all unique. They were a melting pot of sorts, most drawn to the meeting by similar pains. A woman Joelzi had just met, started the meeting promptly at 6:00pm.

"I think I've met each one of you," she said making eye contact with each woman as she visually circled the group. "But just in case you've forgotten, my name is Candace. This group is required for any volunteers wanting to serve in the clinic, and it's for any women who have had an abortion and might be wanting to talk out their experience. We also have a class for men." Several women raised their eyebrows. "Yes, ladies, even men can be affected by abortion choices."

That was definitely not my experience, thought Joelzi. *Myron couldn't get rid of our baby fast enough.* She focused back in on what Candace was saying.

"Over the next six weeks we're going to be identifying some of the emotions that can follow abortion. These are common emotions or reactions, but this is not a conclusive list. It's only meant to be a starting point. The goal in all of these meetings is healing and restoration. You can share your 'whys' and we will listen. But we're not here to poke holes in your reasons or your choices. We ask that you agree to honor what is said here by not sharing anyone else's story outside of this room and that you purpose to be present, attentive, and caring. So let's start off by going around the room and introducing ourselves. Please tell us your name and one or two things about yourself that you're okay sharing with the group." Candace turned to Joelzi who was seated on her left. "Joelzi, would you be okay going first?" she asked.

"Of course," said Joelzi, "my name is Joelzi and I'm a nurse at Oklahoma Memorial Hospital in the Emergency Department." She paused wondering if she should say more. *I'm here to get better. I'm not holding back,* she thought. "And I had an abortion in college," Joelzi said. The women continued around the circle, introducing themselves and giving small snapshots into their lives. *All walks of life...*thought Joelzi, as she drove home later that evening.

Fifty-One

Wednesday, October 20th
Joelzi

She had dropped off the letter for Liliana Lopez to sign with Merci at the high school during Merci's lunch and they had discussed the details of Saturday's move, before Merci had to go back to class. Joelzi had gone back to the apartment to work on making room in the bathroom they would share. Amazon had delivered the twin bed linens for Merci's bed so she had thrown them in the washing machine to get the new smell and stiffness out of them. Now Joelzi was waiting on Adam. Grace had texted saying she wasn't feeling great so she wouldn't be coming.

The doorbell rang at 5:55pm. *Right on time*, Joelzi thought, making her way to the front door of the apartment. But when she opened the door, she was surprised.

"I was expecting you, Adam," said Joelzi, her eyes flitting over Adam's face before settling on Carver who stood beside Adam, a tool chest in his grasp. "But not Carver," she added, trying to ignore the uptick in her heart. *Grace...I owe you.* There was a moment of silence as she and Carver stood taking in each other.

"Uh, hey you two," said Adam, looking between Joelzi and Carver with a smirk on his face, "think we could move this inside?"

"Oh, yes," said Joelzi, embarrassed that she had been caught gazing at Carver. "Thanks for bringing the ladder, Adam."

"And the man carrying the toolbox," added Adam with a grin.

"And the man carrying..." Joelzi stopped repeating after Adam as she realized what she was saying. *I've got it bad.* Her eyes flitted back to Carver's, but he didn't seem to think her words were out of the norm. *I am thrilled Adam brought Carver, but I don't want to be too obvious.* "Let me hold the door..." she helped them get inside and then led them to the alcove. "I need this blackout shade put up for some privacy and then the curtain rod goes just above and outside this opening," she explained. The guys pulled out the shade installation instructions and began to discuss the process together while Joelzi texted Grace.

So TWO men showed up to hang my shade and curtains.

Grace's text came back immediately, starting with the laughter emoji.

Sometimes friends need to help friends. You

170

can give me the deets later.

Joelzi quickly texted back before pocketing her phone.

Not complaining. Will do.

In a short time, the shade and the curtain rod were hung and Carver climbed back on the ladder to slide the curtain rings that Joelzi handed him onto the rod. Joelzi arranged the curtains and the shade. *It looks good*, she thought.

"This really looks good, Joelzi," said Carver, looking around, "and if the rest of your apartment is any indication, you've got a knack for decorating."

"Thank you, Carver," said Joelzi, "I admit, I love decorating. Nursing pays the bills; decorating feeds the soul."

"Sorry to run, Joelzi," said Adam, as he folded up the ladder and headed back to the front door. "But Grace is holding dinner for me and I want to see the girls before bedtime."

"I totally understand," said Joelzi, "I'm just grateful you were willing to help and able to get the job done." She turned her eyes to Carver, wondering if he would offer to stay.

"Uh...I rode with Adam, so I need to be going too," said Carver, picking up the toolbox. Joelzi's stomach dropped with disappointment.

"You could always follow us home for dinner," said Adam, his eyebrows lifting in her direction. "Carver is joining us, and Grace always makes more than enough."

Joelzi worked to keep a happy smile on her face. "Thanks for the invite, Adam, but a friend from work is dropping off some furniture any time now, so I

171

need to stay put," said Joelzi.

Not long after Carver and Adam had left, Simone's family showed up with the twin bed, a bedside table, and a dresser they had found in their attic.

"I wasn't sure you needed a dresser and the bedside table, but thought I'd have the guys bring them anyway," Simone said.

Simone's husband and boys assembled the bed with its mattress and brought in the bedside table and dresser while Simone helped Joelzi make the bed with the new linens. When Simone and her family had left, all of the major move details had been finished. Joelzi positioned a kitchen chair so she could sit and look at the area critically. The whole picture was complete. Merci had a safe place, privacy from the outside window, and a side table. She would have to do her homework at the kitchen table, but the apartment would be quiet enough that the kitchen table would work as an interim desk. *Okay, God, I'm trying to do what I think You asked me to do. Lead the way,* Joelzi prayed.

Fifty-Two

Thursday, October 21st
Hope Clinic
Joelzi

"She has no place to go, Carver. I'm letting her move in with me," said Joelzi. "That's why you and Adam hung that privacy shade and the curtains for me the other night."

"If I had known that's why you were installing the shade and curtain, I might have done differently," Carver said with a frown on his face. "You can't just let Merci move in, Joelzi, she's a minor," Carver said bluntly.

"She's going to be homeless by Saturday, Carver, her mom is kicking her out," said Joelzi. "And you would have done *differently* if you had known it was for Merci?" Joelzi asked, her face contorted with confusion as her thoughts scrambled. "How do you reconcile that statement with Biblical principles?"

"You're right," said Carver with a sigh, "that statement was reactionary. I probably would have helped anyway. My concern is that you need to do this kind of thing the legal way," Carver said with disturbing calmness, moving to unlock his car doors with his car fob. "Jump in, Georgie," he motioned to his brother before turning back to Joelzi. "What happens when Merci decides you're an easy solution? She's going to stay with you, through the pregnancy and then until the baby's a year old, and then until she's graduated high school. You're not thinking logically," he concluded, and headed back toward the driver's side of his car.

"Wow," said Joelzi, throwing her hands up in frustration, "that's a lot to digest when I only wanted to discuss the next few months."

"And on a nurse's salary," Carver had turned back from moving to open his car door and continued. "You can't afford that."

Joelzi felt stubbornness crawl up her spine and rear its head. Her family had told her she could be obstinate sometimes. *This might be one of those times*, she thought. She was exasperated with Carver's detached perspective. *When did Carver Ellis add lawyer to his list of accomplishments? Merci is a real human being.* She felt defensive about Merci and little Hope's situation. *He is not focusing on how old Merci is and the life of her baby.* A strong sense of justice rose up in Joelzi and she became aware of an unwillingness to back down. Joelzi crossed her arms over her chest. "I know it's not laid out on a spread sheet, Carver, but I'm choosing to take a stand for life that goes deeper than my pocketbook. Even if it stretches my resources. After all, we are all called to be people of faith. And *if* I'm one hundred percent confident that I can do this on my own—I'm not walking by faith. Moving Merci in with me may not be an easy answer—but it's a simple one for me. Merci needs a place to stay. I have a place for her to stay. I'm choosing between life and death—I'm trying to do the right thing. I'm choosing life."

"I'm not your enemy, Joelzi," said Carver calmly, his eyes flitting from her crossed arms to her face. "I just think there's a better way. You asked me my opinion and I gave it."

"That's fair," Joelzi said, feeling Carver's calm logic begin to lower her defenses. "But I was hoping you'd offer more than a flat 'no'. I was looking for some brainstorming; some other options to consider."

"I don't have any options for you to consider, Joelzi. I admire your willingness to get involved, but it seems risky to me. However, you're an adult. What you do is on you; I've given you my opinion," said Carver and he got into his car and started the engine.

Joelzi climbed into her car and started her engine, waiting for Carver and Georgie to pull out. But their car didn't move. She looked over that way and saw the passenger window was lowered and Georgie had his head stuck out of it. She lowered her window.

"Carver says we can't leave until after you," said Georgie. "Ellis men don't leave women in a dark parking lot by their selves," he added, moving his head up and down in emphasis.

In spite of being irritated with this last conversation, a warm sensation moved in Joelzi's chest. *Carver Ellis is a catch, even if he's a brick wall sometimes.* Joelzi smiled over at Georgie, "Well, I guess I need to pull out then. Have a good night, Georgie. It was fun working with you tonight. "

I need a moment before I can say the same for you, Carver Ellis.

Fifty-Three

Carver

He was frustrated. Why didn't Joelzi listen? What was there to brainstorm? They needed to find a state home for Merci till she could have her baby and get back in school. All of this time spent avoiding the reality of Merci's choices was just setting Joelzi up to have a sixteen-year-old girl living with her for the foreseeable future and draining Joelzi's finances and her time. *And why do you care?* Carver's heart stuttered as the thought wafted through his consciousness. *Because it will affect any relationship that grows between us.* He waited until Joelzi had pulled onto the road before pulling out of Hope Clinic parking lot behind Joelzi's car. His thoughts proceeded to race back to the previous questions when Georgie interrupted.

"Carver?"

"What, Georgie?"

"Is Joelzi going to let that girl live with her?"

"I don't know, Georgie. Maybe." *Probably. She just runs with her heart. She doesn't even think about everything that could go wrong.* He sighed.

"Are you mad at Joelzi?" Georgie asked.

"No. Why would you think that?" asked Carver.

"'Cause you breathed out really loud. You do that when you're mad at me," said Georgie. "I thought maybe Joelzi made you mad."

"I'm not mad at Joelzi, Georgie," said Carver. "She just frustrates me sometimes," he added under his breath.

"That's okay, Carver," said Georgie, "Momma says that about Daddy all the time. Momma says it's a sign of love."

Fifty-Four

Merci's move into Joelzi's apartment was anticlimactic. At Liliana Lopez's request, Merci and Joelzi had gathered Merci's things on Saturday while Ms. Lopez was at work. Merci didn't bring a lot. Her clothing items fit into a large black trash bag. She loaded her backpack with all her schoolbooks, and brought her pillow, covered with a mermaid pillowcase. Shampoo and body wash were shared with her mother so those items were left. *She can share my stuff until I have time to take her somewhere to buy her own*, thought Joelzi. Everything fit easily into the back seat of Joelzi's car with room to spare.

Seeing how little Merci brought with her made Joelzi's heart ache. *I need to take Merci shopping for a few essentials—she's going to need some maternity clothes—but I need to proceed carefully. It won't help if there's no understanding about how much it costs to have a baby. And how much it will costs to keep a baby. We need to research government assistance, sign up for Medicaid, and a whole slew of things that I've never had to deal with. But one thing I'm sure of...I will not leave Merci without support. I want—no, I need—to make sure Merci has the tools she needs to make the hard choices that lie ahead. And number one on the list is love. Merci needs to know she is loved and cared for.*

Fifty-Five

Sunday, October 24th
Church with Merci
Merci

The coffee Joelzi made the next morning made her stomach nauseated. *But I don't want to complain. Joelzi made room for me. And my bed is really pretty,* thought Merci. *I love these sheets with all the colors. I can hear Joelzi moving around in her bedroom. She said we're going to church today. It's been a long time since I've gone to church. Mami is usually too tired after working a late shift on Saturday.* Merci felt little butterflies in her abdomen. *I need to eat something.* She got out of bed and pattered on bare feet to the refrigerator. Joelzi had bought home egg bites yesterday. She said they only had to be microwaved for one minute. *I think I'll try one of those,* thought Merci, pulling the wrapping off of one and sticking it in the microwave.

"There you are. Good Morning, Merci," said

Joelzi coming into the galley kitchen. "Did you sleep okay?"

She sure is happy first thing in the morning, thought Merci. "Yes ma'am," said Merci.

Joelzi smiled at Merci. "Merci, we're going to be living together for the next little bit. I don't think I can hear you call me 'ma'am' all the time. You're barely younger than my sister. Just call me Joelzi, okay?"

"Okay," agreed Merci.

"Can you finish eating and be dressed for church in thirty minutes?" asked Joelzi.

"Yes, ma'—Joelzi," said Merci, "but I don't have a dress to wear."

"Oh, our church isn't like that," said Joelzi, "wear whatever you have to wear. Jeans are fine."

"Okay."

The church building didn't look anything like the Catholic church she and her mom had used to attend, thought Merci. *This building is just a big box—no carvings of the saints, no wooden benches. But there are a lot of people.* Merci watched as someone Joelzi knew stopped Joelzi to tell her something. Merci kept watching the people. Some were leaving, others were arriving...and they all seemed to be happy. Well, the adults seemed happy. That baby over there was crying...loudly...and its mother was trying to get it to be quiet. Merci watched curiously as the woman rocked the baby, but the baby cried louder, if that was possible. The lady then tried to give the baby a bottle, but the baby didn't like this and arched its back, making it hard for the lady to hold on to the baby. The lady tried to give the baby a pacifier but the baby spit the pacifier out. *The lady and her baby do not look happy.* Eventually a man arrived pulling a small boy with one hand and grabbing the baby's carrier with the other. As they made their way out the front doors, Merci could just make out the little boy asking his mom for candy over the baby's cries. *That lady looked old enough to have a family and she was still having trouble*, thought Merci. Merci's hand went to her belly. *This might be harder that I thought.*

Fifty-Six

The music was actually good, thought Merci as they sat down to listen to the guy who was going to speak. This was normally the part where she let her mind wander, but everything was different today. The guy that was speaking was a middle aged, light-skinned man with those glasses you use to read 'cause your eyes were old on top of his head. He was dressed in regular clothes—no robes—and he was reading from a book in English instead of Latin. *It wouldn't hurt to listen a bit,* thought Merci.

"Today, we're talking about mercy," said the man.

Merci's heart started pounding. *We are?* She thought.

"Webster's defines mercy as 'compassion or forbearance shown especially to an offender or to one subject to one's power. also : lenient or compassionate treatment. begged for mercy. : imprisonment rather than death imposed as penalty for first-degree murder. : a blessing that is an act of divine favor or compassion'."[7] The man paused,

---

[7] Merriam-Webster. (n.d.). Mercy. In Merriam-

took his glasses off and looked straight at her. "The Bible expounds on this idea by using the sacrifice of Jesus Christ on the cross to fulfill the requirement of the law for our sins—our offences against God's laws. We messed up, not once or twice, we continue to mess up and God has shown us mercy.

"Let's consider Paul the Apostle. In Romans, he spouts off all his qualifications. He was a Jew among Jews, circumcised on the eighth day, a Pharisee, ...and yet he was killing Christians. He thought he was doing right, he believed he was okay. It took an encounter with God that left Paul blind to change him."

I wonder what that's about, thought Merci. *Maybe Joelzi can tell me about this guy, Paul.*

Merci tuned back in to hear the man say, "God can handle all of our stuff. We let all our mistakes pull us away from the very relationship that can fix us—a relationship with God. It's the only thing that can restore us and put us in right relationship again. We make mistakes and we run from the heart of God as though the blood that Jesus shed for us, the life that He gave for us, the power that raised Jesus from the dead is somehow not enough to cover our badness. But God has more than enough mercy to cover our stuff. The question is, are you humble enough to let Him? I figure if God can turn a Christian killer like Paul into a preacher of the gospel, He can deal with the likes of me." The man paused, "And he can deal with the likes of you, too. Won't you give God a chance to pour His mercy and grace on you today?"

I'm not sure, thought Merci.

Webster.com dictionary. Retrieved January 4, 2023, from https://www.merriam-webster.com/dictionary/mercy

Fifty-Seven

Tuesday, October 26th
Evening, after Hope and Healing

   Joelzi was reflecting on tonight's discussion as she drove home from her second week of the group meetings. The group had started with a question: "Have you grieved the loss of your baby?" *I didn't know I had the right to grieve. I'm the one who made the decision to abort my baby. I told myself I deserved whatever happened to me.* The tears trickled down Joelzi's face and she let them. She let the feelings of loss percolate to the surface of her emotions and flow over the box where she had stuffed them all these years. She remembered the passing of her grandmother and her mom and her search for comfort in the wrong arms. How Myron had taken her innocence. The stress of the pregnancy. There had been so much conflict. She remembered how the fear of that season had led her to the decisions she had made. *I know why I did it.*

But I'm sorry I let you go. I'm sorry I didn't fight for you.

Fifty-Eight

Wednesday, October 27th
Before work
Joelzi

Joelzi waited until Merci had left for school and, as soon as she arrived to work, she found Grace's contact under 'Favorites' on her phone and pressed 'call.' When Grace answered, Joelzi spoke without waiting for any greeting.

"Grace, I'm ready to talk. I *need* to talk—"

Grace interrupted Joelzi, "Yes."

Joelzi continued, "I know it's not the best time for you..."

"Yes, Joelzi, I'm here for you," Grace said. "You know I'm feeling better these days. We've even had coffee—that's a big improvement. Early afternoons are still better as far as the fatigue goes. And if the girls wake up after their naps, we can sit outside and let them play while we talk."

"It's not pretty, Grace. You may not want to be

my friend after—"

"Nonsense," Grace interrupted again. "I promise to listen with love. Joelzi, you have carried me at my weakest. Please. Let me be here for you. Are you working today? You could just come over."

"Yes, I'm in the parking garage now. I signed up for an 11-11 shift. I wanted to call you and set a time before I lost my nerve," Joelzi said.

"Oh, Joelzi, I'm glad you called," said Grace. "I can't get together on Thursday or Friday; I've got an OB appointment on Thursday and the girls have their annual exams with the Pediatrician on Friday. But we could get together on Saturday around one o'clock. Would that work?"

"Okay," Joelzi said.

"Have a good shift," said Grace and they hung up.

Fifty-Nine

It was Thursday morning and Carver could not get away from last Thursday's conversation outside of Hope Clinic when he and Joelzi had discussed Merci moving into Joelzi's apartment. Every morning, the first thing on his mind was how he had handled the conversation; what he had not said. *I gave Joelzi the impression that I'm against her. But that's not really true. I'm for her. I want to protect her and make sure she isn't taken advantage of.* Carver took a sip of his coffee. *How do I show her? I have to point out the flaws...but maybe I could do so with solutions...*Carver grabbed his phone and opened a new 'notes' page. *Maybe a series of suggestions would help Joelzi...and improve our relationship.*

Regular church attendance, he typed.

Shared housekeeping duties.

Consistent school attendance, schoolwork, and grades.

Needs to sign up for Medicaid.

Keep regular OB appointments.

Keep communication with Merci's mother open.

The more he typed, the more relieved Carver felt. *This might work*, he thought. *Hopefully Joelzi sees this as positive input.* He finished the note and texted Joelzi:

Have been thinking about last Thursday. My comments weren't helpful. Sending you my notes on ways to have good boundaries with Merci. Talk about them tonight at Hope Clinic? I do care.

Moments later, Joelzi texted back:

Love these ideas. Thank you for taking the time to write them down and send them to me. Not at clinic tonight. Trying to stick close to home for Merci's first week. I'm glad you care.

Carver's shoulders slumped. No Joelzi at Hope Clinic? Anticipation of Thursday evening's clinic time faded in significance.

Georgie and I will miss you. Carver took another sip of his coffee, his mind racing with options. He set down his coffee and typed again. **Maybe we could meet for coffee tomorrow and discuss the ideas?**

Sixty

Joelzi calls Grace.

As soon as Grace answered the phone, Joelzi blurted her news. "He did it."

"He did?" asked Grace. "Context, please."

"Carver texted about meeting up for coffee." Joelzi said with a squeal, walking quickly to one end of her kitchen before turning quickly and walking back the other way, her phone held to her ear.

"Okay, that's a good, safe start," said Grace. "Did Mister Slow and Deliberate set a time to meet?"

"Tomorrow," said Joelzi.

"Well, I expect you both to have a wonderful date," said Grace, "and I expect details on Saturday."

"In the interest of full disclosure," said Joelzi, slowing her pace till she was trudging back and forth in her kitchen, "Carver made a list of things he thought I should go over with Merci. He suggested discussing them over coffee," said Joelzi.

"Don't get discouraged, Joelzi. I suspect Carver is doing whatever it takes to get alone with a woman he is very interested in. This is a classic Carver Ellis move," said Grace.

"What do you mean?" asked Joelzi.

"Carver likes to have a reason for plausible deniability just in case your interest is not returned...or...I don't know, Joelzi, for safety reasons," said Grace, her voice rising in an expression of exasperation.

Sixty-One

Friday, October 29th
Coffee with Joelzi
Carver

    He had told himself it was only coffee to discuss Merci's situation at least a dozen times...probably more, but when he picked Joelzi up at her apartment, all those excuses seemed to vanish. She was dressed casually in jeans and a red, short-sleeved t-shirt with some kind of sandals that showed off the white polish on her toenails. The large silver hoops in her ears and her natural hair style that was all Joelzi's—all of these were part of the whole picture of this woman. What was it about Joelzi Parker that just scuttled his well laid plans? *Yes, she is pretty, even beautiful,* he thought as he looked across the table into her deep brown eyes and watched her red lips express her thoughts with such animation. There was a depth about her that was intriguing. Joelzi was caring and took the time to validate the 'invisible people'. Even when she gave her coffee order, she was making eye contact with the barista and asking about their day. Carver was pleased to be seen with her and acknowledged as her date. *Is she the one?* The question flitted across his mind and the pros and cons of a relationship with Joelzi Parker became an active PowerPoint slide presentation. *Nope*, he thought, *I don't have time to examine this right now.* He scrolled to his notes on Merci and pulled his wayward thoughts in line. *First things first.*

Sixty-Two

Saturday, October 30th
in Grace and Adam's backyard
Joelzi

They were out by the pool but still under the shade of the pergola, sipping cold drinks. Joelzi's was some kind of fruit concoction that Grace had insisted on making her, but Grace's was simple water with ginger in it. Grace said the nausea continued to improve but all things ginger really helped.

"So give me all the scoop on coffee with Carver," said Grace closing her eyes and lying back on her lounger. A saucy grin escaped her calm affect and she turned her head toward Joelzi, opening one eye. Joelzi felt her face lift into an answering grin.

"Come on," Grace waved her hand at Joelzi, "you promised all the details."

"It was okay."

Grace sat up from her lounger. "That's it?"

"He was wonderful because Carver is genuine and really does care. We talked about his list."

"Yes…"

"It was all very practical. He tends to think with his head and totally bypass his heart. He wanted to talk about things I could imagine a father pointing out to his daughter…"

Grace scrunched her nose, "Carver treated you like his daughter?"

Joelzi laughed, "Not me. Merci. She moved in last Saturday."

"So, how's it going?" asked Grace.

"It's good," said Joelzi. "We're trying to find a rhythm. Merci is used to minimal adult input since her mom works two jobs. So I'm trying to be home when I'm not working. She probably sees me more than she saw her mother, since I work three twelves every week as opposed to working every night like her mom."

"So how did Carver's list become a thing?" asked Grace.

"Because Carver has been against Merci moving in with me. At one point, he told me all the reasons why I shouldn't get involved and then after thinking about our conversation, realized he had been nothing but negative. So he made a list of things that could be addressed early in the apartment sharing."

"It seems like Carver's a little bit invested," said Grace.

"It does, doesn't it?" said Joelzi. "It was a good list—more like bullet points as though Merci was his daughter and he wanted Merci to respect me. You know, clean up after herself, keep her grades up, go to church—that kind of thing," said Joelzi.

"Oh, that sounds like Carver's in protective mode," said Grace, "So that's all you talked about?"

197

"He clued me in on the medical statistics, like Merci's increased potential for anemia, pre-eclampsia, and a high-risk premature delivery...stuff like that. Which was nice, but I had already done the research. Merci's is definitely a high-risk pregnancy."

"Did you talk about anything *other* than Merci?" asked Grace with a frown.

"We talked about Hope Clinic...did you know he has always wanted to do medical missions?" Joelzi asked.

"As a matter of fact, I didn't know that. I find it refreshing that you are both volunteering at the same medical mission. I didn't see that coming."

"Me either," said Joelzi, "but I like that he wants to give back. I really admire him on a professional level."

"And..." asked Grace.

"And I really like him on a personal level. Carver may be difficult to get to know—he doesn't let people in easily—he's private. But when you see him with his family and when he relaxes and lets his walls down...Carver's pretty wonderful," said Joelzi with a sigh.

"You know I have always thought you and Carver would be a good match," said Grace.

"The thought that Carver and I could ever be a match feels so much like preparing myself for a relationship crash..." said Joelzi. "I'm terrified of hoping."

"Okay, my friend, in the interest of helping you save face over your feelings for Carver, I'll change the subject. Letting a high-risk pregnant teenager move in with you seems extreme, Joelzi," said Grace. "What brought on this need to be so involved?" asked Grace.

Joelzi took a sip of her drink and set it down on the side table with determination. *And there is the clincher. The only way is through. So here we are.*

"I had an abortion," Joelzi said, her eyes locked on the pool, waiting for Grace's reaction.

"I'm sorry," Grace said quietly. Joelzi waited, steeling her heart for what would come next, but Grace was silent. Joelzi glanced at her friend. Grace was looking at Joelzi with kindness and compassion.

"Tell me more?" Grace asked.

Joelzi felt the stiffness seep from her shoulders and she turned to look at her friend. "It was my senior year of nursing school, before we were friends. I had been dating a guy on the football team. We'd been 'together'," Joelzi used her hands to indicate air quotes, "since high school. I got to OU on a cheerleading scholarship. Myron made it on a football scholarship. We came from the same small town east of Oklahoma City, and we just stayed a couple when we got to college. Myron was always a little bit wild. My mom and Mema Anna—that's my grandma on momma's side—never liked him. But Myron wasn't bad when we were in high school. He just started hanging out with some of the other football players in college and he changed. He started drinking regularly and just trying things he didn't use to do. Being at college and having all those other girls interested really messed with him. I'd always told him I wasn't going to have sex before marriage. He was fine with that early on, but when we went to college he started pressuring me. Mema Anna and Momma had always been straight with me about sex. And I had really given my heart to God— for real. Not just words, you know?" She glanced over where Grace had swung her feet over to the side of her lounger so she could face Joelzi straight on. Grace held her ginger water in both hands and was leaning forward, listening.

"At the start of my senior year, Mema Anna died. That was hard. Mema Anna was in her eighties. I knew she would probably die before I did. But I didn't expect her to die so suddenly. She had a stroke. Sitting in her chair talking to Momma one minute and then slumped over and gone."

"I remember," Grace murmured quietly.

Joelzi swiped a tear that had escaped the pools filling her eyes and took a deep breath. "I went back to school and wasn't even back one week when I got a call from my dad one night. My mom had had a car accident. She lost control of the car and slammed into a tree. She was dead when they found her."

"This still breaks my heart, Joelzi. I don't know how you made it through all of that. I wish we had been close then—we had just become study buddies," said Grace, scooting her lounger closer to Joelzi's.

Joelzi let the tears fall for a few moments and then patted Grace's hand and pulled out some tissues from the box she had snagged from Grace's kitchen counter before they headed outside. Joelzi had known she would need them. She blew her nose loudly.

"Losing both of the important women in my life within a week really did a number on me," Joelzi continued. "The night Daddy called to tell me about Momma, I went looking for Myron. I needed someone to hold me, you know?" Grace grabbed the hand closest to her and held it in her lap with two hands. Tears ran down Grace's cheeks and Joelzi could see the depth of sorrow in her eyes. Grace had buried her fiancé before she met and married Adam.

200

She was well acquainted with grief.

"Well, I found Myron," Joelzi continued. "I went to his room. He had been drinking and he was happy to comfort me," Joelzi said. "I didn't want to have sex...I tried to get him to stop. But..."

"He raped you?" Grace said, sitting up suddenly, a look of horror on her face.

"...I did go to his room late at night and I knew he was drunk...and I did want him to comfort me..."

"Joelzi, you don't need to justify what happened," said Grace fiercely. "'No' means 'no'. We're not animals. We have reason and restraint. There is no reason to carry the blame for someone else's actions."

"I've always told myself it wouldn't have happened if I hadn't gone to his room," said Joelzi. "That one event set off a series of events. I missed my period. I told myself it was from all the stress of the funerals—although I must have had my head in the sand. I wasn't on birth control. I wasn't going to have sex. Then I started gagging and heaving every time I tried to brush my teeth. And nothing sounded good to eat and I was so tired I could hardly pull myself out of bed. Well, that's when I bought a pregnancy test. And surprise, surprise, it was positive." Joelzi pulled her hand out of Grace's grasp and blew her nose again before continuing. "When I told Myron, he was adamant that I have an abortion."

Joelzi gazed out over the pool, remembering the conversation that had been etched into her memory. "Myron said he had no intention of marrying me so we could raise a mistake. He was angry because I hadn't been on birth control." Joelzi's tone was incredulous and a disbelieving grimace covered her face. "I wasn't going to have sex before marriage.

Why would I have been on birth control?" Joelzi looked at Grace as though Grace had her answer.

Joelzi swallowed. "Anyway, I ended up having an abortion. I don't recommend it. It may seem like an easy out, but the effects seem to go on forever." Joelzi sniffed into a fresh tissue. "For years, I've stuffed these feelings and then my best friend tells me she's pregnant," Joelzi smiled bitterly at Grace, "and I want to be over the moon for her..." Joelzi squeezed Grace's hand, "but I freeze up. Immediately I think about the baby I aborted. Was it a girl or maybe a boy? These feelings of grief and disappointment—they are crushing. And then I meet a young girl who is in a perfect position to make the same mistake I made. Merci doesn't know how much that decision will change her life. Carver doesn't understand, but I need to make amends. I have to help Merci. That's why I let her move in with me."

"Oh, Joelzi, *I'm sorry* seems like such a weak phrase to tell you how I feel about what has happened to you. I'm truly grieved for you," said Grace. The two friends sat in silence giving space for the heartache and disappointment to be observed before moving on. Moments later, Grace shifted on her lounger, a thoughtful look on her face. "Okay, let's back up and break this down, Joelzi...helping this girl..."

"Merci," said Joelzi.

"Merci," repeated Grace with a nod. "Helping Merci is not going to remove what's going on in your heart."

"But..."

"I'm not saying it's right or wrong, Joelzi. I'm saying you can't 'work' your way out of these feelings. Helping Merci is a beautiful service. But service is not going to set you free. Have you ever told anybody?" Grace asked.

"I told Merci when she came to the clinic. It just seemed the best way to communicate that I understood her situation. And Gina at the Pregnancy Resource Center sort of guessed by the things I said to her. But I've never told anyone close to me.

"You've carried this all by yourself? For what—five, six years?" asked Grace.

"Seven."

"Oh, my dear, dear friend. That's a heavy burden," said Grace. "How have you managed?"

"Concertina wire," said Joelzi. They chuckled together.

"You know Jesus died for all of this, right?" Grace glanced over at her best friend.

"I know it with my head. But my heart is so disappointed."

"Seeing the raw truth of our failures is a kind of grace," Grace said, "a painful grace." Both women were silent for a moment before Grace continued with her thought. "It's grace that gives us the space to really see who we really are—to fully face our failures—to own them. And it's grace that forgives our mess-ups. Our mess-ups have been paid in full, Joelzi. Remember who you are in Christ, and don't let your failures incapacitate you. Jesus says you are worth what it cost him to buy back your life. Don't throw that away by focusing on the past and not embracing hope for the future."

"I'm trying, Grace," said Joelzi. "I'm really trying to believe what God has done for me."

"I'm grateful you told me, Joelzi," said Grace. "Not because I want to hear the bad stuff in your life, but because I want to know you and be your friend. The sharing of the hard stuff is a bonding of its own. That's what happened when you walked through Rob's death with me. And that's how this will unfold. I'm here for you...have you considered getting counseling?" asked Grace.

"I started attending a Hope and Healing group at the Pregnancy Resource Center on Tuesday nights," said Joelzi.

"Do you remember taking me to the Grief Workshop after Rob died?" asked Grace.

Joelzi nodded. "It's the thing that gave me the courage to try this group," said Joelzi.

"I'm glad," said Grace.

"I am too," said Joelzi.

Sixty-Three

"Don't be an African impala, Carver," said Adam, leaning back on his booth seat. They were back at their favorite sports grill, grabbing a hamburger and catching up.

"What's that supposed to mean?" Carver leaned forward, frowning across the table at his best friend.

"Oh, we've been watching animal shows with Zoe," Adam said. "Last night was all about the African impala. In case you were wondering, they won't jump unless they can see where their feet will land. They are risk averse." He smirked at Carver. "Kind of like you."

"I'm not risk averse," said Carver.

"Says the guy who only dates a girl once and immediately compiles a list of why things won't work. You're not willing to fail, Carver. Even in med school you studied twice as long as any of the other med students."

"As I recall, you were right there in the library with me."

"It's true, I was. But I was there because I needed to be there. You were there that long for unnecessary review. Carver, you aced every exam. Your fellow med students hated what you did to the curve. I remember them complaining."

"I think there was a compliment in there somewhere," said Carver dryly.

"Carver, you're brilliant. But you're not perfect. And that's good, because no one wants to date, or marry 'perfect'," said Adam.

"I'm not trying to be perfect, Adam, and I don't think it's wrong to plan. The Bible talks about planning before building."

"Planning is good, but Proverbs also says, 'a man plans his way, but the Lord orders his steps' (Prov 16:9). At some point you're going to have to loosen your grip and let God work His plan. It's strangling your dating life."

"I thought we were talking about my disagreement with Joelzi over letting Merci move into her apartment."

"In a roundabout way, yes."

Carver crossed his arms and leaned back, waiting.

"Your determination to manage the details of Merci moving in with Joelzi makes Joelzi feel like you don't think she can make a good decision without you," said Adam.

"I don't think that..." said Carver, his eyebrows crunching inward.

"Well, your actions speak otherwise. Grace says that Joelzi says you think with your head and totally bypass your heart."

"So, is this the way it's going to be if I date Joelzi? Joelzi talks to Grace, Grace talks to you, and you sit me down and lecture me?" Carver pushed his drink to the side and leaned forward. "I don't want a four-way relationship, Adam." Carver stood up and reached for his wallet. "This is a wasted cause and dinner."

"Whoa, Carver, slow down, man," said Adam. *I have never seen Carver this riled.* "I'm your friend. For what it's worth, I agree with you. No more 'he said, she said' on my part." Adam held his hands up in a show of surrender. "Please. Just sit down and let's change the subject." Adam maintained eye contact. "Please?"

Carver stood for a moment with his billfold in hand and then returned it to his pocket and sat back down in his seat, resting his elbows on the table, and putting his head in his hands. "I'm sorry, Adam. I seem to have a short fuse today." There was a moment of silence. "She has really disrupted my well-ordered life."

"I'm assuming we're talking about Joelzi and not Merci?" said Adam.

Carver looked up and nodded. "She leads with her heart. I like that about her. She's real—genuine. But she's not 'safe'."

Adam grinned. "That reminds me of a line in The Lion, the Witch and the Wardrobe."

"C.S. Lewis?"

Adam nodded. "There's a description of Aslan, the Lion, that says something like 'he's a good lion, but he's not a safe lion.' Of course, Aslan is a type of Christ, and Joelzi's not Christ. But still, Joelzi's heart toward Merci is good—and not necessarily safe."

"Exactly," said Carver.

Sixty-Four

Tuesday, November 2nd
Hope and Healing

Joelzi checked her watch. She had about fifteen minutes before her class started. Today they would start reviewing the symptoms shared by many women who had had abortions. Fourteen Common Post-Abortive Symptoms: Caring for the Heart of the Post-Abortive Woman. It seemed like a good start. *Maybe they have something that will help me.* Ten minutes into the class and she was undone. Joelzi sat in the class, tears running down her cheeks. *I don't care who sees anymore*, she thought. The class had opened with a general prayer for each woman to experience insight and healing and had proceeded to list fourteen of the most common symptoms of women who had experienced abortion, with a stated plan to delve into those symptoms in greater detail as the classes continued. *So far I'm one for one*, thought Joelzi. *Guilt, anxiety, remorse, depression, shame—these are all present in my day-to-day life.* She had hidden and denied many of them, but as soon as they were spoken, Joelzi knew; she had experienced them in some form. The real crusher was 'aversion to situations that involved pregnant women.' Grace's new pregnancy crystallized in Joelzi's mind. That day on Grace's front porch, not being able to catch her breath was a signal to her heart. Another symptom was being worried about being able to have kids of your own. *Yes, that's me too. I certainly don't deserve it. Why would God give me children after what I did?*

She pulled her attention back to the front of the room where Candace was speaking. "At this clinic, we focus on God's best for us. We use the Bible to speak truth. If we ask Him, God forgives us," Candace paused. "Many of the women who have shared their stories with me, and it has been true for me personally, have admitted that it has been easier to accept God's forgiveness, than it has been to forgive themselves. The feeling of unworthiness choke our progress to wellness, so we need to know the truth." Candace paused. "I will not diminish what Jesus did on the cross for me. His death is enough. It is more than sufficient to cover anything we have done. When we cling to our badness more than we cling to His goodness, we are basically saying Jesus is not enough and that we will never move beyond our badness. The Bible says He came to give us life, and life more abundantly. So we need to let go of the power that our sin wants to bind us up with. In this regard, our healing starts with forgiving ourselves. God's unconditional love and forgiveness are more than enough."

Sixty-Five

Wednesday, November 3rd
Joelzi

"First, you let Merci move in with you. That was complicated," said Carver. "But now you're encouraging her to keep her baby?" Carver asked, the high pitch of his voice emphasizing his disbelief.

They were sitting in his car outside her apartment after another amazing date. Merci was in the apartment and Joelzi hadn't wanted her to hear this discussion. After Carver's statement, Joelzi was grateful she had broached the subject in the privacy of Carver's car. Joelzi knew it would cause friction, but she valued Carver's perspective and needed to discuss how she might best help Merci deal with this new reality. Carver excelled at identifying potential pitfalls and maneuvering to avoid them. Joelzi just needed to get him to see her point of view.

"I'm being her friend, Carver," Joelzi said. "I'm hoping to gain influence."

"I don't like it," Carver muttered pulling a hand down his face in frustration.

"And I'm not trying to encourage Merci to keep her baby, as much as I'm trying to give her room to make choices," said Joelzi.

"You're approaching this with rose-colored glasses, Joelzi."

"No, I'm trying to send the message that God sees her and God cares and God uses ordinary people to step in the gap."

"You're telling Merci not to worry about taking care of a newborn on her own, that she doesn't need to think about what it will take to finish high school and try to find daycare for her baby while she stays in school, studies for tests, works to provide for her baby. Isn't she a sophomore?" Carver asked.

"Yes," said Joelzi, "she's a sophomore, but that doesn't mean she can't finish school."

"How is Merci going to get a job if she's in school? Most jobs for high school students pay minimum wage," said Carver. "How is she going to go to school and pay for childcare on a minimum wage salary? You are setting Merci up to fail."

"I'm setting Merci up to have a baby, Carver," said Joelzi. "A baby. It's not something you can just dump because you made a mistake." *I ought to know.*

"No, you're right on that count," said Carver, rubbing his hand down his face again, "but have you even discussed what happens after the baby is born? Merci is not in a good position to raise a baby and finish school. She's on the way to becoming a statistic. You need to discuss other options."

"Other options?" Joelzi felt her heart freeze.

Surely Carver isn't suggesting an abortion?

"Like giving the baby up for adoption. There are lots of families out there that would love to have a baby and can't." There was a lull in the conversation before Carver added, "as a matter of fact, I think Adam's sister, Deeni, has struggled with infertility. A couple like that might welcome the chance to adopt a baby."

Tears pooled in Joelzi's eyes. "Oh, Carver, I know you're right in the most analytical way, but you have no idea what you're saying...you're asking a sixteen-year-old pregnant girl to start talking about giving up the most precious thing she has going for her. Right now, no one else loves or needs her. She's seen the ultrasound, heard the baby's heartbeat, and is starting to feel the baby move...this is not the time to pressure her to give up her baby. Even though I can see how that might be an ideal solution."

They sat in silence for a moment, their words used up, and then Carver reached over and pulled Joelzi across the bench seat of his SUV and into his arms, resting his forehead on hers. Joelzi breathed in the scent of him, warm male, like a favorite pullover jersey. She felt her neck muscles relax and was mesmerized by the way their breathing became synchronized.

"I'm sorry," Carver said. "I never seem to handle things with you as easily as just about anybody else. I know my approach seems harsh. I just see all the hazards so easily...I don't want you to get hurt, Joelzi. You're important to me."

"Really?" Joelzi asked pulling back enough to look Carver in the eyes.

"Really," Carver said, nodding his head up and down perfunctorily. "I've been resisting the tug, but you're pretty irresistible."

Joelzi's stomach flipped as Carver's hand cupped her jaw, and his eyes shifted to where his thumb caressed the corner of her mouth. Instinctively, she lifted her face to his, hoping he might...

Carver's mouth lowered to her lips and he gently touched down for a tender moment before pausing. Joelzi thought her heart would pound out of her chest waiting for Carver to decide. Her closest hand found its way over his and the other lifted of its own accord to pull him toward her. *Carver is a quick read,* Joelzi thought with satisfaction as his lips came down on hers again. *For someone who doesn't date much, the man has a way with a woman's lips,* sighed Joelzi, before she surrendered to the joy of kissing Carver Ellis. *This would be the perfect segue to tell him my story,* thought Joelzi, *but I just can't...*

"It will work out," murmured Carver between kisses, "we'll just keep looking."

"Hm?" asked Joelzi. She was distracted by Carver's fine lips, "oh, yes, we'll just keep looking. God has a perfect plan."

Sixty-Six

Thursday, November 4th

I have a new nephew. Carver texted.

Annie? When? How big? Joelzi immediately texted back.

Yes, Annie delivered this morning. BIG boy. 9lb 7oz Carver typed.

What's his name? Are they okay? Joelzi's questions flew over her phone keyboard.

Marshall Winston Ellis. They are both doing well. Carver texted.

Joelzi sent two heart emojis.

Want to go see them in the hospital nursery? Carver asked.

YES! Joelzi's text pinged immediately.

Visiting hours for the nursery are 4-6pm. Swing by and get you? Carver sent.

Absolutely. Can I bring Merci? Joelzi texted.

Great idea. Pick you up in 15? Carver's text came back.

We'll be ready. Texted Joelzi.

Sixty-Seven

Oklahoma Memorial Hospital Nursery Viewing Window
45 minutes later

Carver had gotten them passes to the viewing area and rejoined Merci and Joelzi at the nursery window as the nursery staff had pushed little Marshall up to the window. Joelzi's heart had flipped. Marshall Winston Ellis was a handsome boy with soft brown skin, perfect ears, and little bow lips. Dark curly hair was plastered down on parts of his head and standing up in other parts. Tears swam in Joelzi's eyes. What a precious gift. A bittersweet joy was drowning her when Joelzi felt Carver's hand slide into hers and grip her hand firmly. Joelzi turned to look at Carver, trying to blink her tears away as she smiled shakily. Seeing her tears, Carver pulled her close and wrapped his arms around her.

"I think my newest nephew is pretty amazing...but when I see you that happy about somebody else's baby...well, that's pretty special. I suspect that means you're going to be over the moon about your own kids," he said softly with a chuckle. "That would be fun to see..." Carver added quietly.

Joelzi looked up at Carver from where she stood in his arms, "Marshall is beautiful and..." She took inventory of her heart. Yes, she was sad with her past choices, but she was also hoping, anticipating that there would be a baby in her future—in the right time, with a man who loved her and wanted their baby. "...and you're right, I'll probably be crazy about my own kids."

Joelzi noticed that Merci was glued to the glass viewing area and she pulled out of Carver's arms and moved to Merci's side.

"What do you think, Merci?" asked Joelzi.

"They're all so small." Merci breathed out. "Well, not him," she motioned to Marshall Winston, "he's huge."

Carver came up on Merci's other side. "Marshall Winston is big. But he's also a third baby."

"So babies get bigger and bigger every time you have another one?" Merci asked Carver.

"Well...not necessarily...but that does seem to be a trend."

"Sometimes when I think about having Hope," Merci's hand went to her baby bump, "I get scared."

Carver and Joelzi exchanged a look over Merci's head. "What scares you, Merci?" asked Joelzi.

"Well, to start with...getting her out. But after that, I don't know anything about babies. I'm an only child." Merci took a deep breath and let it out with a big sigh, "I saw a lady with a baby at church." Merci turned to Joelzi, "You were talking to someone...anyway, the baby was crying and crying, and the lady couldn't get it to be quiet...what if Hope is like that? And that lady had someone to help her. I'll be all alone...sometimes I wonder..."

Carver and Joelzi waited for Merci to finish, not wanting to break into the ponderings of the young soon to be mother. "What do you wonder, Merci?" asked Carver after a lull.

"I just wonder about adoption. Would I be a bad person if I gave my baby away?" asked Merci.

Not wanting to press too hard into these musings, Joelzi wrapped her arm around Merci. "Let's keep talking about this. And we'll do some research so you have more information...Carver will help us, right, Carver?" Joelzi asked, looking at Carver over Merci's head.

"Absolutely. I'll help too, Merci, we won't leave you to do this alone," said Carver.

"And no, Merci..." added Joelzi, "...giving your baby to a family that wants to adopt is not being a bad person. Sometimes it means you want the best for your baby."

Sixty-Eight

Friday, November 5th
Joelzi

"I just don't understand what makes you so willing to drop everything and help Merci." Carver said. Once again, they were hashing out the Merci problem. This time they were in Joelzi's kitchen where she was fixing coffee. Merci was still at school, although the bus would be dropping her off in the next ten minutes. *I'll need to warn Carver that she'll be home soon, but we have a few minutes yet,* thought Joelzi. "I can understand your desire to help her at the Hope Clinic, but you've gone way beyond what any normal person would. You picked her up from school and took her to the Pregnancy Resource Center. You took her back to the Pregnancy Resource Center for her ultrasound. When she decides on the spur of the moment, like most sixteen-year-olds would, that she's going to keep her baby, even though she's getting kicked out of her mother's house—you open your apartment to her so she can carry the pregnancy. It just seems over the top..."

This is the moment of truth, thought Joelzi, pouring a cup of coffee for Carver and handing it to him. She took another minute to pour her own cup, adding creamer, and stirring it carefully. *I've been praying for a way to share my past with Carver. Putting it off more than once, but I really love him. I can't keep going without being honest. He will think I waited to get my hooks in him before telling him a past that might change his mind about me.* "Carver...what are your feelings and convictions about abortion?"

Carver looked at her over his cup of coffee, his eyebrows lifted. "Shouldn't we start with my convictions about sex before marriage?" Carver asked.

"Okay, Carver, I'm pretty sure I already know your convictions on that, but we can start there," Joelzi said with a sigh. "What are your convictions about sex before marriage?"

"It's wrong," Carver said.

"Well, yes, I don't disagree. But life is a little grayer and more blurred than just 'It's wrong.' People mess up. We're not perfect," said Joelzi.

"It leads to all kinds of trouble—not the least of which is pregnancy outside of marriage," said Carver.

"So, back to my initial question. What are your feelings and convictions about abortion?" asked Joelzi.

"It's wrong," said Carver, bringing his cup of coffee up to his mouth and taking a long sip.

"We're on a roll," Joelzi said, rolling her eyes at him. "Come on, Carver, press in a bit. How would you handle an unexpected pregnancy between you and a hypothetical girlfriend?"

"Well, hopefully we were planning to get married anyway...so we'd get married."

"And what if you were a sixteen-year-old girl and you were just trying to fit in and essentially were raped? What would you do then?"

"Merci was raped?" Carver paused. "Oh, that just hurts my heart, Joelzi. She's so young. Her whole life is changed."

Joelzi's eyes blurred, hearing Carver's compassion bleed though his black and white statements. *There might be hope for me.* "Would you recommend getting rid of the inconvenience of an unwanted pregnancy?"

"Never." Carver said. "A pregnancy is life. God gives life. ONLY God gives life. It should be valued."

They were quiet for a moment, sipping their coffee. Joelzi tried to get her thoughts together for the next discussion when Carver continued, a far off look on his face.

"I remember when my parents found out that Mom was pregnant with Georgie. He was an unplanned pregnancy. Both of them were older. Us boys were older. There's ten years between Georgie and me. And then they were told Georgie had Down's Syndrome. They sat all three of us older boys down and told us what the next years were going to be like. That we had been given the honor of having Georgie in our family. That Georgie would be another way that God would help us learn to love." Carver looked over at Joelzi. "And that's pretty much the way it has been. They never once talked about aborting Georgie. And having him totally changed their life. My parents were in a season of life where they were socially important, attending

221

Galas to promote hospitals and that kind of thing. Mom had gone back to teaching and was having an impact there...and they walked away from all of that and have never looked back."

"What a statement about the character of your parents. They are lovely people, Carver." Joelzi paused. "So, back to Merci..."

"No, I wouldn't recommend anyone have an abortion," Carver said. "But I would recommend that Merci give her baby up for adoption. And I do believe Merci would be better off in a home with a male and a female influence."

"Point well taken, I'm a single female. And I agree with you about giving the baby up for adoption, but she's not mentioned it since seeing baby Marshall. There's still time. She's only nineteen weeks along." Joelzi closed her eyes and took a deep breath. *It is time.* "Carver?"

"Yeah?" said Carver, his eyes focused on taking a sip of his coffee.

"I'm an older version of Merci," said Joelzi. She waited, her eyes on his face as he processed her words.

"You've had a baby?" Carver's head popped up; his eyes big with confusion as he looked to her for clarification.

"I was pregnant..." Joelzi said, "and...I had an abortion."

"You aborted your baby?" Carver flinched, swallowing hard, before leaning forward. "You? But you're..."

Carver leaned back, closing his eyes as a pained expression flitted across his features. It took a minute and then his lips firmed and his jaw set as he said, "I see." The words were like a dull knife cutting out her heart.

"But..." Joelzi didn't know what she should say next. As many times as she had imagined this conversation, it had never gone like this. *I just want the Carver I had before my confession,* she thought, watching the emotions cross over Carver's face. Instead, the key turned in the lock, announcing Merci's arrival home from school. Joelzi stood and walked to the front door, struggling to control her facial expression. *This is terrible timing,* she thought. "You're home from school, Merci," Joelzi said, the tightness in her chest making her voice shake. She crossed her arms with a nervous laugh as though she could manage the pain by blocking her body. "How was your day?"

"Good," said Merci with a smile. "Hi, Dr. Ellis, I didn't expect to see you here," Merci said, looking beyond Joelzi where Carver had appeared. "Is everything okay?" she asked, looking between Carver and Joelzi.

"Hi, Merci, I was just leaving," Carver said, grabbing his jacket. "Thank you for the coffee, Joelzi," Carver said with a stiff nod of his head. "I'll see myself out."

And he was gone. Just like that. Joelzi firmed her lips as reality hit her full force. *All hope of remaining a shining example of womanhood in Carver's eyes vanished in the space of a breath. Why do I even try? So much for finding a man who could look past her faults and find the woman that God had forgiven.* Joelzi flipped the lock on the door and turned back to Merci. Pasting a smile on her face she said, "So tell me about school, Merci."

Sixty-Nine

Carver

Carver slammed his car door, threw his car gear in drive, and quickly made his way to the apartment complex exit. It wasn't until he reached the first light that he realized he hadn't buckled. *Calm down. Just because you're disappointed doesn't mean you take it out on your car or forget to buckle,* he thought. He concentrated on driving until the thoughts pressed in again. *Joelzi had an abortion?* Dread buried him like an avalanche. *Of course, something would come up to interfere with the woman I finally took a chance on and let into my life.* What would his family say? Ellises didn't get pregnant before getting married, and Ellises definitely didn't have abortions. His fingers began beating a jarring rhythm on the steering wheel. Was it too difficult for God to bring him a woman without a sordid past? Was there no one out there who could live a good Christian life? Logic shuffled into his thoughts. It didn't line up with the woman he knew. Joelzi came across as a life of the party at the ER but he remembered her trembling hands and saying she was 'terrified' to meet his family. Was she faking the genuine, fun-loving Joelzi that he had grown to care for? She had been reserved when he had tried to get her to talk about Meeker, but he hadn't thought too much about it. He'd watched her with Merci. No, it didn't add up. Joelzi wouldn't fake moving Merci into her apartment. If she was trying to get on his good side, she'd have avoided helping Merci at all. *He* wouldn't have done anything for Merci but what was required of the law. *If we were discussing the parable of the Good Samaritan, I would definitely be one of those guys who passed on by—didn't want to get involved. Not Joelzi. She didn't care what anyone said, she was going to help.* That thought settled some of the acid indigestion bubbling up from his stomach...and what about Georgie? Joelzi could not pretend her way through a relationship with Georgie. She never talked down to Georgie, Joelzi always treated Georgie with respect. And they were always cutting up, laughing, telling jokes. Carver had a hard time believing that was an act. If it was, Joelzi belonged on Broadway. *I always thought I would marry a Godly woman, God.* The story of King David came to mind. *Yeah, well, I guess he wasn't my definition of Godly either...but You did call King David a man after Your own heart. And he royally messed up. And I don't even know the details of Joelzi's past. No...I don't want to know the details. But maybe the details would help me move on. Well, it's too late now. That opportunity crashed and burned when I walked out like I did. What if it was all a ploy and she was just pretending until he was good and caught? Because the real Joelzi had a*

225

history of...well, she had a history. Maybe Joelzi wasn't the one for him. Maybe she was just a test from God. The thoughts spun and twisted, becoming a tangled mess.

Seventy

Work was unbearable. Joelzi clocked in and went to her duty station, avoiding the Physicians area like it was the shark pit. She was getting report from Kelli-Lynn who was now a full-fledged staff nurse. "Wow, Joelzi, if I didn't know you weren't a drinker, I'd say you were hung over. You look terrible," Kelli-Lynn said bluntly. "What's going on? Are you okay?"

"Oh, just some sleepless nights," Joelzi said. If she gave any additional details, the entire ER would be privy to her and Carver's demise before the end of the shift. *I prefer my drama with a new dress and mani/pedi—not as the fodder for the ER gossip,* she thought. The break-up with Carver had been gut-wrenching. He hadn't called or texted in days. Carver Ellis had ghosted her. She wasn't sleeping, she wasn't eating, it was taking all her focus to stay actively involved in Merci's day-to-day activities and to get to work.

"Is it love trouble with Dr. Ellis?" Kelli-Lynn asked cheekily. "He is such a dish. And he can't seem to take his eyes off you."

"Oh, I'm confident he's cured of that by now," said Joelzi firmly.

"Not that I can tell," said Kelli-Lynn looking over Joelzi's shoulder towards the Physician's area. "And he's not looking too good for the wear either. In fact," Kelli-Lynn said, studying Joelzi again, "y'all look like a matched pair." Kelli-Lynn's eyebrows lifted in question.

He's not looking good? thought Joelzi. *Oh, I've got to move on.* Joelzi firmed her lips, "How about that report, Kelli-Lynn? Tell me about my patients."

Seventy-One

"Carver." Joelzi sprinted out of the staff entrance to the Emergency Department, desperate to catch up with Carver. *I will say my piece*, she thought as she jogged toward Carver. She had had enough and decided to have it out with him, but Carver was avoiding her. He hadn't been at Hope Clinic for the past two weeks and had probably switched shifts with some of the other physicians because tonight had been the first time they had worked together in over a week, and that was probably only because she had been called in at the last minute. The providers' shifts were staggered roughly an hour after the nursing staff. Knowing this, Joelzi had camped out in the break room until a few minutes before she knew Carver would get off. At that point, she had moved out on the floor to sit at the charge nurse desk until she saw him leaving.

She and the night charge nurse had been engrossed in a new system for starting IVs when she had glanced up in time to see him passing through the first set of automatic doors out to the area where the ambulances pulled in.

"Carver Ellis!" She suspected he heard her the first time but had just kept walking, but after the second time she had yelled his name, Carver stopped and halfway turned, before waiting for her to reach him. He didn't make eye contact, just looking to the ground around his feet. Breathless but determined, she stopped in front of Carver and locked her eyes on his bowed head. "I know I'm not 'good enough' for you, Carver," Joelzi said with conviction, "but I'm accepted by Jesus." She had simply wanted to clear the air between them, but the chase out the Emergency Department doors had challenged her calm, and now she could hear anger in her tone. She took some slow steady breaths to try to tone her anger down, before starting again. "But I'm 'good enough' now," she continued, "because Jesus paid for me. He said, 'It is finished' for me." As she spoke the words out loud, Joelzi felt them resonate deep in her heart again. Peace soothed the bitterness of loss and she was aware of letting those feelings go. She was letting go of other people's perceptions of what God had done for her. Letting go of the desire for Carver to see her as valuable and worth pursuing.

Carver stood there quietly, not moving with his eyes on his feet. *He won't even look at me.* Tears of sadness and relief leaked down Joelzi's cheeks and she wiped at them with a sniff before continuing, "I did a terrible thing, Carver. I took the easy way out of a difficult situation. I killed my baby. And I suffered the consequences until I finally gave it to

God. I know...you would never do anything like that...but I did, Carver. I need a Savior. And Jesus did that for me. When Jesus died for me, that made me valuable. Priceless. Worth being loved..." Joelzi stepped back and looked at Carver. "So, as much as I really like you—I'm done hoping you might see me as worth loving. I'm going to step back and wait for the man God brings—if He brings me one." Joelzi smiled, feeling stronger, as she took another step back..."I'm God's treasure," she said in awe as new understanding permeated her heart. "The man God brings into my life will recognize that..." Joelzi took another step as though to head for the parking garage but turned back.

"Here's a little food for thought...you can't give what you don't know. I know the grace of God in and over my life. I understand what Jesus's sacrifice means for me. Because He has extended mercy and grace to me—it is in my hand to extend His mercy and grace.

"I made some major mistakes. And I have lived with the consequences of those choices. I thought I was alone. I thought God had left me. I made decisions without asking Him. And I have suffered. The shame and guilt have eaten me up until I avoided my family and my friends. But I finally started counseling. I heard what God had to say to me. And I'm learning scriptures that remind me who God says I am so that when the condemnation comes, trying to diminish what God has done in my life, I remember. God is a redeemer. He saves us. He came to give us life. And I for one, am not going to keep staring at the gift without receiving it. I choose to honor His sacrifice and change my life to reflect that. Yes, I had sex outside of marriage. Yes, I got pregnant and yes, I decided to abort my baby. I will never be able to change my history. But my future is full of hope. Jesus made it so." There was a pause as Joelzi thought over her words, deciding she had said what she had come to say. At her pause, Carver looked up. "Be at peace, Carver. I'm not going to derail the Ellises' 'Godly history'." Joelzi's face quivered, but she held Carver's gaze, straightening her shoulders as she continued, "Have a good life, Carver Ellis. God has the perfect woman for you." Joelzi gently patted Carver on his arm, before letting her hand drop and turning to walk toward the staff garage.

Seventy-Two

Carver

He stood and watched Joelzi until she disappeared into the concrete staff parking garage. He had heard her call his name the first time and God help him; he had wanted to turn and open his arms to her. Hold her, comfort her, give in to his desire to have her in his life. It had taken sheer grit to keep walking, to hope that she would give up chasing after him. But Joelzi Parker was not a fragile, helpless, or wilting flower. Life had made her strong, determined, and resilient. How could he not be attracted to that? She had confronted him, with truth and honesty, so they could move on. As painful as the conversation had been, he admired Joelzi even more for the way she had handled herself. *Why would you bring someone like Joelzi Parker in my life, knowing I would fall for her?* He rubbed the back of his neck with a hand, aware of the tension there. It hadn't been that hard of a shift tonight, but suddenly he was exhausted in a deep, bone-chilling way. He had never suffered from depression, but if this mind-numbing sadness was any semblance, he didn't know how people survived. *I'm so conflicted. I should have told her how wonderful she is,* he thought. But he was raised to be a gentleman. He wasn't going to make her stop and listen to his side of things, and he certainly wasn't going to chase her down to say his piece, even if he *could* think of something to say. Sadness cloaked him in the still night, drawing his shoulders down in defeat. Back to the drawing board. *Number Six has been a monumental flop...no, Joelzi would never be a flop,* he thought.

Seventy-Three

Thursday, November 18th

Carver had called the home phone and asked to speak to Georgie. He had decided for the second week in a row to skip Hope Clinic. *I just can't see her,* he thought. *It's like we're connected and I can't control my emotions when I see her. I just want to go to her and hold her. Tell her I'm sorry and we'll figure it out. I probably need to start looking for a job at one of the other hospitals.* Georgie came on the line and Carver started in with the excuses he had used the last time.

"Hey, Georgie, I'm not going to be able to make it for Hope Clinic tonight..." Carver said.

"Again?" whined Georgie. "Why aren't we going this time?"

He didn't want to lie, so Carver tried redirecting, "Why don't we go out for pizza, Georgie? Get in some brother time?" Carver suggested.

"Because tonight is Hope Clinic night and we're

supposed to be there. Joelzi's gonna be there, and we're part of the team," said Georgie.

I should never have brought Georgie to Hope Clinic in the first place, thought Carver. "I'm sorry to disappoint you, Georgie, but I just can't make it." *I'm definitely in the doghouse now. The whole family is going to suspect...*

Seventy-Four

"Carver how are you, Honey?" his mother asked as she slid a fresh glass of her specialty iced tea his way.

He really didn't want to have this conversation. But his mother was nothing if she wasn't persistent. Still, it was worth a try. "I'm fine, Momma," Carver said with a sigh and lifted his glass to take a sip of the smooth iced tea with a hint of herbs.

"Are you?" Momma asked, a thoughtful look on her face. She paused, "There for several weeks I thought you had found the one. And you seemed to have found your place, volunteering at Hope Clinic. You seemed...energized." Sharon Ellis took a slow drink of her iced tea.

She wasn't wrong, Carver thought.

"But you haven't been back to Hope Clinic in

two weeks," his mom continued. "I know Georgie misses going. Georgie misses seeing Joelzi. As a matter of fact, we all miss hearing about Joelzi. What happened, Carver?"

"She's not who I thought God would bring me. She's..." Carver's eyes closed as he tried to contemplate the right adjective. He didn't want to throw Joelzi under the bus and he didn't want to come across as too particular, but..."

"Broken?" Momma asked gently, breaking into Carver's thoughts.

"Well, actually, yes, she's been broken, wounded. I don't know all the details—she confessed the basics to me the other night..."

"Confessed?" pressed Momma, a small frown appearing between her eyebrows.

"Well, I guess I make her feel 'less than'..." he was groping for the right way to explain their conversation.

"Less than?" a sad look flitted across Momma's face, almost like disappointment. *But how could she be disappointed? She didn't even know what little Joelzi had told him, so was she disappointed in him?* Carver paused. *Yeah, maybe I didn't handle that conversation right,* he thought.

"But she's made a huge change," Carver offered. *I don't want my family judging Joelzi.* "She's been different in the last couple of weeks. It's like she's standing up. Like she knows who she is in Christ." Carver sat back, nodding matter-of-factly, confident he had gotten it right. Somehow, saying the words out loud helped with clarity.

"I see," Momma said quietly.

Uh-oh, that didn't sound good. Somehow, he didn't think Momma 'seeing' was working in his favor.

"She's not who I thought I would marry, okay?" Carver said.

There was a pause in the conversation. Carver examined the sweat drops sliding down the side of his iced tea glass. He thought about Joelzi. He loved her. He could actually think those words without cringing. He'd never been able to think that about any woman he had dated. But he couldn't marry her. He couldn't be the one to mess up the family's generational reputation. *Ellises are strong, godly, and represent the goodness of God*, he repeated to his inner self.

"Carver," Momma said gently, her words breaking into Carver's thoughts again, "we don't tell the story often, and I'm not sure why, but the Ellises have skeletons in their closet too. Honey, no one is perfect. If we aren't physically or verbally making mistakes, be sure we are proud and needing the Lord to humble us. Your Grandma Ruby is a perfect example."

"Grandma Ruby?--but Grandpa Daniel said they knew each other as kids—grew up together."

"They did. But Grandma Ruby had a hard home life. She ran away from home when she was in high school and got caught up in some bad stuff."

"But Grandpa was a preacher; they pastored together."

"Carver, you're seeing the redemption picture. The layers of grace on our lives are like the layers of paint on a masterpiece—the work of the Master. Sometimes, it takes years for the intention of the artist to be fully appreciated. Grandma Ruby came back to town broken, abused, and pregnant. But your Grandpa Daniel had always loved her. He saw the treasure in the broken vessel, and he married her and took in her baby as his own."

There was a pause as Carver did the math.

"Auntie Jemimah wasn't Grandpa Daniel's biological child?" Carver asked. "I never knew."

"Today, we see the beauty of the sacrifice. Back then, there was no beauty. From what your Grandma Ruby has shared with me, she was a bitter, broken mess. Early on she was angry. But God..."

"But God?" Carver waited.

"God got under her rough edges and changed her heart. When Grandma Ruby finally accepted that God loved her—had always loved her—and would always love her, well, then the hard shell crumbled. And God used your Grandpa Daniel to work in her life. I've watched Grandpa Daniel get a funny smirk when Grandma Ruby would tell the story of a disagreement they may have had. He would just sidle over to her and wrap her in his arms, snuggling down into her neck. He would whisper something in her ear, and she would soften. Just like that. She would turn into his arms and would hold on to him like a flower turning into the sun...you ought to go see her. Talk to her. Ask Grandma Ruby to tell you her story. The power of real love is an incredible thing."

Seventy-Five

Saturday, November 20th
Grandma Ruby's house
Carver

"Carver, my handsome doctor grandson," Grandma Ruby said in her southern accent. "It's so good to see you." Grandma Ruby wrapped Carver in a warm hug, and the smell of lavender he always associated with her wafted up into his senses.

"Momma suggested I come," Carver said.

"Yes, she mentioned it on the phone. Come on in, Carver."

Carver walked into the small two-bedroom home that his grandparents had lived in from his earliest memories. It was neat and clean with everything in its place. Grandpa's Bible was lying on the small end table over by his rocker, where it had maintained its place of honor for the past five years since his grandfather had passed. On to greener pastures, as Grandma Ruby liked to say.

"Come on into the kitchen, Honey. I've got water on to make tea. You'll join me for a cup?" Grandma Ruby shuffled toward the small kitchen. Carver followed, taking in the familiar pictures and items that family had given them over the years. They made small talk while Grandma Ruby fussed with the kettle and pulled out a package of Oreos—a favorite cookie they had both shared since he was a boy. When the hot liquid had been poured into the teacups and the small, white ironstone plates had been set in front of each of them, Grandma Ruby sat down in her regular place nearest the kitchen sink and Carver took his place at the side. Grandpa always sat at the head of the table, and it didn't seem right to sit in his place, besides, this was the place Carver always sat when visiting his grandparents.

When she had settled into her seat, Grandma Ruby took a careful sip of her hot tea and then placed it on the table in front of her, firming her lips and nodding her head at Carver. "So, you want to hear the story," she said.

"Momma says I need to hear it. But it's not what you may think. I'm not trying to dig up your past. I..." Carver leaned forward, placing his elbows on the table and cupped his face in his hands. He moved his hands to both sides of his face and peered at his grandmother seriously. "I'm having trouble. I've met someone..."

"Oh, a young lady." Grandma Ruby's face lit up. "Carver, you have no idea how I've been praying the Lord would bring you a young woman to love you and mess up that 'perfect thing' you've got going on. Your grandpa was like that when I left town. Um hum. That perfect thing is not that perfect. Trust me."

242

It's always like this when I talk to Grandma Ruby, he thought. *What perfect thing?*

There was an uncomfortable quiet spell where Carver waited for Grandma Ruby to start talking. But she seemed content to sip her tea, and watch him, waiting for him to make the first move. He squirmed in his seat, faked a sip of his tea, and tried to outlast her...finally she had mercy on him and started.

"Your grandpa Daniel and I were childhood friends. We lived two blocks from each other. Dan was such a tender boy then..." Grandma Ruby seemed to fade into her memories for a moment and then she focused on Carver again.

"If your Grandpa had approached me in pride—you and I would not be having tea and Oreos at this table today. Yes, there are consequences to who you marry, but no one is perfect but Jesus. All parties are broken, Carver. Some of us see our brokenness clearly. And some of us still think we can do everything right. But my Bible says we're saved by grace—not things we do, so that none can boast. And as far as marrying the perfect person, only God can hold us together—both individually and as a married couple." Grandma Ruby took a slow sip of her tea and then nodded her head as though she had decided something and pierced Carver with her gaze. "Tell me about this young woman," she said.

"Joelzi Parker is..." Carver's eyes narrowed as he pictured Joelzi "... she's a one-of-a-kind, diamond in the rough, beautiful soul. She lights a room and when she talks to you, you feel like you're the most important person in the room. She cares about people...and it just oozes out of her." Carver looked over at his grandmother. "And she's pretty too."

"Hmm," said Grandma Ruby, taking a nibble of her Oreo. "Have you had any disagreements?" Grandma Ruby asked, taking a sip of her tea.

"Well, yes. She didn't like how I wanted her to handle a situation she's dealing with right now. She says I think too much with my head," Carver said, reflecting on the conversation. "She straight up challenged me to 'think with my heart', but she wasn't disrespectful."

"I see," said Grandma Ruby, nibbling a bit more of her Oreo. "How about God? Do ya'll talk about Him?"

"That's the funny thing. She talks about God more than I do. First date and she wanted to talk about the sermon and what I got out of it and if I was going to change anything in my day-to-day as a result. It was wonderful and awful at the same time."

Grandma Ruby gave him a smirk, her eyebrows lifted, "Go on."

"We work together, so she sees how I act at work and...it's like being challenged to be all I could be...but it's a little off-putting. Like she sees me. Really sees me. Sometimes I feel like she sees me so well that, well, it's good because I can't pretend, but she's not above confronting me."

"Would you say she's a giver?"

"Oh, absolutely," Carver started confidently, "she opened her home to Merci, a sixteen-year-old pregnant girl whose mother kicked her out of their home because she was pregnant. Joelzi didn't even consider the ramifications of such a decision—she just jumped in. Who does that kind of thing? That was one of our disagreements. She said I was only launching from my head and she wanted to move from the heart."

"Well, to my thinking, she sounds like an exceptional young woman," said Grandma Ruby.

"Well to be fair, that needs to be balanced with her history. She's made some mistakes."

"Yes. All of us have Carver. If you haven't made the actual mess-ups that she has, at the minimum you've been proud that you haven't done so."

He felt his face go slack as the truth of Grandma Ruby's words scraped across his consciousness again. First his mom mentioned pride and now Grandma Ruby brings it up again. *Oh, that burns*, thought Carver. *Are You trying to tell me I'm proud, God?*

"The Bible says none are righteous—not one," said Grandma Ruby. She finished her Oreo while Carver digested her words.

"Carver," said Grandma Ruby, "it seems to me you're looking for a romance novel kind of love story. Those books have none of the things that make up real love. Real love is messy. It involves giving up what you thought was your due. It requires a humility that may look like weakness to some—but is really a sign of great strength. Love comes in the strangest ways." Grandma Ruby got a faraway look in her eyes as she closed her eyes and rocked her head back in thought. "It could show up through a virgin girl who understands she could be ridiculed by all her close friends for having anticipated her wedding night with her groom. Or it might look like the young groom who knows he was not his intended's first. But he takes the rap—gives up his reputation—carries the shame because God said. Love comes in dirty places. That stable was no place for a baby. Love shows up to the least of the least—the bottom of the barrel—they get to share the news of who Love is.

245

Carver was on her track now. She was talking about Jesus coming as a baby. He nodded his understanding.

"But that sweet baby came to die. He stayed quiet for thirty-three years acting like he didn't know what was going on. But he did. Imagine how trapped he had to have felt. Knowing he had the words of life, but he waited for the plan. Now that's humility and strength. Everybody in that village knew him and knew the circumstances surrounding his birth. There had to have been knowing looks passed across the table or across the church aisle if he ever gained any attention. But he waited for the plan."

Grandma Ruby paused and let the words settle, taking another sip of her tea. "But I'm getting sidetracked. Love is messy, Carver. People are not like God. We should be. We want to be. We try to be. But we just aren't perfect. Your Granddaddy decided to love me. When I came back from my wild livin', he wanted me. I told him I was too broken. I told him I might have disease. I did my best to convince him I was not the one for him. So did others in the church. They weren't wrong. I don't hold anything against them. Knowing the truth allows us to make choices with all the information." A tear rolled down Grandma Ruby's wrinkled cheek and caught in one of the creases. She wiped it with a trembling hand as a beautiful smile lit her face. "Your Granddaddy loved me back to Jesus." She paused again, leaning over her teacup, before looking back into her grandson's face. "I guess, what I'm trying to say is: go ahead and find out the details. Those details are going to change your life because they have changed the life of the one you're considering. Get wise counsel. Pray. And if you've done all of that and still have peace—take the next step." She pushed her empty teacup to the center of the table, indicating that this discussion was over and then paused, looking back at her grandson with wise eyes. "And Carver?"

Carver looked up at his grandma where she waited for him to finish his question, "Yes, ma'am?"

"While you're examining all these things in the woman—it might do you some good to examine yourself. Does she see any of these qualities we've discussed in you?" Carver's jaw dropped in surprise. "It's a fair question, Carver. These things go both ways."

Seventy-Six

The drive home from Grandma Ruby's had been a sober reflection of their conversation.

Joelzi may have had some missteps, but she is also the one living out grace. She is alive and joyful and I'm regimented and careful to the point it's choking me. "God forgive me," Carver prayed out loud as he drove his car toward his apartment. *She makes me want to break out of my careful plan and risk my heart. Who am I kidding, Joelzi's already captured my heart—I've just been pretending. Is there any possibility she would give me another chance? And how is an uptight perfectionist supposed to get through to her?* He made a U-turn and headed the car toward his parents' house. *I need an intervention.*

All the Ellis men sat around the kitchen table. His dad, Lincoln, sat at the head of the table where he always sat. His brothers, Winston, and Luther-Martin, sat across the table from each other, alternating smirks with outright grins as they eyed Carver. And Georgie sat to his dad's left, focused on the two large unopened pizza boxes in the center of the table. Carver had shown up on his parents' front door about two and a half hours ago and simply said the words that expressed his heart, "I've messed up." His mom and dad had exchanged 'the look', something they had perfected over their forty-one years of marriage, that must have communicated his dire need for male input. Before she left to 'spend time with Aunt Jemimah,' Mom had called in an order for pizza to be delivered to the house. Carver heard her tell his dad to "make the boys be nice, Honey. It's hard to realize you're in love and a little out of control. You remember how it was for us..." Mom gave Dad a quick peck on the lips, even as Dad got that smile on his face and said, "I remember." So, the troops had been called in and were all seated around the table, most of them more interested in Carver's situation than the pizza.

"Okay, son," said his dad, "your brothers and I are here for you. How can we help you?"

Carver closed his eyes and dropped his head in his hands, rubbing his forehead with his fingers. *I don't even care if they roast me over a pit, I'm desperate to find a way out of this.* He looked up and made eye contact with Winston. "I messed up. I hurt Joelzi." His eyes turned to Luther-Martin, "I thought I was doing the right thing. But really I was protecting my heart. I was scared..."

"You're scared of Joelzi?" asked Georgie, his elbows propped on the table with his face held in his hands, a frown on his face.

"No...maybe...yes..." Carver couldn't seem to get the right words out.

"Joelzi's nice," Georgie said. "She loves me."

"Joelzi is nice, Georgie," Carver smiled reluctantly at his brother, "but I mixed up a real understanding of what it means to love God and let God love me back. I've made Joelzi believe she is not good enough for me. Truth is, she's been a much better example of a godly woman, than I have been of a God-fearing man. Joelzi loves with her whole heart. I had the chance to have a love like each of ya'll have..." he looked around the table, "and I botched it."

"I think it's safe to say that each of us has botched something in our relationships with the women we love," said his dad with an understanding smile.

"What is it you need from us, Carver?" asked Luther-Martin, "Why did you call a family meeting?"

"I want her back," said Carver bluntly. "I need advice on how to get Joelzi back."

Both Winston and Luther-Martin chuckled and looked at each other. "Oh, how the mighty have fallen," Winston said quietly to Luther-Martin and they reached across the table for a fist bump.

Carver rolled his eyes. "Could we focus on getting Joelzi back?" he asked.

"How serious are you about Joelzi?" Winton asked, raising his eyebrows in Carver's direction.

"She's the one," said Carver without hesitation. It felt good to say it out loud in front of the men of his family.

"She's the one," repeated both brothers, a look passing between them. "Well, that changes everything."

"In that case, my best advice is to never underestimate the value of an apology," said Winston.

"And it has to be genuine," added Luther-

Martin, "women seem to have a second sense about whether you're being honest or not."

"And if you're NOT wrong—and that scenario is highly unlikely," Winston continued, "but in the event it does occur—don't bring up the need for an apology on their part." Winston and Luther-Martin exchanged a look and nodded their heads up and down in agreement.

"But I *am* wrong," said Carver.

"Yes, you are, Carver. So, make it a good apology, heartfelt, something that costs you your pride, something that Joelzi can see as a demonstration of how future disagreements will be handled," said his dad.

"You should be ready to crawl across broken glass for the woman God made for you. Grovel," added Luther-Martin.

"Okay, apologize, crawl across broken glass, grovel...should I send flowers...or maybe take flowers with me?"

"No, no, no Carver, that's too cheesy. Joelzi's liable to throw them in the trash if you send them before you apologize or better yet, throw them at you if she opens the door when you take your sorry self to her apartment door. Save the flowers for when she loves you again." Luther-Martin laughed sheepishly. "Catherine had to dig flowers out of the trash after I sent flowers ahead of my apology. In my limited experience, women tend to have strong feelings about these things."

"You're not wrong," said Winston, "and I wouldn't have it any other way. Nothing like a strong woman who loves her man..." There was silence in the kitchen as the married men pondered their wives.

"Hey, guys, don't forget the reason we're here. I

need advice on how to get Joelzi back," said Carver when the men seemed to be taking too long.

"Hmm, *How to Woo a Woman 101*," said Luther-Martin, "this could take a while."

"Can I have some pizza while y'all talk about wooin'?" asked Georgie.

Lincoln Ellis passed the pizza box to his youngest son with a grin. And then cleared his throat. "Well, let me start by saying, a woman doesn't want to be a project. So what's discussed around this table—stays here. Right, Georgie?" Georgie grinned back at his dad around the pizza he had stuffed in his mouth and gave his dad a thumbs up. Lincoln Ellis continued, "What you're starting on, Carver, is a marathon that will last a lifetime. Winning a woman's heart is not a sprint. It's a lifelong pursuit and it is worth all the effort you devote to it."

"Hear, hear." Winston and Luther-Martin raised their iced tea glasses and clinked them together in agreement.

"Marriage is an 'As Is' venture," his dad continued, "you'll both change..." he paused, "just don't assume it will mostly be Joelzi. After you give her your heartfelt apology, Carver, it might be good to have some items in your playbook."

Carver's mouth dropped open and his voice hit a high note as he asked, "You have a playbook?"

"Not like you're thinking son," replied his dad. "It's more like things I've learned to pay attention to... like...listen to learn about her. What does Joelzi like? Your mom loves flowers—but she'd much rather I buy her flowers with roots, so she can work in the yard and harvest flowers year after year." He pointed to the hydrangeas on the countertop. "I bought her that hydrangea bush five years ago for no particular reason," his dad said. "You'd have thought I had bought her a new diamond ring."

"He might need to start with a diamond ring," said Winston.

"Before he gets to the diamond ring he needs to convince her he loves her," said Luther-Martin.

"Good point," said Winston, "study her; listen to her—not just the words she says, listen to the meaning. What do you think she's saying? Say it back to her to see if you got it right."

"Make her laugh. It will require some work, but find ways to make her laugh," added Dad.

"And don't get stuck in your head—be real," said Winston, "you tend to get a little focused sometimes."

"Maybe you should talk to Grace. Isn't she Joelzi's best friend?" said Luther-Martin.

"I was kind of hoping to keep it in the family," said Carver, "unless it doesn't work out."

"Go big or go home, brother," said Luther-Martin. "Winning the love of your life is worth any potential humiliation. I'm pretty sure Grace would know some things that would help your cause."

"Momma says we should always smell good," said Georgie. "I think Joelzi would like you if you smell good, Carver." They all laughed. Carver was fastidious about cleanliness.

"Yeah, Carver," said Luther-Martin with a smirk, "you could work on your hygiene."

"You should send her something at work. That would be a big statement. The whole ER would get the drift."

Carver felt his stomach muscles tighten. That would be a monumental shift. Acknowledgement of his feelings in the ER setting would be a 'no turning back' moment. *Maybe that's one way of showing*

Joelzi how serious I am about us.

"But first things first," said Lincoln Ellis. "You need to apologize and ask Joelzi to forgive you."

The comradery of the moment changed as the men turned their attention to the pizza. But Carver remained focused on his next step. How to persuade Joelzi Parker to give him another chance? How to convince her he loved her?

Seventy-Seven

Sunday, November 21
Carver

He had called last night, hoping to beg forgiveness as soon as he had finished talking to all the men in his family. But Joelzi's phone had gone to voicemail. He had tried again this morning with no satisfaction. Then he had tried going to church and waiting for her, but she didn't show—at least not in the section she normally sat, and he had sat through both services.

I deserve this, he thought. *How many times now have I pushed Joelzi away, only to have to beg forgiveness. And she just kept giving me chances. I don't deserve her, but she's worth fighting for.*

He tried texting. It was harder to beg forgiveness by text, but he was willing...

But he got no response. Zip.

His mind kept telling him to give up, but when he thought about how valuable Joelzi was to him and felt the crush of disappointment over losing her, he rallied. *I can't give up. Not until she tells me there's no chance. I guess I'll just have to drive by her apartment tomorrow and see if she'll answer the door.*

Seventy-Eight

Monday, November 22
Joelzi

When the doorbell rang, Joelzi checked her peephole and saw Carver standing there. Her heart started pounding and she could feel her face flush. *He's here. Outside my door.* Tears burned her eyes as she stood there trying to decide what to do. *I can't talk to him right now—I'm too broken. I'll cry and I don't want him to see me cry...but he's here...what does he want? I ignored his calls and texts on purpose. I thought that would be enough.* Joelzi set her forehead on the door and heard Carver speaking through the door.

"Joelzi, I know you're there—I saw your car in the parking lot. We need to talk. I owe you an apology. I messed up badly. I let you believe things that aren't true. I was trying to protect my heart from you being able to hurt me, but that's just an excuse. I shouldn't have reacted the way I did. I should have given you a chance to say what you wanted to before I left so abruptly." Carver paused and she could hear him clearer—*he must be right at the door on the outside.* Joelzi peeked through the peep hole and saw the side of Carver's head, propped on the door. His dejected posture moved her. He cleared his throat, "I don't deserve you, Joelzi, but I need you in my life. Please give me another chance."

"Okay," Joelzi said softly, unlocking the door and opening it slowly. Carver stood there quietly; his eyes steady on hers.

"Can we t...t...talk?" Carver asked. Joelzi just nodded her 'yes' and let him in. "Can we sit on the couch?" he asked. "I have a lot to say..." Joelzi nodded again. They moved to the couch and he waited for her to sit before moving to sit beside her and bending over with his head in his hands. He turned to face her. Joelzi blinked the tears back while looking for her box of Kleenex. *I might as well get the box. Can't imagine getting through this conversation without a few tears.* She rose from the couch and grabbed the box of tissues before returning to her place.

"Okay, I'm as ready as I can be." She indicated the box of tissue with a sigh, pulling one out and dabbing the tears that had started running down her cheeks.

"I'm not here to hurt you, Joelzi. I'm here to apologize. No, that's not it. I'm here to ask you to forgive me. Again. For the way I handled our last conversations. For not caring about what you have gone through. And for just generally being a jerk."

Joelzi looked up from her tissues in disbelief. "You are?"

Carver continued as if she hadn't interrupted

258

him. "I'm really sorry you went through all of that. I didn't even ask you if you're okay." He looked up at her and reached for her hands, holding them together in his. "Are you okay, Joelzi?"

Joelzi swallowed the lump in her throat. *This is the real Carver Ellis.* "Yes, believe it or not, all of this stuff with Merci has exposed things in my heart that I hadn't dealt with. I'm better than I've been in the past seven years."

Joelzi watched Carver's eyes tracking over her hair, her eyes, and her face as if he could assure himself of her wellness by looking at external things. A small smile traveled his lips as he seemed to finish his assessment. Joelzi smiled back and her eyebrows lifted in question. Carver cleared his throat again, seeming to realize the conversation ball was in his court. "I really care about you, Joelzi."

Joelzi became aware that his hands were trembling.

"You're the first woman that I've wanted to know better—that I could say I have feelings for." Carver squeezed her hands before continuing. "You're the first woman that makes me want to be a better man. The first woman I've wanted to protect. And the abortion and all the stuff that led up to that decision—I just want to fix it. I don't want it to hurt you." Carver paused and took a deep breath, "But Grandma Ruby reminded me that it's part of your story. I can't take it away. So I want to press into the bitterness of those moments and be with you. Do I wish it hadn't happened to you? Absolutely. Will it impact our lives? I'd be a fool to pretend something as impactful as an unwanted pregnancy and an abortion won't impact our lives. But does that history prevent me from wanting you in my life? No.

I want you in my life, Joelzi. I need you in my life. And I want to know all about you. I don't want you to feel you have to hide anything from me. And I want to be open with you. I've never wanted to say that to anyone before you. You're pretty special to me. Would you have mercy on me and forgive me for how I handled all of this?"

Tears streamed down Joelzi's cheeks, and loud hiccups of joy bubbled out of her. Joelzi pulled her hands out of Carver's grasp and threw her arms around Carver's neck, burying her face in his shoulder. His arms wrapped around her, pulling her to him and he held her as sobs shook her frame.

"I thought you would never want to be my friend again." The words were muffled as she spoke them into his shoulder.

"Oh, Joelzi, I don't think I could ever get to that place. I...I...I love you, Joelzi."

"You do?" asked Joelzi.

"I do," Carver nodded his head, "I think I just avoided you back then because I knew you would wreck me for anyone else. You've smashed through my carefully prepared and protected 'list' with your joy for life. Your laughter moves me away from my stringent rules to a place of meaning and joy like I haven't known before. I didn't know what I was missing until you barreled into my life. Do you think you could give me another chance? Let me have a place in your heart?" Carver asked.

"Oh, Carver, you've been rooted and planted in my heart for a long time. I've been trying to get over you. It's been tearful work and hasn't happened yet."

Carver released her enough to gently kiss her. "Could you stop working to get over me? Please."

Joelzi leaned in for another kiss. "I could try...it

might require some convincing."

Carver pulled her into his lap and got serious about convincing her. After a while, when they were both breathless, Carver pulled back and settled her against his chest.

"I'm ready to listen, if you want to tell me the story," Carver said.

"It's not pretty, Carver."

"No, life isn't always pretty. But you are so much more than a beautiful image. I'd like to really know you, if you could trust me with the real you, Joelzi."

Joelzi paused. *Do I chance it? This is what I really want—someone to accept me with all my history—good and bad. Someone who clearly sees me and chooses to love me, knowing God is working all things for my good.* Yes, she could trust Carver, but...She took a deep breath. "Can we do it another day? I don't want to mess this up." She pointed between the two of them, her index finger lingering on Carver's lips.

"Okay," Carver said, kissing the finger over his lips, "I'm not going anywhere; I'll be here when you're ready."

Seventy-Nine

Wednesday, November 24th
Carver

Grandma Ruby opened the door, a big smile spread across her lips, "Well, now. Here you are. Back so soon. Don't know as I've seen you two times in one week since you were a little boy and your momma needed me to watch you."

Carver stepped forward and hugged his grandmother. "Well, it's special circumstances."

"I can see that," Grandma Ruby said, leaning around Carver with a smile. "And who would I be having the pleasure of meeting?" she asked with a smile and her signature left eyebrow lift, never taking her eyes off of Joelzi.

"Grandma Ruby," Carver pulled Joelzi into his side and wrapped his arm around her. "This is Joelzi, the girl I told you about, well...wo-wo-woman," Carver stuttered over the 'woman' part.

"I remember her name," Grandma Ruby

interrupted, moving to stand in front of Joelzi. Grandma Ruby wrapped Joelzi in a warm hug and then stood back, letting her hands slide down Joelzi's arms until she was clasping Joelzi's hands. "Let me look at you."

Joelzi's beautiful brown eyes widened until Carver thought he could see the white parts showing and she straightened her posture and seemed to paste a forced smile on. She looked petrified, but she stood quietly as Grandma Ruby gazed steadily into Joelzi's face, her knobby hands firmly holding Joelzi's.

"Um hum," Grandma Ruby said after a quiet moment. "Come on in, Honey. How about a cup of tea? We've got some talking to do."

"Yes, of course, I'd love to have some tea." Joelzi's wide eyes looked to Carver for assurance, but he had nothing to give her. Grandma Ruby was doing her thing again and he wasn't sure he felt smooth about it.

"Carver," Grandma Ruby said in her southern way as she started toward the kitchen before turning back around to Carver, "your car is looking dirty. I think maybe you've got time to go get a car wash."

"A car wash?" Carver repeated after his grandmother, "But I just..."

"And maybe you could swing by and pick up some fried chicken while you're out." Grandma Ruby patted his shoulder as she maneuvered him back out the front door. "We need some time, Son, don't ask questions."

When she had maneuvered her grandson out her front door, Grandma Ruby turned to Joelzi. "You sit right here, Joelzi, while I get the kettle going." Grandma Ruby shuffled over to the stove, grabbing the kettle and moving to the sink to fill it. When it was on the stove and two teacups were sitting at the ready, she came back to the table and sat down in her chair. "There now," she clasped her hands in front of her and smiled gently at Joelzi, seated to her left across the square table. "So you are the young lady my grandson came to see me about," she said.

Even though she was disturbingly frank, Joelzi felt an immediate connection to this woman. There was a worn humility in Grandma Ruby's bearing. Joelzi knew instinctively that this woman, like Mema Anna, would filter all her failure through the lens of love. The longing to be known and accepted as she was, pulled on Joelzi's heart. Joelzi felt tears welling up and cresting her eyelids. Ever since she had started the Hope and Healing classes, her feelings were always close to the surface. Emotions she had carefully locked down now easily breeched her crumbling barriers. Memories that had been stuffed away with rigid determination broke loose from her restraints and percolated to the surface. She had let go with Grace and had gotten some relief. Would telling Carver's grandma her story be cathartic? Joelzi felt the moan of remorse rising from her gut. "I...I...I'm a failure," Joelzi whispered the last. "I've given it to God, and I know I'm forgiven. Some days are really good. But then my past rears its ugly head and makes me afraid to move on." Joelzi lowered her head in defeat.

Joelzi felt Grandma Ruby reach across the table and cover her hand, "I'm listenin'. Just talk it out."

"I...I had sex with a guy that I thought loved me. I was in a bad place—but that's no excuse—I knew better—I was raised for better." Joelzi felt Grandma Ruby pat her hand in comfort.

"Go on," murmured Grandma Ruby.

Joelzi raised her head to look into the kindest, gentlest eyes she had known in what seemed like an eternity. Joelzi felt her lips tremble as she sucked in a shaky breath. "I just told this story to my best friend Grace. You'd think I would get over it..."

"Sometimes the process takes time," said Grandma Ruby. "We don't get too worked up over the method; we take as many times tellin' as needed to find peace." Grandma Ruby paused. "One day, the experience becomes part of the arsenal of the Lord, and He uses it to help others. Like today. The Lord has turned my sorrow into joy. Now I can walk with you through your sorrow. The Lord doesn't waste anything, Honey," said Grandma Ruby. "Now, you were sayin'?"

"Mema Anna had passed the week before. She was my rock..." said Joelzi.

"Ain't no one the Rock but Jesus, Honey," Grandma Ruby murmured, "No one." Grandma Ruby paused, "Keep tellin'."

"I could tell Mema Anna anything and she would read me like a book and tell me the truth," Joelzi smiled, remembering. "So, I was already low. Then Momma died in a car accident..." Joelzi swiped at the tears that seemed to be gathering force as they flowed down her face. She sniffed to stop the snot that wanted to run also.

"Here, Baby." Grandma Ruby handed her a tissue. "Tears are important work. Let 'em flow."

"I needed someone to hold me, so I went looking for my boyfriend, Myron. He had been drinking. We went up to his room. I was crying and Myron was holding me and...things went too far. I tried to get him to stop, but he wouldn't," Joelzi gasped a sob. "I hadn't ever had sex. I was waiting for marriage. But...it was the worst experience for my first time.

Myron didn't care. He was drunk and just out for what he could get." Joelzi laughed derisively, "he said something about 'being grateful to Momma for finally getting his due after waiting all these years.'" The piercing whistle of the water boiling in the kettle interrupted Joelzi's story.

Joelzi blew her nose as Grandma Ruby retrieved the kettle and poured hot water over the tea bags, setting the cups on the table in front of Joelzi and herself. She sat back down, nodding her head thoughtfully, before looking Joelzi in the eye. "I'm sorry, Joelzi." Then Grandma Ruby lifted her teacup, its gentle rattle on the saucer exposing the fine tremor in her hands before she cradled it securely in her gnarled hands. Grandma Ruby's lips firmed and she nodded Joelzi's way.

"Honey, you need to call that what it was so you can get through it. That selfish act by a drunken young man was rape." Grandma Ruby paused. "I am truly sorry that happened to you." She took a careful sip of her hot tea, before firming her lips again and looking Joelzi in the eye. "Now," she said, "what are you gonna do about it? You can hold it close, sweep it under the rug, hide it, and not let it go. Or you could get it out in the open where God can shine some light on it. Share it with people you love and trust and get some healing." Grandma Ruby took another sip of her tea before setting the cup back down on the saucer. "God is most concerned with our hearts...um hum." Grandma Ruby paused a moment. "I think it was Helen Roseveare. She was a missionary to the Congo during a time of great unrest. The short of it is she was gang raped. She went back to the UK to get some counseling...some healing. Years later, during an interview she was asked about the rape. Her answer was telling. She said something like, 'We don't fear what they can do to the body; we fear what can be done to the spirit—the spirit of a man or woman is eternal.' Now that is worth some meditation," said Grandma Ruby. "By all means, we get counseling and wisdom about these things, but these things don't have the power to keep us from life...unless we let them..." Grandma Ruby seemed in no hurry. She sipped her tea and let the silence sooth before asking, "What else do you need to get off your heart?" Grandma Ruby asked.

Joelzi wrapped her cold hands around the hot teacup, taking a moment to reflect. "So, I'd lost the two women who meant the most to me, and I'd lost my virginity to a drunken boyfriend who clearly didn't care for me. I was numb. How could my life have derailed so quickly? I left Myron's place when he fell into a drunken sleep and drove back to my apartment. The weeks that followed are a blur. I went back home for Momma's funeral. Losing my momma was devastating. Just trying to keep up with schoolwork and fighting through the grief—it was eight weeks later before I realized I had missed my period." Joelzi took a sip of her tea. It soothed the raw spots in her throat but did nothing for the raw places in her heart. "I panicked; but I knew." Joelzi looked up at Grandma Ruby, prepared to see disappointment on her face. But Grandma Ruby's face was a picture of compassion. "Deep in my gut I knew. I bought a pregnancy test and it was positive." Joelzi's laugh was high pitched and self-deprecating. "I was pregnant. Just one more thing to have to deal with. I felt like God had deserted me. Like I was hidden from Him. I couldn't tell my dad—it was too much to pile on him. He was trying to get through my mom's death, and he had my younger brother and sister still at home. I couldn't drop out of my nursing program—I only lacked one year. And if I dropped out and went home, I would become two more mouths to feed? I didn't dare tell Grace. She's my best friend now. But we had just met each other then and she is so clean. She would never do the things I've done. And I didn't want Grace to stop being my friend because I had done those things. So, I called Myron. I didn't want to, but it was his fault I was in this position." Joelzi sighed into her cup, "Myron made it clear he wasn't up for 'being a baby daddy'".

Joelzi sipped her cooled tea. "That positive pregnancy test started a whole new set of problems." She looked at Grandma Ruby with honesty. "You know how the Bible says, 'the truth will set you free'? I rethink how things could have been different if I had just faced the truth. We tell ourselves we can get rid of the problems and we'll be free. But the problems just pile up. They get heavier. I am better. I've been going to a post abortion counseling group, and I've shared a brief version of my story with Merci and a more detailed version with Grace. I told Carver the basics, and now I'm telling you, but I'm so tired of carrying my problems." Joelzi firmed her lips and faced Grandma Ruby. "I killed my baby, okay? I had an abortion. And I cannot get away from it. There is not a day that goes by that I don't wonder what my baby would look like. Was she a girl? Or maybe he was a boy. And on my bad days I wonder how Jesus could stand to look at me. I'm no better than a murderer."

"Well, I guess that's as good a place to start as any," said Grandma Ruby. "Our sin is what took Jesus to the cross. No way to get around that. And when we've faced ourselves—and we all have to face ourselves—no one is able to live a sinless life.

Yes, you've done terrible things. I have too. Yes", Grandma Ruby's left eyebrow rose in emphasis and her gaze pierced the tender places in Joelzi's heart, "I have too." Grandma Ruby carefully set her teacup in its saucer before continuing, "Carver's Granddaddy was God's tool in my life. We grew up in the same town. He was from a good God-fearing family. I grew up next door, but worlds apart as far as family life. We attended the same schools from grade school through high school. I had family problems and I dropped out before finishing. I was going to find a better way. Daniel, that's Carver's Grandaddy, begged me not to leave. But I thought I was a strong, independent woman." Grandma Ruby smacked her lips, "But I was really a hurting, broken, young soul." Grandma Ruby paused, eyes closed as though watching a movie in her mind, before shaking her head side to side and continuing. "I was even more broken when I came back to town. Much like the prodigal in the Bible except I was penniless when I left and penniless and pregnant when I returned. And Carver's Granddaddy loved me anyway. He looked at this broken, pregnant woman and knew he could love me. He married me. Even though he was called to preach and I was less than the kind of woman he was expected to marry if he was goin' into the ministry. Daniel Ellis took on me and my pregnancy with a passion and zeal that was heart-stopping. Daniel was like that until he took his last breath. That man was a giver." Grandma Ruby paused, her eyes rummy with memories. "Just a minute," she said, getting up from the table and shuffling her way into the living room. When she returned, Grandma Ruby held a small bowl in her hands. It was pale blue with lines of gold in an inexplicable pattern intertwined in the bowl.

Setting the bowl on the table between them, she took Joelzi's hands and wrapped them around the bowl.

"What is it?" asked Joelzi, holding the bowl gently in both hands.

"It's a Japanese bowl that was broken. Carver's Granddaddy bought it for me early in our marriage. He saw it in a secondhand store and said it reminded him of me."

"A broken bowl?" Joelzi asked tipping her head to the side and squinting her eyes in confusion.

"But it is no longer broken," Grandma Ruby said gently, a knowing look in her eyes. "The pieces have been glued back together. Filed. Scraped. Heated. Glued. And then gold has been used to cover the repairs. According to the Japanese, it makes the broken places stronger—more resilient. They call it "Kintsugi." The Bible says, 'Come, buy gold refined in the fire.' (Rev 3:18) You and I are like this broken bowl, Joelzi. But if we choose to, we can bring our pieces to the Potter. I'm talking about Jesus. Only Jesus knows how to fit us back together. Only Love can take our broken pieces, mend them with gold, and make us beautiful and functional again. And when God does it, He uses the pain and sufferin' and He makes it like this bowl." Grandma Ruby ran a gnarled finger down one of the veins of gold on the bowl. Jesus takes that gold and strengthens the cracks making a new design. The vessel is stronger and more beautiful than before. The bowl doesn't hide its imperfections, it simply lets the light of the Holy Spirit shine through."

The front door opened and Carver strolled in with a bag labeled "Get N Go Chicken." He made his way into the kitchen, setting the bag down on the counter and turned to eye the two women carefully.

"Ya'll okay?" he asked, his eyes clocking back and forth between the two women before settling on Joelzi.

Joelzi felt the strength of his questioning gaze and tucked her head down into her chest, trying to furtively blot her cheeks and hide the tear streaks on her cheeks. *My eyes are probably a swollen mess. I've done nothing but cry buckets. What must Grandma Ruby and Carver think of me?*

"We've had a good visit," Grandma Ruby said matter-of-factly, setting her teacup into its saucer and pushing her way out of her chair, "but I think you need to take your girl somewhere and feed her."

"But I just got back with the fried chicken you asked for," Carver said, his mouth going slack and his eyes widening as he lifted the bag of chicken up as evidence and looked between the two women.

"Well, I can keep that for when Georgie comes to see me," Grandma Ruby said, taking the bag out of his hand and setting it back on the counter. "That boy loves fried chicken." She paused. "Ya'll go on now," Grandma Ruby waved her hand toward the front door, "I'm feeling tired and Joelzi needs some fresh air." Grandma Ruby came around the kitchen table and wrapped Joelzi in a warm hug. "You pray on what we talked about now. God doesn't give us pain to leave us there. You leverage that pain and get you some gold, Honey." She reached down and grasped the Japanese bowl, placing it in Joelzi's hands. "I want you to have this."

"Oh, I couldn't take your bowl..." said Joelzi.

"Grandma, that's a family heirloom..." said Carver, his mouth sagging and his eyes bulging.

"Carver, I believe I'm aware of that," said Grandma Ruby firmly without taking her gaze off of Joelzi.

"Honey," Grandma Ruby said, looking Joelzi in the eye, "I believe I'm to give this to you. Please take it and let it remind you."

Joelzi's eyes filled with tears and her throat clogged with emotion, "Thank you, but I just couldn't. It's a family heirloom."

"Hmp," Grandma Ruby pursed her lips in a line. She dipped her head as she set the bowl back down on the kitchen table. "Well...you know where I live now. I believe I would enjoy having you visit," Grandma Ruby said, her eyes locked on Joelzi's.

"Well that would be nice." Carver said. "Joelzi and I will check our schedules and try to come over when we both have off." He glanced at Joelzi for her agreement. "I wouldn't mind being present for some of the conversation," he added with a frown.

"I would love that," Joelzi agreed with a smile.

"Thank you for taking me to meet your grandmother, Carver," said Joelzi quietly. "She's wonderful...and a little bit terrifying."

They were driving home from the strangest, most wonderful encounter Joelzi had had in a long time—since Mema Anna had passed. Carver had been quiet and for good reason. Grandma Ruby had sent him on an errand so she could speak plainly to the broken woman sitting at her kitchen table. Grandma Ruby's personal history had made Joelzi's pain clear to her and with Godly directness, Grandma Ruby had gone straight to the core issues.

Carver chuckled and then let out a bark of laughter, a grin stretching across his face. "Grandma Ruby is terrifying and wonderful. And I can't believe she offered you her bowl from Grandpa. She treasures that bowl, especially now he's gone."

"Well, you can relax about the bowl," said Joelzi, "I didn't take it."

"Oh, I'm not really worried about the bowl," said Carver, reaching over to take Joelzi's hand in his, "I was just surprised. So, tomorrow is Thanksgiving. Are you going anywhere?" asked Carver.

"Thanksgiving is one of my assigned holidays for work this year," said Joelzi. "So you're off?"

Carver nodded, "Yes, it will be a full-on feast at Mom and Dad's place. I was hoping I could bring you."

"I hate to miss it," said Joelzi, "I really like your family, Carver."

"What about Merci?" asked Carver.

"Grace asked her to join them for Thanksgiving," said Joelzi, "I love that about Grace, she just oozes hospitality...well, when she's feeling good."

"So she's feeling better?" asked Carver.

"Grace is back to being Grace. She's eighteen weeks along now and seems to have more energy than before she was pregnant," said Joelzi.

Eighty

Because Joelzi had missed out on spending Thanksgiving with the Ellises, Carver had taken her out for brunch today. They were back at Joelzi's apartment and since Merci was still at school, they had the place to themselves.

"I'm ready to tell you the rest," said Joelzi watching Carver for his reaction.

Carver stilled and looked at her. "Then I'm ready to hear it," he said, holding out his hand. Joelzi let Carver draw her over to her couch. He settled in with his back to the corner of the couch, turning his body towards her and pulled her to sit close to him. Joelzi repositioned herself to face him, her inside leg bent under her. Carver paused a moment before reaching out and capturing Joelzi's hands in his. "This is better," he said. "I want to look at you while you tell me," he said. "Just...tell me what you want me to know...I'm listening with my heart."

Joelzi took a deep breath and plunged in. "My grandmother and my mom died within a week of each other," she started.

Carver's eyes widened and he squeezed her hands. "I remember you said something about this at Saturday supper. That had to be hard."

Joelzi nodded her head, "It was. Really hard." She looked at Carver. "Mema Anna was old and she was showing signs of decline. Her passing was not unexpected. Just terrible...but Momma's passing was totally out of the blue. It was a single car accident." Joelzi blinked the tears that wanted to well up even seven years later. Carver squeezed her hands and waited quietly for her to continue. "Anyway, I was messed up over hearing that momma was gone and I made some bad choices. The guy I had been dating since high school was a football player at the same university. We were still together, although I'm not sure how long we would have remained that way. Myron was enamored with being known on campus for his prowess on the field. He didn't have the godly raising I had had. In hindsight, I see that he was getting deeper into drinking and partying. But he was 'my guy' and when Daddy asked me not to drive home the night he told me momma died, I went looking for comfort." Joelzi stopped and looked Carver in the eye. "I went to his fraternity house and told him what had happened. Immediately he left the frat party they were having downstairs and we went to his room. Myron had been drinking. He had had more than he could handle and it became more obvious as his comforting turned into heavy kissing and..." Joelzi's voice trailed off. "At some point I asked him to stop, but he was out of control. We had sex," Joelzi said flatly. "He fell out in a drunken stupor to sleep it off, and I gathered my things and left. I was such a fool," Joelzi whispered, her eyes focused on their interlocked hands, waiting to see how Carver would react.

"Joelzi, that was rape," Carver said tersely as he leaned forward.

"That's what Grace and Grandma Ruby said. But I take the responsibility for going to his room when he was drunk."

"Joelzi, you don't need to give excuses for why this guy did this to you. Did you report him?"

Joelzi shook her head 'no.' "I was just in shock. I went home and showered—erasing all evidence, then climbed into bed and cried myself to sleep."

"Oh, Joelzi, I'm so sorry," said Carver.

"So, I'm in my senior year of nursing school, my mom and grandmother are dead, my dad and younger brother and sister are devastated, and I just hide what happened. I throw it in the back closet of my mind and just keep doing the necessary things. About eight weeks later, I realized I was pregnant. I had avoided Myron after the fiasco, but when I realized I was pregnant, I called him and told him. He made it clear he wasn't up for a baby or marriage, but he would pay for an abortion. He even talked to his teammates and located 'the best clinic to get rid of the problem'. I couldn't see any other way, so I went along with it." Joelzi paused before looking straight into Carver's eyes. "I had an abortion, Carver. It has been a dark secret that I have hidden for seven years. I just finished a counseling group for people who've had abortions, I've told Grace, I've spilled my guts to Grandma

Ruby, and now I'm telling you. I've held this in for seven years and now I just keep telling people. Talking about what happened has been freeing. That's why I was crying that day at your grandma's. Grandma Ruby really talked straight to me. She helped me to see Jesus is the only one who can put me back together. It's why she offered me her Kintsugi bowl."

"Kintsugi bowl?" Carver asked.

"The bowl that your Grandpa Daniel gave her—it's a Kintsugi bowl. Repaired with gold. That's what God does for us when we let him—He repairs us better than new. The script that was running in my head insisted that I deserved what I got. The belief that I failed God, that God failed me and that I couldn't trust anyone with what had happened were just lies. You and Grace are right, Myron did rape me. But God didn't fail me—He was with me in that dark place. And it's obvious after sharing my story with Grace and Grandma Ruby and now you, that I can trust the people who care about me. And more people care about me than don't. Anyway, I'm owning my life—my choices. And I'm learning to put what God says about me in my heart and not just my head."

"I want to be here and walk through this with you, Joelzi. If I'm honest, I'm angry that I couldn't be there to protect you when all that was happening," said Carver.

"You didn't even know me then, Carver," said Joelzi.

"I know that with my head, but my heart...not so much," said Carver quietly.

"So the tables are turned," said Joelzi with a smile. "Your heart is alive and leading...it's not bad to feel, Carver," said Joelzi.

"But it is painful," Carver said.

"Maybe that's one of the reasons you like logical things," said Joelzi, "They don't have the same power to hurt."

"But logic doesn't make my heart lift when you are near me, Joelzi," said Carver.

"I make your heart lift?" asked Joelzi.

"You make my heart do all kinds of things I never knew it was capable of," Carver said, leaning forward. He slowly brushed her cheek with his hand, using his thumb to trace her lips. Joelzi smiled and closed her eyes, relaxing with his touch. Carver slid his hands on either side of her face, before moving one hand to cup the back of her neck and pull her toward him. Then he leaned forward and kissed her. Joelzi couldn't stop the smile that bloomed under his lips. *The details didn't change him*, she thought. *This must be real love.* He pulled her closer and she opened her eyes and wrapped her arms around his neck until they were face-to-face, lip-to-lip, and nose-to-nose. Joelzi watched Carver's eyes clocking over her face as though drawing it in his mind so he could map it with his lips. Carver kissed her bottom lip. Then he moved to her eyes. Joelzi closed her eyes to better assist him. Carver kissed the ear lobe above his hand, and then made his way back to her lips.

"Okay, that's enough for now. We've got to stop," Carver said, easing off the kissing and setting his forehead on hers.

"Okay, change of subject..." said Joelzi.

"That's my girl. What are we talking about?" asked Carver.

"My history is what motivates me to help Merci. I want to take what has happened to me and use it for good—let it be a catalyst for change. Can you

278

understand?"

Carver nodded his head, "More than ever before."

"I don't want any other young woman to believe her only choice is abortion, especially after rape," said Joelzi, "and I'm willing to be uncomfortable to do it. Not that Merci makes me uncomfortable but having her in my apartment has impacted my choices."

"How is it going, having Merci here?" Carver asked.

"Good. Different. It's like living with Mary Margaret again. There's stuff all over the bathroom and her room would be a total disaster if she had enough clothes to be really messy. What is it with teenagers and their inability to pick up?" asked Joelzi, rolling her eyes at Carver with a smile.

"I'll have you know I was a very neat teenager," Carver replied.

Joelzi collapsed with laughter, pushing her shoulder into his, "Of course you were, Carver Ellis. I may have to make it a life goal to help you have one thing out of place on occasion," she teased.

"It might be worth the discomfort," Carver said with a knowing grin.

Eighty-One

Carver
Driving home

She just takes my breath away, God. All those terrible things happened to her and she is still determined to let her life shine for You. I don't deserve Joelzi. She's worth waiting for. I want to protect her. I know You brought her into my life so I could protect her. Show me how to love her well, Lord. How to help her see how wonderful she is. And so help me...if I ever see that guy, he'd better be wearing a face mask or he won't be looking the same. Carver felt pain in his hands and realized he was gripping the steering wheel too tightly. He relaxed his hand. *Calm down. You'll probably never meet him.*

Eighty-Two

Later that day
Joelzi's apartment
Joelzi

Because Carver had made a list of all the things Merci should be learning, she and Joelzi were in the kitchen making fried chicken. It was one of the things Joelzi remembered her mom and Mema Anna teaching her. *I can at least show Merci how to do this.* She and Merci had laughed while preparing mashed potatoes. They were peeling their potatoes over the trash can and Joelzi kept dropping her potatoes in the trash can and having to dig them out. Fortunately, it was a new trash bag with only potato peelings, so far. Merci had no difficulty with her potatoes and seemed to find extra joy in watching Joelzi's struggles. Joelzi had purchased chicken that had already been skinned and cut up, and they had followed her family recipe, dunking the chicken pieces in the flour and batter and back into the flour.

By the time the oil was hot, Joelzi and Merci had fingers thick with batter and somehow there was flour everywhere. But, eventually, the green beans and almost all of the chicken had been cooked and were warming in the oven. Joelzi had just finished washing her hands when the doorbell rang. Her heart took a leap.

"I'll get the door while you wash up," said Joelzi as she walked to the door and opened it, revealing a spiffed-up Georgie and Carver. "Just in time," said Joelzi, "and looking good."

"My flowers are for Merci," said Georgie, pulling a bouquet of flowers from behind his back as he stepped inside. "Where is she?"

"Merci's in the kitchen, Georgie," said Joelzi, "right over there." She pointed to the kitchen before turning back to where Carver waited just inside the doorway.

"And my flowers are for the lovely lady who is cooking me dinner tonight," said Carver reaching out for Joelzi's hand before bending over and brushing it with a kiss. A beautiful bouquet of his mother's hydrangeas appeared from behind his back.

"Oh, they're beautiful, Carver, did you get them from your mother's yard?" asked Joelzi, struggling not to pull the kissed hand to her cheek.

"As a matter of fact I did," said Carver, "with her blessing."

"I love the thought that Sharon was willing for you to share them with me," said Joelzi. "Come on in," she said, closing the door behind Carver. "I need to put these in water and then check the chicken."

"It smells good," commented Carver.

"After you shared your list of things Merci

should be learning while living with me, Merci and I agreed to try fried chicken and mashed potatoes with cream gravy," said Joelzi. "We're grateful that you guys were willing to be our guinea pigs tonight."

"We're happy to be trial guests. Can't go wrong with fried chicken, mashed potatoes, and gravy," said Carver, "I can't wait to taste it. Georgie and I are hungry—right, Georgie?"

"I'm not hungry," said Georgie, "I'm starving."

"Then we need to pull the food out of the oven and eat," said Joelzi. In short order, the food was on the table, iced tea was in the glasses, and they were seated around the table. "Would you say the grace over the food, Carver?" asked Joelzi.

"It would be my pleasure," said Carver, reaching out both hands to hold those beside him.

This is what it would be like to have Carver in my life, thought Joelzi, before she picked up the mashed potatoes and passed them to Georgie.

That meal was the start of frequent suppers with Carver around Joelzi and Merci's little kitchen table. Sometimes it was just Carver, but other times Georgie joined them. If it was a weeknight, Merci would help with dishes and go to her 'area' to study. Those nights, Joelzi and Carver got comfortable on her couch and talked about their friendships with Adam and Grace, their favorite ER stories, college days, and God. But weekends, when they were not working, Carver and Merci made an effort to include Merci which translated into playing board games, catching a movie, and just spending time together.

Eighty-Three

Saturday, November 27th
The Ellis home

From the moment Carver had asked Joelzi to forgive him, he had taken every opportunity to be connected. He called her, texted her, Carver had even sent a huge bouquet of flowers to the ER on a day Joelzi was working. The note had said 'Thinking of you—grateful you're in my life—Carver.' The ER had been awash with sentiment.

"Are those from Dr Ellis?"

"Oh, wow, when Dr Ellis makes a move, he goes all out!"

"I thought there was something going on between you two!"

"I guess that means another good one bit the dust," said one nurse. "I'm happy for you, Joelzi— but sad for the rest of us."

Joelzi couldn't bring herself to be sad for the other women in the ER. She clearly understood the message Carver was sending; he was all in. She was too.

She was attending her second Ellis Family Saturday Supper and had noticed a change in all the family members. Knowing looks passed between Winston and Luther-Martin. And Annie and Catherine treated Joelzi like she belonged, asking her opinion on all manner of things and giving her hints on things that Carver liked. And even more telling, when the family decided to watch a movie together and Winston and Luther-Martin had moved to sit close to their wives, Carver grabbed Joelzi's hand and moved them into a corner of the couch, promptly wrapping his arm around her possessively. "Is this okay?" he asked Joelzi quietly, looking down at her there at his side. The feeling of being home, right where she belonged, invaded her core. Happy shyness made Joelzi smile up at Carver. "This is perfect," she said quietly.

"We're all right here watching you two. Keep those hands where we can see them..."

"And no stealing kisses in the dark..."

Winston and Luther-Martin were in fine form, ribbing Carver. But Annie and Catherine quickly intervened.

"Y'all leave them alone," said Annie with a laugh, leaning forward to mouth a silent "sorry" to Joelzi.

"It's payback time, Honey," said Winston to Annie. "Don't you remember what Carver put us through when we were a new couple?"

"That was years ago," said Annie, "besides, I thought you wanted Carver and Joelzi to be a couple. Annie lifted her eyes to the ceiling like she was trying to remember and then said, "'Joelzi is just what Doc Brown needs—someone to shake him up till he's happy—like me'."

"Doc Brown?" Joelzi asked Carver quietly.

"A nickname from high school. I was...studious. They named me after..."

"...Back to the Future," finished Joelzi. "It's a favorite. Maybe I'll adopt it."

"From your mouth it might sound special," Carver said.

"Are you wooin' Joelzi?" asked Georgie, standing in front of them, his arms crossed, head angled to the side, watching them carefully.

Everyone laughed.

"I'm trying," said Carver boldly, looking down into Joelzi's eyes. "Is it working?" Carver asked quietly.

Joelzi grinned up at Carver and snuggled into his side. "I think so, but you might need a little more practice."

Eighty-Four

"So, tell me about your family…" Carver said, reaching over to take Joelzi's hand in his. Joelzi still couldn't believe it. She and Carver Ellis were officially in a relationship. She turned her face to smile at him, taking in his firm jawline, visible under the low-cut beard, his warm brown skin, and the profile of his mouth, his lips turning up at the edges, hinting at amusement. "Are you profiling me?" he asked, keeping his eyes on the road.

"Well…I'm looking," Joelzi said.

"Like what you see?" Carver asked, taking his eyes off the interstate to give her a quick grin.

"Maybe," she said.

Carver squeezed Joelzi's hand. "I like what I see."

"Oh yeah?" she asked.

"You are beautiful to me..." Carver said. Joelzi smiled. "...exactly what I wanted but was afraid to believe God for," Carver continued. "It's hard to believe you've forgiven me and we're in a car headed to see your family..." Carver pulled her hand up to his mouth and kissed it. Then he settled their joined hands to his chest and glanced her way. "I'm not getting sidetracked—what do I need to know about your family to not make today awkward?"

"This is my dad's second marriage. As you know, my mom died in a car accident at the start of my senior year of nursing school." Carver kissed her hand again before returning their joined hands to his chest.

"Go on," Carver said.

"My dad remarried. Pretty quickly. Mary Margaret and Sammy Jr. were young—they needed a mom, and my dad was lonely. Christiana was a good fit for the family, even though I was not very appreciative or supportive at the start. Christiana's been good for Daddy and Mary Margaret and Sammy Jr. I was mostly out of the house, so I'm not close to her. But I listen to Mary Margaret, and even though she bemoans having an adult telling her what needs doing, I think she likes Christiana and has bonded with her. Mary Margaret is a little scary in her personality. She's a total romantic. She will probably embarrass us both before the day is out. Her filters are...very thin."

"Good to know," Carver murmured.

"Sammy Jr. is more of a guardian. He is very loyal and protective. He plays basketball—and he's good at it. He's on the Junior High School team. And then there's Handsome."

"That's a unique name."

"He's my two-year-old half-brother, and the

288

glue that pulled me back into the family. He's entertaining and irresistible. His real name is John. But he's so cute, we all just call him Handsome. You'll love him," said Joelzi.

"So, you haven't given me much information about your dad," prompted Carver.

"Daddy..." Joelzi paused, thinking about her dad, "...Daddy is a rock. Steady. He's an electrician for OG&E. He refuses to give up or sit down—even when faced with the death of his wife and the raising of his young children. He's a wonderful man."

"Steady, rock solid, respectable. I've got it," said Carver.

"Carver?"

"Hmm?" murmured Carver.

"Daddy doesn't know what happened to me after Momma died," said Joelzi.

"He doesn't?" asked Carver, turning to look at Joelzi quickly.

"And I don't want him to know. Not yet," Joelzi said softly.

"And yet you told me." Carver said quietly, squeezing her hand. "Thank you for trusting me enough to tell me. It helps me know you. I want to be there for you when bad stuff happens—I mean, I'm not saying that's going to happen again..."

"I know what you're saying, Carver. Thank you," said Joelzi.

"And your dad's new wife?" asked Carver.

"Christiana is a good woman. She's done wonderful things for my family, and I like her...she's just not my momma," said Joelzi. "It's times like these...bringing my boyfriend home to meet my family...that I really hate Momma's not here."

"I'm sorry, Joelzi," said Carver quietly, glancing

her way. "So, I'm elevated to boyfriend level?"

She looked at him and raised her eyebrow. His glance her way and the grin that covered his face as he focused back on the road ahead, indicated he had caught the lifted eyebrow. "Are you suggesting you'd like another level?" she asked innocently.

"Maybe," he said. After a moment of silence, Carver added, "would you be okay with a higher level?"

Joelzi grinned, "Maybe," she said scooting closer to him.

Eighty-Five

Carver

As they pulled into the driveway, Carver noticed the curtains in the front window ripple closed. *They've been watching for us.* He looked over at Joelzi and she smiled mischievously.

"They've been watching for us," Joelzi said. And she laughed out loud, her irresistible, feminine soprano pealing out.

I love her laugh. It's like a call to come home. Carver couldn't help the grin that stretched his lips and revealed his teeth. He chuckled, "You're enjoying this 'meet the family' moment, aren't you?"

"Probably," Joelzi agreed. "You'll do fine, Carver. They'll love you."

"Let's hope you're right. Shall we?" he asked, nodding his head toward the front door.

"Let's," Joelzi agreed and moved to open her door before Carver's words stopped her.

"Wait for me?" Carver said. "I'm coming to get

your door."

The front door opened before Carver had extracted Joelzi from the car and the family poured out. Well, Mary Margaret and Sammy Jr. came running down the stairs. Mr. and Mrs. Parker stayed on the front stoop watching. And Handsome was in Mrs. Parker's arms, struggling to get down.

Joelzi hugged Mary Margaret first as she was the first one down the steps. Mary Margaret squealed, looking over her sister's shoulder at Carver. He assumed it was something all girls of her age did. He had heard Merci make a similar sound. Mary Margaret stepped aside, eyeing Carver curiously as she waited for Joelzi to hug Sammy Jr. Mary Margaret must have had something in her eye because she kept batting her eyes in his direction. Carver chanced a quick look at Joelzi, raising his eyebrows quickly and hoping she could read his question. *Does your sister need help?* Now Mary Margaret was smiling at him in a funny way. Carver looked back at Joelzi for direction. He hadn't grown up with sisters. Joelzi rolled her eyes and mouthed something to her sister before turning his direction.

"Everyone," Joelzi said to the whole bunch as she reached back and took Carver's hand, pulling him to her side, "this is Carver Ellis. He's..." she turned to look at him shyly, "...he's my boyfriend."

There was dead silence for about five seconds while everyone turned to look at Carver. It seemed to last for ages. Mr. Parker's silent examination was telling. *He's taking my measure*, thought Carver, straightening his posture instinctively. Mrs. Parker had a relaxed smile with a hint of entertainment on her face. *She thinks this whole 'meet the family' thing is amusing*, Carver thought. Next, he glanced at Mary Margaret and was taken aback to see her posing his direction in a blatant way. *Joelzi warned me. Best stay clear of that one*, he thought, turning his attention to Joelzi's brother. Sammy Jr. looked the most normal. *No expectations other than the potential for a game of hoops later.* He could deal with that. Lastly, his gaze fell on Joelzi. He couldn't help the smile that stretched his face as he took in her happiness at being home and bringing him with her. *I'm all yours*, he thought. He hoped his face reflected his thoughts.

The group seemed to take a corporate breath and Mrs. Parker said, "It's wonderful to meet you, Carver. Mary Margaret, Junior, bring him in. I hope you're hungry, Carver. I've made my special enchiladas and beans and rice. I hope you like things hot, Carver," Christiana added casually, "my peppers bring a whole new meaning to spicy." Mr. Parker turned to take in Carver's answer, seeming to wait for Carver's response with lifted eyebrows. "Ah, yes ma'am, peppers sound fine." Carver looked to Mr. Parker and sighed in relief as the man nodded without saying a word. Christiana continued, "We were just waiting for you two to get here. I do hope you're okay with two-year-olds, Carver. Handsome is not shy and he's desperate to meet you."

"I think I can take on a curious two-year-old," said Carver as he and Joelzi reached the top step and Handsome launched himself out of his mother's arms into Carver's. *No fear of strangers from this one, world beware,* thought Carver.

"Watch your beard. He's got an amazing grip..." Immediately, Carver felt small hands grab hold of both sides of his sideburns. *Thank God I just had a trim—not much for him to pull. Ow! He might have a future in hair plucking.* He noticed Joelzi watching him. Carver quickly turned Handsome in his arms so the toddler was looking outward and Handsome lunged for Joelzi. She leaned into the boy and kissed his cheeks till he was giggling with her. *She'll be a wonderful mother.* Carver turned his attention to Mr. Parker. *Don't get sidetracked with possibilities,* he told himself, *you still have to face the lion in his den.*

"Sir." Carver reached out to shake Joelzi's dad's hand.

"Carver," said Mr. Parker slowly meeting Carver's outstretched hand with his, "thank you for bringing my daughter home for a family meal. She doesn't get this way as often as we would like."

"My pleasure, sir," said Carver. *I should have asked Winston and Luther-Martin about their first-time meeting Annie's and Catherine's families—this is surreal.*

They all got inside after lots of noise and commotion, not unlike when his family got together. Other than the initial awkward silence, they were a typical family. Mary Margaret whispered things in her big sister's ear and he saw Joelzi roll her eyes a time or two. Once, he noticed Joelzi turn a deep red, which is hard for a brown-skinned person—he should know. Joelzi gave Mary Margaret a look that said, "that's enough," before getting on the floor to play with Handsome. *I'll have to ask her about that later,* Carver thought, and worked hard to minimize the grin that wanted to escape. Invariably, when he could take his eyes off of Joelzi, Carver caught Mary Margaret watching him. The first couple of times he smiled carefully at her, but then she batted her eyes at him. He blinked in shock. Mary Margaret batted her eyes at him again and he had to duck his head so his smile wouldn't offend her. He looked for Joelzi, she would know what to do. Joelzi's grin said she had seen the exchange. She shook her head slightly and turned her attention to Handsome. She picked up her half-brother and turned to her sister. "Mary Margaret, let's go help Christiana get lunch ready."

"But someone needs to keep Carver company," Mary Margaret said.

"The guys are here. Carver's hardly had a chance to talk to Daddy or Junior. Come on. To the kitchen," Joelzi said firmly. She linked arms with Mary Margaret and pulled her into the kitchen.

Carver breathed a sigh of relief; he was not used to teenage girls. He'd only been raised with boys. Boys didn't flutter their eyes at men. *I'm sure she's just practicing, but that was awkward.*

"So, Joelzi tells me you're on the basketball team," Carver said to Junior.

Junior's face creased into a grin, "Yes, sir," Junior said.

"Ah...just Carver,...if that's okay with your dad," Carver added. "Sir makes me feel like an old man." He looked up to see Mr. Parker's eyebrows raise. "I mean, not that it means someone's old when you use it. It's a good sign of deference..." Carver said, feeling his way around what could be seen as disrespectful. He felt like he was walking a tight rope with Mr. Parker.

Eighty-Six

Joelzi

    Lunch with Joelzi's family was over and they were headed back to Oklahoma City and had just hit Interstate Forty when Carver pulled off at a gas station. "I'm on a quarter tank," he said to Joelzi, "Might as well fill up when it's convenient. Do you need anything from inside?"

    "I'll just run to the restroom, I forgot to go before we left the house." Joelzi climbed out of the SUV and headed into the restroom. When she came out of the restroom she went to look at the cold drinks. *Carver likes...*

    "Joelzi...is that you?" the voice came from behind her.

    Dread soured Joelzi's stomach as she recognized the voice. *It can't be.* Her face felt like a fragile porcelain mask as she turned to the tall, heavily muscled man.

    "Joelzi," he said in excitement. "I thought it was

you. Who would ever have believed I would see you in a gas station off of I-40?" He invaded her body space and swallowed her frame in a bear hug, not seeming to react to her stiff posture. He pulled back and put his heavy hands on her shoulders as he looked at her. "As beautiful as always."

Joelzi pushed against the weight of his hands, straightened her posture, and wrapped her arms around her chest. *What were the chances?* Her heart pounded violently in her chest. *Do I dare?* "Myron," she said in a carefully controlled tone, swallowing hard and taking two steps backwards out of Myron's body space.

Myron just smiled. "So how are you? Did you become a nurse?" he asked.

Joelzi felt the slow burn of anger flare in her gut and silence the rapid beat of her heart. She took a deep breath and held a shaking index finger up. "I'm not doing this, Myron," she said flatly.

Myron's eyes widened and his arms lifted off her shoulders to raise to his side, palms opened, "You're not still mad over all of our history are you?" he asked. His eyebrows drew together and his face tightened. "That's water under the bridge, Joelzi."

Joelzi glanced around the gas station. The area they were standing in was empty, with most customers at the checkout line. *This is not where I would choose to have this conversation. But it doesn't have to be long. I just need to get to the point. Hopefully Carver doesn't come looking for me.* Joelzi took a slow steady breath and then looked Myron in the eye. "You raped me, Myron," said Joelzi quietly. "After all these years, I can finally say it."

Myron's head went back like she had punched him in the nose before he recovered and stepped toward her. "Joelzi, you wanted me. You told me so," he said.

"Myron, I wanted comfort because I had just lost the two most important women in my life. I was asking for comfort, for consolation. What you gave started as comfort and escalated. I asked you to stop, Myron, and you didn't. That's called rape." Joelzi said firmly.

"Joelzi, you don't just get a guy all riled up and then shut him down. You let me kiss you, you knew where it was going..."

"Myron, we had dated for four years and you had never taken kissing that far. I had no reason to believe you would cross the line that night."

"Joelzi, you can't blame me for what happened," insisted Myron.

"Here's the truth, Myron. I needed your comfort that night, and you took advantage of the situation. Your actions that night took something precious from me that I can never recover—that I was saving for my husband. I have faced reality, Myron, whether you can face it yet or not. The rape resulted in pregnancy—as you already know because you paid for the abortion. I take full responsibility for what I did to my baby. I've gotten counseling and have talked through what happened. But I won't deny what actually happened anymore."

"I don't need to listen to this, Joelzi," said Myron defensively. "I'm somebody. And no one would believe you anyway, even if you made a fuss. I'm in the NFL now. Girls are lining up to be with me."

Joelzi a sense of relief washed over her, blowing a clean breeze through the dank edges of her heart. She had said what needed saying. *I'm only in charge of me. I can't change him, but the honesty about the rape—facing it straight on was strangely freeing.*

Joelzi pursed her lips as she considered how to continue. She was no longer angry. But she was very sad for the man whom she had considered a friend for so many years until that night. *He is messed up.*

"Myron, I have no interest in 'making a fuss'," said Joelzi. "But you've forgotten that God is *always* watching. God cares about his children. I'm God's kid, Myron. And you will not get away with what you've done. You are doing things that will catch up with you someday. When that happens, and your life falls apart...don't forget about God. He always loves us, especially when we're messed up." *He's in your hands, God. I don't want anything to do with him.* Joelzi turned and headed for the entrance to the gas station just as Carver came in through the glass door.

Eighty-Seven

Carver

Carver made his way into the gas station, his eyes sweeping the area over by the restrooms until they found Joelzi. She was headed toward him with a pensive look on her face. Carver's eyes took in the tall, athletic man over by the drink refrigerators, before clocking back to Joelzi. *Did I interrupt something?*

"Do you know that guy? He looks like he could play in the NFL," asked Carver, sliding his arm around Joelzi's shoulders as he opened the door and led them back out to the car. Joelzi was quiet, letting him open her door and wait for her to get settled. Carver stood inside the opened car door and waited.

Joelzi settled her purse on the floor beside her and then turned to look at Carver. She reached her right hand out and brushed his face, before letting her hand reach around to the back of his neck. He could feel the tremble in her hands. She leaned toward him as he felt the pressure of her hand gently pulling him to her. Joelzi kissed him, but it wasn't the happy kiss he expected. There was a sadness in her lips. He became aware of her trembling body and concern prompted him. "Joelzi?" Carver asked quietly. "What is it? What happened?"

"That was Myron Davis. He was my college boyfriend," she said quietly.

The words registered in slow motion before crystallizing into a deep red rage. Carver pulled back and said the first thing that came to mind, "I'll kill him." He moved to pull away from her grasp, but one look at Joelzi's face gave him pause.

"Don't leave me, Carver," Joelzi said, holding on to his arms. "He's only the past," Joelzi said.

Carver struggled to pull his emotions back under control and felt his body shudder with the strain. Joelzi was his priority. She needed him. Confronting her ex-boyfriend was not going to comfort her. "I'm sorry, Joelzi," pulling her back into a tight embrace. He felt Joelzi nod her response, as she pressed into his embrace. Carver stood there, holding Joelzi, his mind racing with thoughts of how to fix this. But there wasn't any way to make it go away except God and time. Joelzi loosened her grip on his torso and patted Carver's shoulder. "There's a line of cars waiting for this pump," she said with a small smile, "we should go."

"They can wait," said Carver pragmatically, holding his stance at her side.

Joelzi set her jaw and smiled determinedly. "Somehow I don't think they see it that way. Let's go, Carver. There's nothing else we can accomplish here."

301

"You're sure?"

"I'm sure," Joelzi said, "let's go back to the city."

"Okay," said Carver, kissing her swiftly on the lips, before pulling back, and closing her safely inside the SUV. He walked around the car and quickly climbed into the driver's seat, struggling to come to grips with what had just happened. He grabbed Joelzi's closest hand, needing to maintain contact, and pulled it to his chest. *God, what do I say? How can I tell her how much she means to me? How I would like to pummel that guy into the ground for what he did to her. To remind her how You see her.* The next twenty minutes were silent as they both processed what had happened. "How are you doing?" Carver asked eventually.

"Surprisingly well," said Joelzi.

"Really?" he asked, chancing a quick glance her way.

"Really," Joelzi said with a firm nod of her head. "It's like...telling him the truth...calling that night a *rape*...it's fully in the light. I can breathe."

"I'm sorry it came at the end of a stellar day. I really enjoyed meeting your family, and that really put a damper on the fun day."

"It did. Temporarily," Joelzi agreed. "But I choose to not let my past mar today. Let's move on, Carver." Joelzi turned to Carver, her eyebrows lifted in question. "Deal?"

"Deal," said Carver.

There was another moment of silence before Joelzi spoke, "So, about today...are you going to be able to maneuver the maze that is Mary Margaret?"

Carver grinned, "You did warn me, but she's got nothing on her sister." He repositioned her hand in his and catching her eye, motioned to the radio.

302

"Find us some music?"

"Do you like R&B?" Joelzi asked, leaning toward the radio.

"That would be the saved station on number two," he said with a grin.

Joelzi punched the number two on his radio and the sound of Etta James's smoky contralto came floating over the airwaves. "A*t last...my love has come along...*"[8] Joelzi leaned in and turned the volume up making full use of the SUVs excellent sound system.

Carver chanced a quick glance at Joelzi pulling her hand to his lips and solemnly kissing it. The grin stretching Joelzi's cheeks energized him and he relaxed, letting his head move with the sultry rhythm until he hear himself playing backup singer..."ooh yeah yeah..." with the radio. Her giggle gave him courage and he wiggled his eyebrows at her. Joelzi laughed out loud and scooted toward him. He channeled his best version of Etta and let his voice fill the car as he poured out his heart for Joelzi. *Did she understand that he meant the words? She was the one he had dreamed of...would*

[8] At Last · Etta James At Last! ℗ A Geffen Records Release; ℗ 1960 UMG Recordings, Inc. Released on: 1960-11-15 Producer: Phil Chess Producer: Leonard Chess Associated Performer, Recording Arranger, Conductor: Riley Hampton Associated Performer, Vocals: Etta James Composer Lyricist: Harry Revel Composer Lyricist: Mack Gordon. Lyrics for "At Last" by Mack Gordon and Harry Revel, copyrighted by Warner Chapel. All reasonable efforts were made to contact the copyright holders.

she be his? He made eye contact with her and noticed her trembling chin and shiny eyes. And when he looked back at the road it was blurry before he was able to blink it back into clarity. He took a deep breath and let Etta finish the song, the lyrics solidifying his next steps.

Eighty-Eight

Tuesday, December 7th
Coffee with Grace

"So...meeting the parents went well?" asked Grace.

"Yes, Carver really made a good impression," said Joelzi. "My dad was a bit standoffish at first. But Carver handled it well. Carver was polite and interested. And Daddy eventually relaxed."

"Go on," said Grace.

"My stepmom loved him—he ate everything she put on his plate. He even ate the hot peppers." Joelzi giggled, "Carver was sweating and his face was turning red, but he finished those peppers and Christiana was beaming. 'See, he even eats my hot peppers with no complaining,' Joelzi mimicking her stepmother's voice. Carver did drink a lot of tea that day," Joelzi laughed out loud.

"And what about your brother and sister?" asked Grace.

"Sammy Jr. was thrilled because Carver played HORSE and was real competition. I guess Carver didn't let him win. And Mary Margaret...oh my gosh, she is a flirt. She kept making eyes at him," said Joelzi.

"Mary Margaret flirted with Carver?" asked Grace her eyes bugged out and her hand went to her chest as though to calm herself. "Tell me more...inquiring minds and all that..."

Joelzi chortled as she remembered. "We had barely arrived, when Mary Margaret started flirting."

"More details please," said Grace.

"She started by sort of staring at him over my shoulder, like she was super curious—which she was. Carver is an exceptionally good-looking man," said Joelzi.

Grace grinned at Joelzi, "an *exceptionally* good-looking man," she parroted with a knowing smirk.

"Then Mary Margaret looks back at me—I was trying to have a conversation with her and I notice she's looking at Carver again; except this time I watch as she pauses and holds eye contact with him. And *then* she kind of blinks her lashes down and then looks back up at him and smiles—like you see girls do when they're trying to pick up a guy."

"Your sister is trying to pick up Carver?" asked Grace.

"Oh, it's not what it looks like, Mary Margaret had just gotten some of those magnetic eyelash extensions and was trying them out for the first time. I don't know, maybe they were heavy and she was trying to keep her eyes open...but I caught her flashing Carver with them. The look on his face was priceless. He looked like a deer caught in the headlights—just stunned. And then he looked at me with a 'help me' look and I couldn't help it—I just

306

laughed and told Mary Margaret to stop it." Joelzi demonstrated Mary Margaret's eyelash maneuvers and Grace and Joelzi laughed until Grace was wiping tears from her eyes. "I can just imagine Carver's reaction. He's so quiet and calm. I'm sure he felt out of his league."

"Do you have any other Mary Margaret stories?" Grace asked.

"Just one other..." said Joelzi.

Grace's eyebrows rose in question, "Don't stop now, I haven't had a good laugh like this in a long time."

"We had gotten into the house and Mary Margaret was sitting on the couch beside me and across from Carver. She was whispering crazy questions in my ear..."

"Like?" asked Grace.

Joelzi's face felt hot, "Like if he kissed good..."

"That Mary Margaret is a bold one," said Grace, her lips puckered like she was trying not to laugh out loud, "and does he?"

"Grace."

"Well if you told Mary Margaret surely you can tell your bestie."

"Yes."

"Yes?"

"He kisses quiet satisfactorily," said Joelzi sedately, before clapping her hands and giggling as a slow blush climbed her cheeks.

"Tell me what you *really* think about Carver Ellis?" asked Grace, grinning at her friend.

Joelzi got a serious look on her face before saying, "Carver Ellis is the best thing that has ever happened to me...other than God," Joelzi added, looking at Grace to make sure she understood. Grace nodded her understanding. No one was better than God. "Before I *really* knew Carver..." Joelzi paused trying to come up with a good picture for her feelings. "Okay, here's a good emergency room analogy for you. I thought Carver was like asystole: flat line on the EKG strip, no heart action, he could almost 'calm' you to death. And to be fair," Joelzi held her hands up in a surrendered motion, "I would have also said I was more of a ventricular tachycardia heart rhythm: erratic, unstable, and unsustainable. Not that I'm crazy or he was dead, but just the places our hearts were."

"And?" Grace asked.

"And together we make perfect sinus rhythm," Joelzi said quietly. "I'd say we're a good balance for each other."

The two were silent for a moment before Joelzi continued. "On the trip home we stopped at a gas station for Carver to fill up. I went inside to use the restroom. When I came out he was there..."

"He?" asked Grace. "Carver?"

"No," said Joelzi. "Myron, my ex-boyfriend from college—the guy who raped me."

"Oh Joelzi," said Grace, "what did you do?"

"What are the chances of that happening, Grace?" asked Joelzi, looking at Grace with disbelief on her face. "The more I think about it, the more I feel like God set it up."

"I don't think God is mean like that Joelzi," said Grace.

"He's not," said Joelzi. "It wasn't what you're thinking. Yes, it was uncomfortable...but I got to tell Myron that I know what he did to me was rape. It was strangely freeing."

"What did he say?"

"Oh, he blamed it on me, basically gaslighting me, and then told me other girls were glad to have

308

him in their beds."

"Joelzi, I'm sorry," said Grace.

"I'm not. That conversation shed new light on all that history. I'm free. I'm well. I'm in a relationship with a guy that really cares about me."

"Did Carver meet him?"

"Not exactly. He didn't know who it was until we were in the car."

"How did Carver react?"

"He was very angry. Turns out that saying 'slow water runs deep' is true. Carver wanted to go back in the gas station and have words. But that wouldn't have solved anything. Myron is not at a place to change, so it would be like beating your head on a brick wall. The important thing was that I stood up to Myron. And I would not recommend Myron find himself in Carver's presence anytime soon," Joelzi added. "But Carver was more interested in getting me out of there than making a scene. That's who Carver is—he takes care of first things first. And I was first to him, Grace. Me. Joelzi Parker. I really like him" Joelzi said, lifting her eyes to solemnly look at her best friend. "Oh, what am I hiding? I love Carver Ellis."

Eighty-Nine

Carver beat an unknown rhythm on the steering wheel. The closer he got to Meeker, the more he kept having to wipe his sweaty hands on the thighs of his jeans. *The air conditioning isn't working well either. I just had the car in the shop. I guess I need to take it back in and have some more refrigerant put in the system.* He had called Mr. Parker last week to set this meeting up, simply asking if Mr. Parker would be willing to meet with him for about an hour. Today was the only day they both had off. So, as much as he would rather be spending time with Joelzi and maybe getting a kiss or two, he was on his way back to Meeker. He caught his reflection in the rear-view mirror; he was grinning like an idiot. Joelzi Parker made him want to throw off every restraint, run out in the rain and yell something silly like 'I love Joelzi Parker.' His Waze app interrupted his thoughts, reminding him the next turn was his. He settled in for the last two minutes of the drive. It was midday. That was good because he didn't want to do this in front of Mary Margaret and Sammy Jr. He parked in front of the modest ranch house and walked to the door, taking a deep breath as he rang the doorbell.

Mrs. Parker answered the door, Handsome in her arms. "Hello, Carver," she said with a smile on her face," Sam said you would be swinging by today." Carver hadn't told Mr. Parker exactly what he wanted, but by the look on Mrs. Parker's face, she and probably Mr. Parker, had a strong suspicion. "Come on in. Sam's at the kitchen table reading the paper." She turned and walked toward the large opening that led to the kitchen. "Would you like a cup of coffee? Or maybe a glass of tea?"

"No ma'am. Thank you, but..."

"Well, that's fine, come on—you know the way...Sam," she called as she led the way, "Carver Ellis is here."

Mr. Parker stood up from his chair as Carver came into view. "Carver, it's good to see you again. And so soon..." Mr. Parker made his way over to Carver.

"Sir." Carver said, stepping forward and reaching out his hand to shake Mr. Parker's hand. He felt a slow deep burn on his face as he watched Mr. Parker wipe his hands on the thighs of his jeans after shaking Carver's hand. He didn't blame him; Carver's hands were sweating profusely now. Carver's face felt so stiff he thought it would crack if he opened his mouth. He gave up any pretense of being calm and wiped his hands on his own jeans pants.

"Handsome and I'll just go check on the laundry and leave you two to talk," Mrs. Parker said with a smile, and she turned and left the room."

Carver stood there awkwardly for a moment.

"Carver, come sit down at the table and tell me what I can do for you," said Mr. Parker, indicating the chair beside his.

Carver took a moment to get his thoughts together. He was grateful that Mr. Parker simply held his readers in one hand and waited. "Sir...I...ah...I...lo...lo...love your daughter." He closed his eyes in frustration. *What grown man stutters when he asks his potential Father-in-Law to marry his daughter?*

"Hmm," murmured Mr. Parker eyeing him carefully. "Which daughter would that be?" he asked, watching Carver steadily. "Mary Margaret seemed pretty taken with you last Saturday, but she's a little young..." Mr. Parker glanced up with a smile on his face.

Carver chuckled and a calmness settled over him as he sat up straighter and looked Mr. Parker in the eye. "I'm in love with Joelzi, sir. She's the only girl for me. She...she's the loveliest woman I have ever met. I want to ask her to marry me and I'm here to ask your blessing."

Mr. Parker looked at Carver quietly for a moment before saying, "Joelzi is special to me."

"Yes, sir," said Carver, nodding his head.

"She's my first daughter. And when they put her in my arms the first time, I was instantly in love with this baby that the Lord had given my wife and me—" he continued.

"Yes, sir," said Carver, leaning forward. He wanted this picture of a father's love for Joelzi. *I'll have to be sure to tell her.*

"I'm the first man in her life. I'm her first human protector. And those distinctions come with responsibility. So, I've got some straight questions

312

for you, Carver. I'm looking for honesty here—not perfection." Mr. Parker paused. "Will you consider my questions?"

"Yes, sir," said Carver.

It had been an insightful day, Carver reflected on the drive back to Oklahoma City. The first thing Mr. Parker had delved into was Carver's relationship with God. When he was satisfied with Carver's answer, Mr. Parker had asked Carver what 'forever' meant to him. Mr. Parker had briefly talked about his first wife, and their marriage. "If you're looking for marriage to solve your problems, Carver, you need to drop everything right here and drive back to the city. Marriage is beautiful *work*," Mr. Parker had said. "It's my experience that women are very intuitive. As a man, you need to respect that, cherish it, rely on it. A godly woman is a helpmeet. I heard Jordan Peterson describe it as a 'benevolent adversary'. Benevolent because if you're blessed, they love you; adversary because they will go toe-to-toe with you over things they consider to be important." Mr. Parker leaned forward with a thoughtful look on his face. "Have y'all had a fight yet?" he had asked.

Carver had felt the blood drain from his face, remembering the time outside of the Emergency Room when Joelzi confronted him. "Yes, sir."

"And how did that go?" Mr. Parker had asked.

"She called me on my actions," Carver had said. "She chased me down to do it, too."

Mr. Parker leaned back in his chair with a chuckle. "Joelzi's a lot like her momma. Her momma was fierce but loving. Tell me why you love Joelzi. What do you see in her?"

Carver had thought a minute before beginning. "Joelzi sees me. She's not overly impressed with my job description. She sees *me*, Carver Ellis, the kid who stuttered as a child. The guy who gets caught up in the details in his head and forgets to live with his heart. She balances me in a way that is enriching. I love how she loves God. She's strong, but tender. She's giving. She cares about people. She's—"

"Not perfect," Mr. Parker had interrupted.

"No, she's not perfect," Carver had said, "but...she's perfect for me."

Two hours and two glasses of iced tea later, Carver had left with Mr. Parker's blessing. "Carver, if Joelzi will take you, we'd be pleased to welcome you into the family."

Carver was relieved and excited. *Now to ask Joelzi to marry me. Maybe it's time to call Grace.*

Ninety

Carver scrolled through his contacts until he found Grace Noble's name. He checked his watch; it wasn't too early for a call. Adam said Grace was feeling better these days. Hopefully, he wouldn't catch her in the middle of trying to put the girls down for a nap, it was after lunch. He pressed 'call' and waited for the ring.

"Hello?" said Grace.

"Hi, Grace, it's Carver," he said.

"Carver Ellis. How are you?" asked Grace. "I feel like I hardly get to talk to you these days. At least you and Adam still hang out regularly."

"Yes, it's been a slower schedule since your good news happened—congratulations!" said Carver.

"Well, thank you, and we need to improve the regularity of your 'man time'," said Grace.

"Are you feeling better?" Carver asked.

"Yes. Thank God. I felt like I was constantly

examining the cleanliness of the toilets in the house. Not pleasant being a toilet inspector," Grace added with a laugh.

"No," Carver said with a chuckle, "that doesn't sound fun."

"But the end result of all that inspecting is pretty exciting," said Grace.

"Yes," Carver said, "it is."

"So...I don't usually hear from you, Carver. What can I do for you?" asked Grace.

"Well," said Carver, "I'm pretty sure you're aware that Joelzi and I are in a relationship..."

"Yes, Carver," Grace said in a happy tone, "I thought you two would never see the obvious connections you share. Adam and I would've already had you two over for dinner, but I've been off my game."

"We'll take you up on that when you're feeling good, but right now I need help," said Carver, "I need to know things that Joelzi likes. At this point, you know more details than I do. That will change with time, but..."

"Details about what Joelzi likes...Joelzi does not like sweating or getting her hands in dirt," said Grace. "She wants her flowers without roots."

"Flowers without roots," said Carver, typing a quick note in his phone. "Got it."

"She loves interior decorating—and she's good at it," said Grace.

"Interior decorating—I noticed that when she pulled all that stuff together for Merci moving in. And her apartment has a really nice vibe, that's good to know," said Carver.

"Joelzi loves being pampered. That means a mani-pedi or a spa day or getting her hair done."

"Nails, spa, and hair. Got it," said Carver.

"It might help to know exactly what you are planning, Carver," said Grace.

"Uh...well...I'm trying to plan my proposal," said Carver.

"Your proposal!" Grace shouted.

Carver pulled the phone away from his ear with an understated smile, not fully understanding all of Grace's exclamations. He waited until he could hear her saying, "Carver? Carver!" before he put his phone back to his ear. "Sorry about that, Grace, it got a little loud there for a moment," he said with a grin.

"Oh, my goodness, Carver, what can I do to help?" asked Grace.

"I was wondering if ya'll ever discussed what kind of wedding ring she would like..."

"Sort of, but not specifically..." Grace hedged. She cleared her throat, "Have you checked Joelzi's Pinterest account to see if there's a wedding board?"

"Didn't even think of that. Does she have one?"

"Yes. Most women do," said Grace, "so don't read too much into it. That might be a good place to start. What else are you thinking?"

"I want the proposal to be private and special, but I don't want to leave out the close family and friends...and I was thinking about a kind of scavenger hunt the day of..."

"Ah, Carver...remember, Joelzi does not like to be sweaty or get her hands in the dirt..." said Grace, "I hate to say this but I don't think a scavenger hunt is really Joelzi's thing."

"Not that kind of scavenger hunt," said Carver, "I have something a little more elegant planned..."

Ninety-One

"Grace, what's up?" asked Joelzi, swinging her legs over the side of the bed and sitting up.

"Good Morning, Joelzi. Is it too early?" asked Grace.

Joelzi yawned. "No, eight o'clock is a good time. I worked swing last night, but it wasn't a crazy shift so I got in bed at a decent time—not a lot of de-stressing needed."

"Oh, good," said Grace. "I wanted to talk about a girls' day."

Joelzi perked up, "You know I'm always up for a girls' day. What are we doing?"

"We're going to the spa—mani, pedi, and massage..."

"Yes, please," said Joelzi.

"And then girls' lunch at that little Bistro we like..."

"I like the way you think," said Joelzi.

"We need to have our hair done. I'm desperate for a haircut—I haven't gone since I got pregnant and could do nothing but hang over a toilet. But I don't think we'll have the time on our Saturday. I'm just saying we should do that ahead of time," said Grace.

"When are we doing all this pampering that takes all day?" asked Joelzi. She could hear a paper being handled in the background.

"Um...it looks like we have three options. They're all Saturdays... Are you off next Saturday?

Joelzi put Grace on speaker and pulled up her work calendar on her phone. "I work 11am to 11pm today...and I'm off the next Saturday. That will work," said Joelzi.

"Um...do you still have that raspberry dress you wore to my wedding?" Grace asked. "And those stilettos you wore with it?" asked Grace.

"Yes," said Joelzi, dragging out the word.

"We're going to need those," said Grace.

"Grace, what are you planning? This is becoming very specific," said Joelzi. "I've got to get my hair done ahead of time, we're doing mani/pedis, I'm bringing my raspberry dress and my stilettos. Are we going to a concert?" asked Joelzi.

"Joelzi, I've been sidetracked as a friend since marrying Adam, becoming a mom to Zoe and Remi, and then getting pregnant. Could you just relax and enjoy a girls' day out with me? There's a lot planned, but Adam is up for watching the girls and I'm feeling good. Just let it be a surprise?" asked Grace.

"Of course, I can," said Joelzi. "It's been a long time since we had a girls' day. It will be fun."

Ninety-Two

"I like that one," said Carter, pointing to a large oval solitaire. Carver, Adam, and Georgie had already visited every jewelry store in the mall and were now at RTL Family Jewelers, a small, privately-owned, stand-alone jewelry store with one-of-a-kind items.

"This one?" The jeweler pulled the ring Carver had indicated out from the locked case. The oval stone was encased in a half bezel platinum setting and secured on a wide platinum band. The large diamond's longer dimension ran horizontally across the finger.

Carver took the ring and moved it around in the overhead lights. It lit up the room.

Adam whistled softly. "Not much in love, are you, Carver," Adam said with a grin. "That's a rock."

"I thought Carver was buying Joelzi a ring," said Georgie.

"He is, Georgie, but your brother is *loco* in love..."

"*Loco* in love?" asked Georgie.

"It will look good on her," said Carver, engrossed in his discussion with the jeweler.

"Head over heels..." said Adam.

"He's gonna do a summersault? Carver's not good at summersaults," said Georgie, a frown on his face.

Carver turned to the jeweler, "I'm a little concerned about the diamond falling out, as there's only two sides covered."

"Oh, probably not, sir," said the jeweler, "it looks exposed but the longer sides are in the bezel. The stone is in the setting very securely."

"You don't know the kind of work we do. I want her to wear it, and I don't want her to lose it in body parts," said Carver.

The jeweler paled. "Are you in the mortuary business, sir?"

"No, we work in the emergency room. You can never tell what's going on there," said Carver moving the ring in the light.

"I see," the jeweler said thoughtfully.

"Anyway, can you add an additional partial bezel that runs down the open sides in yellow gold? Just a simple line here," Carver indicated what he was thinking.

"Well, that would be an additional service. I don't think we have a setting like that..."

"But you make jewelry, right?" Carver asked.

"Yes, I make settings," the man replied.

"Can you add something like that?" asked Carver.

"Yes. We would need to draw it out so you have an idea of how it would look. And adding the gold will make it easy for your fiancé to wear gold or platinum jewelry. Yes, it could look very nice...although you might consider just wearing the wedding band at work...I mean, I'm assuming this is an engagement ring.

"Yes, an engagement ring," said Carver. "But I want everyone to know she's spoken for until we get married and then she can wear the band."

"Of course," said the jeweler.

"I thought about maybe using gold in the wedding band to coordinate..."

Adam turned to Georgie, "Let's go sit in those chairs," Adam indicated the two chairs along the wall of the small shop. "We may be here awhile, Georgie, your brother is suddenly becoming a jewelry connoisseur."

"I'm glad we ate already," said Georgie. "Carver is really interested in the ring. He wants to make sure it's good enough for Joelzi. Winston told him to buy the biggest one he could pay for."

Adam smiled, pulling out gum for him and Georgie, "Did Winston say why?" Adam offered Georgie a piece of gum.

"Yeah," said Georgie, taking the gum, "Winston said Carver was never gonna be able to afford anything so big after he had babies and worked in a medical mission. He said Joelzi was gonna need to see that big ring and remember Carver loved her," said Georgie.

"Well, if you know you also want a ruby ring guard, you could just..." Adam heard the murmurings of the two men as they worked out what Carver wanted.

He's so in love, the man is going to buy the whole

322

store, thought Adam. They were there another twenty-five minutes when Carver turned to Adam.

"Did Grace have Joelzi try on her wedding ring?" Carver asked perfunctorily. "We need a size."

"We're up, Georgie," said Adam before standing and walking over to Carver and the jeweler. He pulled Grace's wedding ring out of his pocket and handed it to Carver. "I don't know how they do it, but women try on each other's rings. This is Grace's wedding band and she says it fits Joelzi perfectly." Adam turned to the jeweler, "But it's not staying. You can use it to measure, but it's going home to my wife and on her finger where it belongs."

"Of course, sir, I'll just slip it over the ring sizer and we'll have our measurement," said the jeweler. He quickly measured Grace's ring and gave it back to Adam.

"And you'll have it before Saturday, right?" Carver asked the jeweler for the third time.

"Yes, sir, it will be ready for you on Saturday," said the jeweler.

"Morning," insisted Carver.

The jeweler smiled at Carver, "I will begin working on it today and I guarantee it will be finished on Saturday morning."

"Okay, then." Carver seemed to come out of hyperfocus and notice Georgie and Adam. "I did it," Carver said with a satisfied lift of his shoulders.

"Yes, you did," said Adam clapping his friend on the shoulder, "Come on, jewelry man, let's get you out in the fresh air. How about ice cream all around?" Adam said looking at Georgie.

"Yeah, ice cream. That was hard work waiting for you to find the right ring," said Georgie.

Ninety-Three

Saturday, December 18th
Girls' Day Out

Grace had insisted on driving and had just picked Joelzi up. It was ten-thirty and they were on their way to Joelzi's favorite spa for manicures, pedicures, and massages. Joelzi could hardly wait. She got her nails done regularly, but she didn't often splurge on a massage. The spa had assured Joelzi that they could accommodate a pregnant Grace, and Joelzi could feel the tension from the last three nights of work seeping away with just the knowledge of the approaching day of pampering. Joelzi's phone began pealing out "At Last" sung by Etta James and she grinned. The stress of encountering Myron at the gas station had been trumped by Carver singing "At Last" to her on their way back to the city. She had officially designated the song as Carver's ringtone. Joelzi caught Grace's raised eyebrows and smirk before Joelzi turned to look out the car window and answered the phone.

"Hey," Carver said.

"Hey, yourself," said Joelzi.

"Are you and Grace going to the spa like you planned?" Carver asked.

"Yes, Grace just picked me up and we're headed there now," said Joelzi.

"What's it called?" asked Carver.

"Echelon Day Spa and Bistro," said Joelzi.

"Sounds interesting," said Carver.

"It is," said Joelzi. "It's in a huge building but offers all kinds of different services. We'll start with the spa services. They have hydro pools and hot and cold pools and they serve complimentary detox drinks while you sit in the pools and let your pores open. Then we'll move on to our massages. I signed up for a hot stone massage," said Joelzi. "After the massages, we go sit in the sunken waterfall room in our robes and just chill. We'll get our nails done last and then we'll stop and eat in the bistro," Joelzi sighed in satisfaction.

"So, you're looking forward to it?" Carver asked.

"Absolutely," said Joelzi, "it's a dream to get away with Grace and do all of this."

"Well, that's good. It sounds like a long day," said Carver. "Did you leave Merci at the apartment? I hope she's cleaning up around the place," said Carver.

"As a matter of fact, she got her chores done last night. Her mom called yesterday and asked to take her to lunch," said Joelzi. "Merci is really trying to keep up with your list, Carver. I think it's really helping her feel like she belongs," said Joelzi.

"Well, that's good," said Carver, "it's important to feel a part. That's pretty exciting that her mom is picking her up. We want to nurture that relationship."

"I totally agree," said Joelzi. "Carver, we've just pulled into the parking lot, I'm going to have to let you go..."

"Okay, I just wanted to call and tell you 'Good Morning' and 'I love you'," Carver said. "I hope all that pampering doesn't wear you out too much..."

"Oh, it won't," said Joelzi, "it's relaxing in an invigorating way."

"So, you might be up for a visit later tonight?" Carver asked. "I have some things I have to get done today, but maybe I could swing by your apartment this evening?"

"That would be a wonderful end to the day, Carver," said Joelzi.

"Okay, then, I'll see you later tonight," said Carver. "I love you. Have a great day."

"I love you too, Carv," said Joelzi making a kiss sound to the phone before hanging up. Joelzi turned back in time to see Grace roll her eyes and grin in her direction.

"Let's go, my lovesick friend," said Grace, "we've got personal care therapy waiting."

It was 4:00pm before they were finished at the spa. And when she thought they were done, Grace had taken her across the way to a hairstylist who had added some pizzazz to Joelzi's hair. Grace had gone to her car and grabbed the raspberry dress Grace had insisted Joelzi bring while Joelzi's hair was being touched up. As soon as Joelzi's hair was done, Grace held out the dress and insisted Joelzi put it on.

"What is going on, Grace?" asked Joelzi.

"If you don't want me to lie, you need to avoid asking me questions I can't answer," said Grace.

The hairstylist smiled at the two friends, before turning to Joelzi.

"You trust her?" she asked, her head tilted to the side and one hand on her hip.

"Yes," said Joelzi slowly, her eyes squinting at Grace as though it would help her understand why her friend was acting like this.

"Then you better get that dress on. Looks like you got places to be—and from the looks of that dress—it's gonna be good."

Joelzi looked at her friend. Grace had pulled Joelzi's dress back to her core, the dress lying over her twenty-week pregnant belly as she stretched her neck, moving her shoulders back and waited for Joelzi to decide. *Grace is tired. She's been with me all day without complaining once. If my beautiful pregnant friend can manage today without complaint, then I can meet her in the middle of the adventure,* thought Joelzi.

"Hand it over, Grace," said Joelzi, "I guess we're going to see this to the end—whatever *this* is."

Grace held out the dress solemnly with one hand while supporting her belly with the other. Joelzi almost felt sorry for her until she noticed the spark of excitement that lit Grace's grin when she thought Joelzi couldn't see her reflection in the mirror. *Hmmm.*

Ninety-Four

Grace drove to the front entrance of the Oklahoma City Museum of Art and pulled in.

"Grace, it says 'no parking'," said Joelzi, pointing to a No Parking sign to their left.

"I'm not parking," said Grace, "I'm dropping off."

"You're dropping off?" asked Joelzi.

"Out you go," Grace said, motioning with her right hand for Joelzi to get out. "And there's your date," said Grace indicating a man walking their way in a dark blue suit with a raspberry tie that matched Joelzi's dress. "Right on time."

Joelzi's heart started pounding for no reason as she recognized Carver coming her way. Carver reached the car and opened Joelzi's door with a smile. He held his hand out to her and without thought, Joelzi placed her hand in his, letting him pull her out of the car and to his side.

"Hi, Beautiful," Carver said quietly.

"Hi, Handsome," said Joelzi, leaning in closer.

"I thought that was your brother's name," said Carver.

"So it is. But you *are* handsome. How about

charming?" Joelzi asked.

"It might work," Carver said, "I'm certainly trying to be."

"Okay, you two, I'm out of here. Have a wonderful time," Grace said with a grin and a wave of her hand as Carver closed the car door and she drove off.

"Surprised?" asked Carver.

"Definitely. This is definitely over the top. Are we going to attract attention walking through the museum dressed up like this?" Joelzi asked, smoothing down the raspberry dress she had worn to Grace and Adam's wedding.

"Maybe," Carver said, "but I have dinner planned and we won't be overdressed for that."

"Nice tie," Joelzi said, reaching up to adjust it. It didn't need adjusting, she just wanted to touch him.

"So, have you been here before?" asked Carver.

"No, but I've wanted to. They have a Chihuly exhibit that I've always wanted to see," said Joelzi.

"The really tall one?" Carver asked, tucking her hand in his elbow and making his way to the front doors.

It seems the planner has planned, thought Joelzi when the staff person at the entrance greeted him by name.

"Welcome to the Oklahoma City Museum of Art, Dr. Ellis. We hope you have a pleasant evening."

"Dr. Ellis," Joelzi said with a raised eyebrow. "You were expected...well this should be a treat. I think I'll enjoy myself," Joelzi said with a grin.

"That's the plan," said Carver.

They spent about an hour wandering through the museum. "Are you sure they don't have one of your paintings, Carver? Your work would totally fit in this place," Joelzi commented.

"No, I have no paintings here," said Carver.

"But they know you, Carver," said Joelzi.

"So they do..." said Carver enigmatically.

Finally, they rounded the corner and there it was—the large Chihuly exhibit the museum was known for. "Oh my goodness, Carver, isn't it beautiful?" said Joelzi, letting go of Carver's arm and walking up to the rail that kept viewers away from the fragile glass structure. She gazed at all the pieces so carefully placed to make this large tree-like structure. "Amazing. Just amazing," Joelzi said, holding on to the rail.

"Yes," said Carver from behind her, "you are amazing, Joelzi."

Joelzi turned and noticed Carver only had eyes for her. Carver took Joelzi's hands in his, never letting his gaze waver from her face.

"Why are you looking at me like that, Carver?" Joelzi asked breathlessly.

"I'm captivated with the woman that I hope will be my future wife...the mother of our children...the helpmeet that God provided for me...the one who I hope will come alongside me and make the hard places bearable and the good places sweeter." Carver's smile faded and his lips firmed, "I've made mistakes, Joelzi. I've been proud where I had no right to be." He squeezed her hands in emphasis, "you know I love order and planning and control. And I'll likely drive you batty, but...I love you, Joelzi. I've never said that to any woman but my momma. I've never felt the way I feel about you—like you're my missing rib—like you fit in my arms and beside me. Like my life would be so much richer if you were in it." Carver went down on one knee and Joelzi felt her face get wobbly and her eyes fill with tears. "Joelzianna Parker, will you marry me?"

"Okay," she said.

"Is that a 'yes'?" Carver asked, as though making sure the answer had been answered properly.

"Yes," said Joelzi holding his face with her hands as she leaned down to kiss Carver. It was a minute before Carver said, "Joelzi, honey, this floor is killing me, let me stand up and kiss you properly." Joelzi was in total agreement and they spent some time blessing each other with holy kisses, before she heard a young child say in a not so quiet voice, "Momma, why are they kissing so long? I thought the museum was where you're supposed to look at things?" Joelzi and Carver pulled apart long enough to glance at the mother of the child. Both women silently mouthed "sorry" to each other and then the mother pulled her child to another part of the museum.

"I bought you a ring." Carver said.

"You did?" asked Joelzi.

"Yes. I had help from Adam. I'll buy you another one if you don't like it," said Carver.

"I'll like whatever you picked out," said Joelzi.

"I checked your Pinterest board."

"You did?"

"Grace suggested it. I bought the engagement ring that I thought you would like and then picked out a wedding band that was simpler—something that wouldn't catch on things at work and...later when we have kids..." Carver looked at her shyly, "I'm not trying to rush things...I just..."

"You're not rushing things, Carver," said Joelzi. "I want to have kids with you and I would love a ring that won't catch on stuff when I'm at work and won't scratch our kids when I'm changing diapers. I'm just getting a little anxious about you putting it on my finger."

"Oh yeah?" said Carver.

"My ring finger is feeling really naked," she wiggled her left hand at Carver.

Carver grabbed her hand and kissed her ring finger before sliding the most beautiful solitaire diamond ring over it. The platinum band was wide and held a large sparkly oval solitaire in a beautiful platinum setting that partially covered the long sides of the diamond. Two small yellow gold commas added support on the exposed ends.

"Oh, Carver," Joelzi struggled to catch her breath. The ring was stunning. More beautiful than any ring she had believed she would ever receive. "It's beautiful," Joelzi said, examining the ring on her finger appreciatively.

"The wedding band is platinum with little diamonds," he said. "I figured you'd wear that at work after we're married. We can take it back if you don't like it...I want it to be perfect for you."

"You, Carver Ellis, are perfect for me, and I love the ring you picked out. I'm honored." Joelzi stretched up to kiss him again, before holding her hand out to look at her ring again.

"Does it fit okay?" Carver asked.

"Perfectly. How did you do that?" Joelzi asked.

"Do you remember trying on Grace's wedding band?" asked Carver.

"Yes, that was a ploy?" asked Joelzi.

"I asked her for help," said Carver.

"I'll have to be sure and thank her," said Joelzi, leaning in to kiss Carver again. He kissed her back.

"I guess we need to move on before we burn the eyeballs of the next little kid coming our way," said Carver.

Joelzi laughed. "He was funny. Reminded me of

Zoe at Adam and Grace's wedding." They chuckled together at the memory.

"We do need to get going," Carver said, "we have reservations for dinner."

"Wow. When you decide to ask a girl to marry you, you just go all out," said Joelzi. "So were all of today's events on you?" Joelzi asked.

"I had Grace's help...but yes, today was about making a memory for you," said Carver.

"First the mani/pedi, then the hair, shopping, lunch with Grace. I owe her. Poor pregnant Grace dragged me to all my favorite spots. I kept telling her we had done enough and she just kept pushing. Now I understand; she was the Matron of Honor on a mission."

"I definitely owe her," said Carver, "I made the plan, but she executed it."

Joelzi wrapped her arm around his as they began making their way to the exit, "I think your new moniker needs to be Charming Doc Brown."

"Not bad," said Carver, "but currently, I'm enjoying 'fiancé'."

Ninety-Five

They made their way back to Carver's car slowly because Joelzi kept slowing down to look at the ring on her finger that was nestled on Carver's forearm. Before long, they pulled into valet parking at Ludivine's.

"Our first date," Joelzi said with a smile of recognition, "you remembered."

"I will always try to remember, Joelzi. You're on my 'listen-and-take-notes-most-important-person' list."

Joelzi kissed Carver right there in front of the maître d' for those words of affirmation. The maître d' cleared his throat and looked at Carver formally. Carver straightened his tie, "Ellis party, please." The maître d' led them to a private room in the back, opened the door with a flourish, and waved them in.

"Surprise!" the shouts came from all over the room. All of the Ellises—even Grandma Ruby were there. Grace, Adam and their kids, and Merci were present. And Joelzi's family had driven from Meeker to be here and celebrate. Joelzi stood there, shocked, thrilled, and amazed at all the planning Carver had done to make this a special day. Joelzi turned to Carver. He stood there calmly at her side, a smile of satisfaction on his face. "I love you," Joelzi said quietly. "You made a way to have our families and friends here. Carver Ellis, I love you. Fiercely." Joelzi stepped up to her fiancé's chest, gently grabbed him by the lapels and pulled him down to her lips. Carver required minimal coercion to move into Joelzi's best kissing zone. The occupants of the room erupted in hoots of joy as Carver made himself available for Joelzi's lips.

Ninety-Six

It was mind-blowing how twenty-four hours could change the trajectory of your life, thought Joelzi, reflecting on last night. Grandma Ruby had brought them a gift last night.

"I tried to give this to you earlier, Joelzi," Grandma Ruby had said, handing a wrapped box to Joelzi. "But Carver here," she had smiled at her grandson were he stood beside Joelzi, "was worried about keeping the Kintsugi bowl in the family—a family heirloom—he said." Grandma Ruby paused, "as I suspected on first meeting you, Joelzi, there was no danger of the family heirloom leaving the family," Grandma Ruby grinned. "I hope it sits in a place of honor where it reminds you both that only God puts broken things back together better than they were."

"Yes, ma'am," Carver and Joelzi had said in

unison.

"And put it high enough so that all those children you two will have can't break it again."

She and Carver had stayed up late after yesterday's engagement party, talking about the logistics of getting married. Carver did not want to wait a long time. Neither did she. Carver had a large two-bedroom unit in the Aberdeen and he had suggested they all move in there after the wedding until he and Joelzi could buy a home. Obviously two bedrooms was plenty, even though having Merci with them would definitely dampen their newlywed freedom. But Carver had agreed it was the right thing to do. Merci was twenty-four weeks pregnant now. They needed to see Merci through her pregnancy and delivery, and hopefully her return to her mother's home. Merci and her mother had been talking and Liliana had taken Merci to breakfast yesterday. Currently, communication was open between the mother and daughter. Liliana Lopez had even asked to take Merci to her next OB appointment. Those were all good signs for the future.

They were sitting at a booth waiting for their food to be served. Joelzi smiled over at Carver as Merci grabbed Joelzi's hand to look at her engagement ring again.

"It's so pretty," said Merci, moving Joelzi's ring finger so the light would catch the facets of the diamond.

Joelzi could not pass up this mentoring moment. "This is what happens when you wait on God, Merci. I'm not saying my path was perfect. It wasn't. But when we decide to wait for God's plan—regardless of how impossible it seems—God's plan

337

is always better," said Joelzi.

Merci waited while their food was served before commenting. "So if I wait, I'll get a big rock like this?" she asked with a smirk.

"No," said Joelzi with a laugh, "if you wait on God, you will get God's best plan for you." Joelzi looked to her right where Carver was sitting and watching them. "Carver is more than I hoped or imagined, Merci." Carver lifted his eyebrows at Joelzi's quiet statement and winked at Joelzi. Joelzi felt her insides turn over in that new sensation of being known and loved for who she was. "What I'm really trying to say, Merci, is 'wait on God.' God's way is always better."

Merci's gaze clocked between Carver and Joelzi and she grinned. "I think I can be okay with waiting on God," she said before turning to her plate piled high with food, "but I'm not fine with waiting on this food to get cold. Are we going to pray? I'm starving."

Ninety-Seven

It was a simple wedding, more elaborate than Grace and Adam's courthouse wedding, but still understated in an elegant way, Joelzi reflected as she watched all the women she loved prepare for her big day. *Today I'm marrying Carver Ellis,* she thought. When Carver had admitted he didn't want to wait a long time to get married, Joelzi had enlisted Grace's help to look for a wedding dress that was available sooner than the standard nine to twelve months. And God had provided.

Joelzi looked at her reflection in the full-length mirror. Her dress was a classic A-line ball gown. Its corset bodice came to her natural waist and was covered in dense ivory lace, from the scoop neck to the dainty cap sleeves. The skirt was covered with tulle that had been sprinkled with lace and floated to the floor and the back of the dress spread out behind her in a chapel length train. Although Joelzi had found the dress in a bridal resale store, it fit her like it had been made for her. Joelzi wore a simple silver and crystal headband in her hair that had been pulled up in a natural updo, and a veil trailed behind her.

Grace managed to cajole Remi into leaving her floral crown in place and made her way over to Joelzi's side. "You look beautiful, Joelzi," said Grace, a smile of satisfaction on her face. "You don't know how happy it makes me to see you marrying Carver today. I've always thought you were the one for him. And today it becomes official." The two friends stood side by side, Grace's peach Matron of Honor dress displaying her now distinctive thirty-two-week pregnant baby belly. *Maybe someday, I'll get another chance to be a mother*, thought Joelzi. The thought did not cause the old angst. She was forgiven. *But first things first*, she thought, *I've got to marry my man.* A grin of joy erupted across her face at the thought before a commotion behind them had Joelzi and Grace turning to watch Mary Margaret attempting to place eyelash extensions on a very pregnant Merci. Merci kept blinking at inopportune times causing the fake eyelashes to fall off. After lots of laughter and failed attempts, the lash extensions were in place, pictures were taken, and the church wedding coordinator stepped inside the room.

"Joelzi," the wedding coordinator said with a smile, "your Groom and his groomsmen are in place and waiting for your entrance." Joelzi tried not to cry even as her face crumbled. *How can I contain this joy?* she thought. She wiped a tear, took a deep breath, and nodded at the wedding coordinator, "We're ready." Joelzi bent down to the little girls that Grace, Mary Margaret, and Merci were cuing

340

up. "Okay—remember to throw your flower petals out on the ground and smile," said Joelzi. As Etta James began belting out "At Last," Zoe, Remi, Marti, Angie, and Winnie began making their way up the aisle to the front of the chapel. The older girls reveled in their task and threw their flower petals with abandon. But Remi didn't seem to understand the concept and kept picking up the scattered petals, and putting them back in her basket, to the delight of the audience.

"I may have overdone the 'clean up what you drop' rule in our house," said Grace as she relayed the antics to Joelzi.

"It only makes the day sweeter," said Joelzi with a grin as the sound of laughter filtered past the open door. "These are the stories we will remember and tell during anniversaries and when these girls grow up and get married...this is what makes life rich."

"I'm up," said Grace as Mr. Parker appeared at the door. "Enjoy your day, Joelzi," Grace said. "You deserve it."

Ninety-Eight

Carver

We've been standing at the front of the church waiting for ages, Carver thought, checking his watch again. *No, not even a minute has passed.* Carver ran his finger inside the collar of his tux shirt and stretched his neck again. The shirt collar felt tighter than it had when he had first put it on. He bounced on his feet until Adam caught his eye and raised his eyebrows.

"Excited?" Adam whispered with a satisfied grin on his face. Carver chuckled. That was an understatement. As Etta James began singing "At Last" and the little girls began making their way to the front of New Life Community's wedding chapel, Carver's thoughts wandered. He had waited a long time for today. He had botched this relationship several times and truth was, he'd probably mess it up again. But God had seen fit to give him an exceptional helpmeet. What was it Mr. Parker had called it?—a benevolent adversary. Joelzi was exactly who he needed by his side. Carver noticed that Merci, Mary Margaret, and even Grace had made it down the aisle during his musings. The music changed again and Carver's heart stuttered as he caught a glimpse of his bride on her father's arm. Carver hadn't expected to cry, but tears dripped down his cheeks unchecked. *Joelzi is beautiful. And she's mine*, he thought, *to love, honor, and protect*. His chest ached. His throat was clogged. He swallowed. Carver tried covering his face with his hand, as his features morphed between joy and incredulity, but he couldn't stop looking up to watch Joelzi as she made her way to him. Once their eyes locked, he couldn't look away. Carver felt Adam lean over and press a clean hanky in his hand. The closer Joelzi got to where he stood, the faster she seemed to be moving, until it looked like she was pulling Mr. Parker down the aisle. He grinned. *I'm glad she's in a hurry. I am too. And my face probably echoes hers.* Joelzi's smile was big, but her lips warbled as though she couldn't decide whether to laugh or cry. By the time Joelzi and Mr. Parker reached the front of the chapel, Carver and Joelzi were both weeping freely. He was vaguely aware of sniffing and laughter from the audience. He found himself beside Joelzi without being aware of moving. He reached out to take Joelzi's hand before the pastor had even had time to ask Mr. Parker who gave this woman. Laughter erupted again when Mr. Parker smiled at Carver, patted him on the shoulder and asked, "You in a hurry, son?"

Yes, Carver thought, as he held his bride's hand and looked down at her face, *I've waited a lifetime*.

The ceremony was surreal. His favorite parts were the vows and the ring exchange. They had

343

cried through those parts too. Before their first kiss and being presented as husband and wife, the pastor had stepped back and told the congregation, "Carver wants to say a few words to his bride. Carver…"

Carver reached into his pocket and pulled out the ruby ring guard he had purchased the day he bought Joelzi's engagement ring.

"Joelzi, Proverbs 31:10[9] talks about a wife of noble character being worth more than rubies. It says her husband trusts her without reserve. That's the way I feel about you, Joelzi. I bought this ring guard of rubies to remind you. You are precious to me. Carver slid the additional ring on her finger and instinctively moved to kiss Joelzi.

Pastor Tommy moved to the side of the stage, "…you may kiss…" But Carver had already taken Joelzi in his arms and was making his commitment known. "…your bride," Pastor Tommy finished with a chuckle. When Carver and Joelzi came up for breath, Pastor Tommy turned to the congregation, "Let me be the first to present to you, Doctor and Mrs. Carver Ellis."

The entire church audience stood and cheered.

---

[9] NIV

Additional Items

I could not have completed this book without the unique skill set of my editor, Maria Mountokalaki. Your expertise in the Greek language was a lifesaver!

I'm humbled by husband's consistent belief in my ability to put words on the page. David, you convince me to keep trying, even when the learning curve is steep. I love you.

To the reader, thank you for taking the time to read Joelzi and Carver's story. I hope it encouraged you. If you have been impacted by rape or abortion, or love someone who has been impacted by rape or abortion I hope you understand the love of the Father for you. This book is my attempt to open up discussion about the difficult issues of rape that results in pregnancy and abortion. I have listed some additional references should you want more information.

As always, I value your feedback. Your online review on Amazon/ Kindle helps the book stay in a position to be found more easily. Thank you in advance.

And for those who are wondering what happens to Merci—stay tuned, the rest of her story is Book three.

According to the National Sexual Violence Resource Center (nsvrc.org/saam/campus-resource-list) 90 percent of college rape victims knew their offenders. Of the completed rapes, fewer than 5% of the victims notified the police.

https://www.nsvrc.org/sites/default/files/publications/2019-09/Rape-Related%20Pregnancy_Final508.pdf

The CDC's fact sheet on Rape-related pregnancy (RRP) reports that about "3 million women in the U.S. experience RRP during their lifetime."

https://www.cdc.gov/violenceprevention/sexualviolence/understanding-RRP-inUS

https://www.godeeperstill.org

https://www.focusonthefamily.com/get-help/post-abortive-recovery-resources/

For more information about Dr. Helen Roseveare:

http://www.christianfocus.com/item/show/958/

Give Me this Mountain Christian Focus Publications

About the Author

Cindy Luke spent years in multiple Emergency Departments as an RN before heading back to school to become a Nurse Practitioner. Her Emergency Department experiences, the joys and challenges of raising four children alongside her very own knight in 'mostly shiny armor', and her love for the Lord Jesus compelled her to write her first novel.

She and her husband had a wager competing to see who would finish their dream project first. She lost that wager, but finished the first book, Saved by Grace, and in the process became so invested in her characters that she delved into Book two. Here Comes Mercy-- Joelzi and Carver's story.

Cindy continues working as a nurse practitioner and writing on the side. She has moved back to sunny Florida with her husband and their one-hundred-pound mutt, Booker. And is hopeful the warmer weather will improve time spent writing.

Yes, for those who wonder, Book Three, the rest of Merci's story, is in the works.

www.ingramcontent.com/pod-product-compliance
Lightning Source LLC
Chambersburg PA
CBHW051945240626
47153CB00005B/1635